Willi

An Outline of the Necessary Laws of Thought

A treatise on pure and applied logic. Four edition

SALZWASSER
VERLAG

William Thomson

An Outline of the Necessary Laws of Thought

A treatise on pure and applied logic. Four edition

Reprint of the original, first published in 1863.

1st Edition 2022 | ISBN: 978-3-37500-798-0

Verlag (Publisher): Salzwasser Verlag GmbH, Zeilweg 44, 60439 Frankfurt, Deutschland
Vertretungsberechtigt (Authorized to represent): E. Roepke, Zeilweg 44, 60439 Frankfurt, Deutschland
Druck (Print): Books on Demand GmbH, In de Tarpen 42, 22848 Norderstedt, Deutschland

AN OUTLINE

OF THE

LAWS OF THOUGHT.

AN OUTLINE

OF THE NECESSARY

LAWS OF THOUGHT:

A TREATISE ON

PURE AND APPLIED LOGIC.

BY

WILLIAM THOMSON, D.D.

FOURTH EDITION.

NEW YORK

1863.

PREFACE.

SOME account of the exact position which this work pretends to occupy amidst a crowd of valuable treatises on the same subject, may not be an unfitting introduction to its pages. The system of Pure Logic or Analytic that has been universally accepted for centuries past, is very defective as an instrument for the analysis of natural reasoning. Arguments that commend themselves to any untaught mind as valid and practically important, have no place in a system that professedly includes all reasoning whatever; and an attempt to reduce to its technical forms the first few pages of any scientific work, has generally ended in failure and disgust. The consequence has been that the more popular writers on Logic have begun to treat its strictly technical parts with a certain coyness and reserve. They have denied to the rules of the syllogism that prominent place once assigned to them, yet at the same time they have refrained from rejecting as cumbrous and unnecessary an instrument which did not subserve any practical end in their systems.

The present work is an attempt to enlarge the science of Pure Logic, so that it may be adequate to the analysis of any act of reasoning. How far it has attained its object ought to be decided by the application of its principles to many miscellaneous examples from different sciences; and whilst I have rigorously and frequently applied this test to it for many years, I cannot hope that the partiality of an author will be a sufficient guarantee of its pretensions, and therefore commend the same line of examination to any one who believes, with me, that a sedulous practice of logical analysis will richly reward the understanding with accessions of strength and clearsightedness. If the result should be the detection of many errors and omissions on the author's part, enough of matter may perhaps be left unshaken, to prove that Pure Logic is not the mere *officina veteramentaria*—the warehouse of useless relics—it is too often taken for, but a practical system—an important branch of mental culture.

To Sir William Hamilton, of Edinburgh, whose death every student of philosophy may deplore as a personal loss, I am greatly indebted for valuable assistance, freely and generously afforded, at the cost of much time and trouble. There is no longer any fear that such an acknowledgment will be misconstrued into an admission that the present work only reports the opinions of that illustrious philosopher; as he has himself recognized its claim to an independent position.* In truth, the extension of the syllogism, the enlarged list of immediate inferences, the doctrine of the three aspects of propositions, in Extension, Intension, and Denomination, and the grounds for rejecting the Fourth Figure of Syllogism, which serve, with other things, to give this little book its character, were worked out originally without assistance from any living author, from such materials as any student might command; and it may perhaps be permitted me, without seeming to court a damaging comparison, to point out that the twelve affirmative modes of Syllogism in each figure, which here replace the much more limited number of the old system, are precisely those which Sir William Hamilton has found it necessary, on his own principles, to adopt. This will be an evidence to the reader that the alteration in question is not rash and arbitrary.

To Professor De Morgan, who has put forth, besides many excellent Mathematical Books and Essays, an elaborate and acute *Treatise on Formal Logic*, my best acknowledgments are due for his kind and patient explanations of certain parts of his system. Other obligations to him are notified in their proper places.

The Appendix *on Indian Logic*, by my friend Professor Max Müller, of Oxford, whose philological pro-

* Sir W. Hamilton's Discussions in Philosophy, p. 126.

ductions have already made his name known over three continents, although they are but the first gatherings of a harvest rich in promise, is intended to call attention to the interesting resemblances between the Greek and Hindú systems, which have never yet received the consideration they deserve.

The favour with which this book has been received, has far exceeded the expectations of its writer. It is now adopted as a class-book in several places of education; and the careful revision of the present edition may perhaps have rendered it more fit for such a use.

W. T.

Queen's College Oxford: June, 1857.

TABLE OF CONTENTS.

INTRODUCTION.

LANGUAGE.

OUTLINE

OF THE

LAWS OF THOUGHT.

INTRODUCTION.

Εἴπωμεν οὖν διὰ βοαχέων τίς ἡ πρόθεσις καὶ τίς ὁ σκοπὸς πάσης τῆς ἀναλυτικῆς ἐτιστήμης.

ALEXANDER APHROD.

OUTLINE

OF THE

LAWS OF THOUGHT.

INTRODUCTION.

"Nullam dicere maximarum rerum artem esse, cum minimarum sine arte nulla sit, hominum est parum considerate loquentium atque in maximis rebus errantium." CICERO.

EVERY process has laws, known or unknown, according to which it must take place. A consciousness of them is so far from being necessary to the process, that we cannot discover what they are, except by analyzing the results it has left us. Poems must have been written before Horace could compose an "Art of Poetry," which required the analysis and judicious criticism of works already in existence. Men poured out burning speeches and kindled their own emotions in the hearer's breast, before an Art of Rhetoric could be constructed. They tilled the ground, crossed the river or the sea, healed their sicknesses with medicinal plants, before agriculture, chemistry, navigation, and medicine, had become sciences. And wherever our knowledge of the laws of any process has become more complete and accurate; as in astronomy, by the substitution of the Copernican for the Ptolemaic system; in history, by a wiser estimate than our fathers had the means of forming, of civilization and its tendencies; in chemistry, by such discoveries as the atomic theory and the wonders of electro-magnetism; our progress has been made, not by mere poring in the closet over the rules already known, to revise and correct them by their own light, but by coming back again and again to the process as it went on in nature, to apply our rules to facts, and see how far they contradicted or fell short of explaining them. Astronomers turned to the stars, where the laws they sought for were day and night fulfilling themselves before their eyes; historians collected facts from the records of different countries, watched men of many races, of various climates, differently helped or hindered, for there, they knew, the true principles of history were to be read; and chemists, in the laboratory, untwisted the very fibres of matter, and watched its every pulse and change, to come at the laws which underlaid them. "Even geometry," says the great chemist, Justus Liebig, "had its foundation laid in experiments and observations; most of its theorems had been seen in practical examples, before the science was established by abstract reasoning. Thus, that the square of the hypothenuse of a right-angled triangle is equal to the sum of the squares of the other two sides, was an experimental discovery, or why did the discoverer sacrifice a hecatomb when he made out its proof?"

§ 2. The same applies to Logic, or *the science of the laws of thought.* The process of thought, or that active function of the mind by which impressions received from within or from without are described, classified, and compared, commenced long before the rules to which it adheres with unfailing strictness, had been drawn out. And though they do not *depend* on experience—*i. e.* their truth may be tried and made manifest without recurring to examples—still without experience, without the power of watching our own thoughts and those of others, there could never have been a science of Logic, which had its origin when some reflective mind, that had for years performed the various acts of thought spontaneously, began to lay down the laws on which they take place, or to give rules for repeating them at pleasure. The clearest reasoner cannot with propriety be called a logician, so long as he disputes spontaneously and without rule; whilst the man with the humblest reasoning powers may lay claim to the title, in so far as he reasons according to laws, ascertained by reflection upon the process of thinking. If, for example, we call Zeno of Elea the inventor of Dialectic or Logic in Greece, it is not in virtue of his marvellous ingenuity in arguing against the possibility of motion, because this might have been the result of natural acuteness; but because his arguments, all constructed upon one type, that of forcing his antagonists into an absurd position by reasonings drawn from their own views, seem to indicate the possession of a logical rule, the same which now has the name of *reductio ad absurdum*. He had reflected upon those modes of argument which his position led him to adopt spontaneously, and had formed a general rule or plan which assisted him in forming like arguments in future. Logic then, like Philosophy, of which it is a part, arises from the reflection of the mind upon its own processes ; a logician is not one who thinks, but one who can declare how he thinks. This important distinction, which has been too often neglected, must govern all researches into the history of the science.

§ 3. Logic has been defined to be *the science of the necessary laws of thought.* But this definition, the correctness of which shall presently be examined more particularly, requires a few words of general explanation. Our thoughts are formed indeed by laws ; and when we conceive, abstract, define, judge, and deduce, we put in practice so many ascertainable principles. But does Logic simply explain these laws *in themselves*, or contemplate them *in their uses*, as assisting and regulating our efforts in seeking after knowledge ? This distinction is analogous to that which is drawn between Anatomy and Physiology, the former of which simply examines what are the parts of the human frame, and the latter, the Science of Life, dwells upon the uses and developments of the parts : the one declares that I have a brain, and the other determines that it is the principal seat of passion, sensation, and reason ; and that it is weak in childhood, strong and constant in mature life, and subject to a gradual decay in age. It is competent to us unquestionably to consider the principles of thought under this twofold aspect of their nature and their employment. Thus, if we take a judgment ; say, "The happiness of the human family will increase in proportion to the increase of mutual love," and consider it in its own nature, we shall decide that it is a judgment correct in form, that certain other judgments may be gathered from it, that it has some qualities which may belong to a judgment, and wants others; and so far we are only looking at the judgment *in itself*, by what we know of the laws of judgment. But if we consider this example in connection with truth and knowledge, we are led to examine further, whether it is false or true, whether in forming it we fulfilled those conditions, of observation and reasoning, without which we have no right to expect a true result; to what region of thought it belongs, and what is the method, be it testimony, deduction from principles, or observation of facts, by which judgments are to be obtained in that region. In the former case we only put in requisition what may be called *pure* Logic, which is defined to be *the science of the necessary laws of thought in their own nature;* whilst the questions in the latter case belong to *applied* Logic, or *the science of the necessary laws of thought as employed in attaining truth.*

§ 4. But is this distinction worth preserving in our exposition of the science? Many logicians, believing that they must undertake to teach men "the art of reasoning," do not attach any value to the laws of thinking, except in so far as the employment of them may help men to think, and so to enlarge their stock of truth; that is, they do not regard pure Logic as a distinct branch of their subject. But there is one grand reason for the opposite course. Truth is a wide word, and denotes all that we can ever know of ourselves, the universe, and the Creator. The science which explains how the mind deals with truth, must be loose and indefinite, as its object-matter is of infinite extent; so that applied Logic can never attain perfect completeness and precision, because it can never affirm that it has shown how the mind deals with every part of truth and knowledge. But the laws of thought themselves are few in number, and lie, in examples of perpetual occurrence, under every thinking man's observation; and therefore it may be declared with tolerable correctness when a full and accurate view of pure Logic has been taken. To secure that which we have completely mastered, it is desirable to keep it separate from that in which perfect completeness is hopeless; and therefore we purpose to consider Logic under two distinct lights, first as a science of laws, and next as a science of laws applied to practice.

But here a caution is necessary (which we shall have to repeat in connection with the tripartite division of pure Logic itself), that as the distinction is in a measure arbitrary, for the laws of thought are always put in force with a view to the attainment or communication of knowledge, it will be impossible to maintain it with perfect consistency throughout our labours. Occasions constantly arise when the line of demarcation becomes blurred and confused; when the bare laws of thought cannot be explained without the mention of that truth, in the search for which they are always employed: thus, in treating of Definition, which is one form of judgment, we imply the existence of a person *for* whom it is necessary to define a given notion that he may possess the true meaning of it, and be able to identify the things for which it stands. All that can be expected from us is, that, even if we find it necessary to repeat the same truths in the two divisions, we do not desert our point of view, but explain the laws of thought, first mainly for themselves, and then mainly in relation to truth, which is the object of all thought and inquiry.

§ 5. Pure Logic (which is later in the order of discovery than applied, inasmuch as it is formed by abstracting from that more general science) takes no account of the modes in which we collect the *materials* of thought, such as Perception, Belief, Memory, Suggestion, Association of Ideas; although these are all in one sense laws of thought.* Presupposing the possession of the materials, it only refers them to their proper head or principle, as conceptions, as subjects or predicates, as judgments, or as arguments. It enounces the laws we must observe in thinking, but does not explain the subsidiary processes, some or all of which must take place to allow us to think. Metaphysics is the science in which these find place; but they also belong to *applied* Logic, because they are so many conditions under which the human mind acquires knowledge. Again, in pure Logic, the dif-

* "Now universal Logic is either pure or applied Logic. In the first we make abstraction of all empirical conditions, under which our understanding is exercised; for example, of the influence of the senses—the play of the imagination—the laws of memory—the power of habit, of inclination, &c.; consequently also of the sources of pre judices, nay, in fact, in general, of all causes out of which certain cognitions arise to us or are pretended to do so, since they merely concern the understanding under certain circumstances of its application, and in order to know them, experience is requisite."—*Kant's Critique,* p. 58, English transl. 1st ed. The ground here taken is different from that in the text. I do not say they are *contingent,* for memory, for example, enters into every act of thought; but, that they are *subsidiary;* thought is not complete without them, but at the same time thought is never complete with them alone.

ferent processes of the mind are regarded in their perfect and complete state; whilst in applied, the imperfect faculties of man, the limited opportunities of observation, the necessity of deciding upon a question when the materials of a judgment are still insufficient, impose many limitations on the perfection of our knowledge. Thus, whilst pure Logic only treats of arguments that are certain and irrefutable, the most important duty of applied Logic is to determine under what conditions imperfect arguments, such as the Example, the Imperfect Induction, the Deduction from a proposition that is not truly universal, and some of the Rhetorical Enthymenes, can be fairly employed, and to show, that though these weaker forms are so many deviations from a perfect demonstrative argument, they are so far from superseding the perfect forms, that in reality each of them appeals to, and attests the cogency of, some perfect form, to which it strives, as it were, to conform itself. As we are anticipating, a very easy example must suffice to illustrate our meaning. Every one is perfectly certain of the truth of the proposition that *men grow infirm and die;* of which we have been convinced partly by our own experience of men, and partly by the experience of others, delivered to us from all quarters, in the sober pages of the moralist as well as in the reckless lyrics of the reveller. Nor does our conviction of this truth permit itself to be disturbed by the consideration, which is likewise undeniable, that the whole aggregate of this experience does not in itself warrant any statement having *all* mankind for its subject: that even supposing the decadence and death of every man in times past had been observed, which is utterly inconceivable, at any rate there are many now living upon whom the common doom has not passed, and whose cases therefore cannot enter into the sum of our experience. In a word, we have concluded from an experience that *many* men have become infirm and died, the much wider truth that *all* men do so; and this is warrantable in the given case, and we are right in rejecting upon the faith of it an assertion, unless supported by evidence that transcends experience, that one man has not died, such as we have in the fable of the Wandering Jew, or a proposal to obviate death in future, such as was involved in the search of the alchemist for an Elixir of Life. But that this mode of argument from a particular to a universal, from *some* to *all*, is not valid in itself, is evident from applying it to another case, in which it is absurdly false—*some men are tall, therefore all men are tall:* and the only form perfectly indisputable in itself would be, "the men whom we have observed have all died, and these men are all men, that is, the only men, therefore all men die," which from the nature of this case cannot be employed. But applied Logic first shows that this perfect argument is the measure of the validity of the other; that our conclusion is only true if we can say, not indeed "these men are all men," which is impossible, but the equally *general* proposition, "These men are (*as good as*) all men;" thus conforming really to the perfectly conclusive argument; and next, how and under what circumstances we can conform the incomplete to the complete enumeration, how *some* can ever be said to be as good as *all* for purposes of argumentation

But it is time to proceed to examine the different parts of the definition of pure Logic, by showing that Logic is a science, rather than an art—that it is a science of the necessary laws or forms of thought—that it has thought rather than language for its adequate object-matter.

§ 6. *Logic is a science rather than an art.* The distinction between science and art is, that a science is a body of principles and deductions, to explain some object-matter: an art is a body of precepts, with practical skill, for the completion of some work. A science teaches us to know, and an art to do; the former declares that something exists, with the laws and causes which belong to its existence, the latter teaches how something must be produced.* An art will of course admit into its limits every thing which can conduce to the performance of its proper work; it can recognize no other principle of selection. The painter may fail of perfect success from employing improper colouring materials, or a muddy and perishable varnish, as well as from incorrect drawing or ill-managed light and shade; the lower defect or the higher is fatal to that perfect picture which he wishes

* *Περὶ γένεσιν τέχνη, περὶ τὸ ὂν ἐπιστήμη.* *Aristotle, An. Post.* II. xix. 4. By Science in the text is meant the *speculative* science of *Plato* and *Aristotle;* by Art the *practical* science. *Plato* seems to use *τέχνη* and *ἐπιστήμη* as interchangeable terms (*Theæt.* 146, C.). Again (*Politicus*, 258, D. E.) he divides *ἐπιστῆμαι* into *πρακτικαὶ* and *γνωστικαὶ*; the latter he would subdivide (260, B.) into *critical*, which end in judging merely, and *epitactical*, which lead us to some practical result. See also *Theæt.* 202, D. Where *Aristotle* distinguishes between Science and Art, which is not invariably the case, he explains them as we have done in the text, adding only that the object-matter of Science is necessary or invariable; that of Art, contingent and variable. See *An. Post.* I. ii; *Top.* VI. viii. 1; *Eth. Nic.* VI. iii.

to produce. So that an art may contain precepts of a very dissimilar character; the painter must be taught Expression, Anatomy, and mixing of Colours; the Rhetorician must learn to manage his thoughts, his hearers, and his hands, with equal dexterity. The science, on the other hand, having the object-matter for its touchstone, admits nothing except what relates directly to it; and so a far greater unity and simplicity naturally belongs to it. Geometry treats of nothing but the properties of space, because it is a pure science; whilst the arts founded upon it, such as Land-surveying, must bring in such topics as inequalities of surface, use of instruments, and the like. The science of Musical Counterpoint teaches the theory of harmonic progressions, and nothing else; but the musician's art, in which it is employed, must add the knowledge of instruments and their compass, of the human voice, even sometimes of the powers of a particular singer. Now in the popular meaning of the word Logic, no doubt the notion of an art is more prominent; to be able to reason better, and to expose errors in the reasoning of others, is supposed to be the object of this study.* But those writers who have followed out this view have been compelled to go over too wide a field for any one system. Logic must be the widest of all arts or sciences; because thinking, which is its object-matter, belongs to all the rest; it is *ars artium*, the art which comprehends all others, because its rules apply to every subject on which the human

* Upon the historical view of the question, whether Logic is an Art or a Science, most valuable remarks will be found in a paper by *Sir William Hamilton. Edinburgh Review,* 115, p. 202, seq.

mind can be engaged. If then it is to be taught as an Art, it should contain specific rules for reasoning or thinking in every region of thought; it must propose to itself nothing less than to enable men of the most various capacities to apply a set of principles to effect the work of thinking correctly, under all circumstances. And the consequences are, an enormous expansion in the first instance, from the huge mass of heterogeneous materials; and a consciousness of incompleteness in the second, since it is impossible to suppose that so vast a work has ever been completely achieved. Works in which the attempt has been made often contain a chapter on Scriptural Interpretation, and perhaps another on Forming a Judgment on Books:—can it be supposed that the precepts under either of these heads can be complete? The one is an epitome of all Theology, and the other, it might be said, of all wisdom. Now Logic may be unquestionably an art or a science; but it seems that all we can do is to lay down the principles of the science and leave each student to form for himself his own art, to teach himself how to employ these principles in practice. In this way we may attain something like completeness in a moderate compass, and may escape those incessant shiftings of the boundaries of the art, which are inevitable where men have to select a finite number of precepts out of infinite knowledge.

§ 7. Those who represent Logic as both art and science are accustomed to assume that all arts, possessing the principles of correspondent sciences, teach their application to practice, so that art is but science turned to account. In the case of Logic this is not very far from the truth; but as a general statement it is false, for it overlooks that notion of *unconsciousness* which is commonly involved in Art. Shakspeare is admitted to be a consummate artist, but no one means by this that his plays were composed only to develop a certain express theory of Dramatic Poetry, such as Coleridge, Horn, or Ulrici have since founded upon them. No: the man of science possesses principles, but the artist, not the less nobly gifted on that account, is possessed and carried away by them. "The principles which Art *involves*, science *evolves*. The truths on which the success of Art depends, lurk in the artist's mind in an undeveloped state,—guiding his hand, stimulating his invention, balancing his judgment, but not appearing in the form of enunciated propositions."* And because the artist cannot always communicate his own principles, men speak of his "*happy* art," as if it were almost by chance or *hap* that his works were accomplished; † and it was the fashion of the last century to speak of Shakspeare himself as a wild, untutored child of genius, not even to be named as an artist, because in truth his plays wanted dramatic *science* and were not obedient to the law of the dramatic unities. So that the praise of being a good logician, or of having a logical mind, is sometimes awarded where there is little or no acquaintance with the science of logic. An understanding naturally clear, and a certain power of imitation, will enable the

* *Whewell's* Philosophy of Ind. Sciences, ii. p. 111.

† So we have the line of *Agatho*, Τέχνη τύχην ἔστεοξε, καὶ τύχῃ τεχνην.

thinker or speaker to pour forth arguments which might serve for examples of all the logical rules, not one of which he has learnt; and without some share of these talents, no precepts would avail to make a reasoner. But when we write upon Logic, the unconscious skill of the artist must be left out of the account, because it cannot be communicated by rules. By the art of Logic we mean so much of the art of thinking as is teachable, and no more. The whole of every *science* can be made the subject of teaching.*

§ 8. In treating of Logic as a science, we shall not forget that the ultimate object of the study is strictly practical, and shall labour to state the principles in such a way as to facilitate to the student their application as an art. If we would redeem Logic from the charge usually brought against it, that it is a system of rules which the initiated never employ, and the uninitiated never miss, it must be by giving it a far more extensive verification in practice than it usually receives. The inconsistency of teaching a science, where we mean that an art should be ultimately learnt, is only apparent, not real; and at any rate is less injurious than that of those who teach an "instrumental art" which is never employed in practice, and which is too often inadequate to the simplest tasks of practical application.

§ 9. *Pure Logic is a science of the necessary laws of thought.* After the remarks already made (in page 23), this subject will need less illustration. Logic only gives us those principles which constitute thought; and presupposes the operation of those principles by

* Διδακτὴ πᾶσα ἐπιστήμη δοκεῖ εἶναι. *Aristotle, Eth. Nic.* VI. iii.

which we gain the materials for thinking. Thus I have a conception of *house*, which sums up and comprises all buildings in which men live; how did I obtain it? Logic answers that it was generalized from different single houses which I had seen, by noticing what points they had in common, and by gathering up these common features into a new notion. It tells us, further, that this conception has various powers, that it may be defined, by declaring what I understand by it, that it may be divided, as into "houses of the rich," and "houses of the poor," that by comparing it with other general notions, as church, quay, monumental pillar, I may form a more general conception, in which all these may be comprehended, that of building. In all this Logic is to a certain extent my guide, because *conception* is one great function of thought; but with considerable reservations. It only tells me what is true of *all* conceptions, and leaves me to apply the principles to this particular one; for about *houses* Logic of course knows nothing, and to know what is a house and what not, I must go to Architecture or to common experience. Logic only tells me what principles I *must* put in practice in forming any general notion whatever; but to her all general notions are alike. She makes no account of the great diversity of the classes of things they represent; king, animal, acid, mammal, are all alike to her, and ranked together as conceptions, though the sets of objects they severally stand for have little resemblance. Logic then takes no account of the *contents* of a conception, of the things from which it is generalized; these are contingent *to her*—if any given class from which a conception is now formed were annihilated, there would still be conceptions. The function of conception is essential to thought; its laws are accordingly laid down, but their particular use must be determined by the particular sciences. Logic teaches me what Generalization, or the forming of common notions from many things, is; but Botany teaches me to generalize upon plants, Political Economy upon the facts of social prosperity, Geometry upon the properties of space, and so on through the whole range of sciences.

§ 10. In another direction also Logic seems to stop short, and to leave to another science what it was incumbent upon it to explain. Our conceptions are formed from single objects; how do we come to know these? The logician replies, that it is not his business to show how, but that for the most part they are derived from the senses, by means of which we are put in communication with the external world. But many further questions arise out of this answer. What are the senses? How much of every notion conveyed by them is new, how much is the result of the experience of past impressions? Does my *sight* tell me that yonder steeple is about three miles off, or is it my understanding coöperating with my sight? Is there no doubt that the senses report truly? Are we even certain that there *is* an external world? To these and many like questions the logician has one answer: "I presuppose a man able to perceive, to receive impressions from the surrounding world, and then merely explain the principles on which he *must* proceed, in combining his impressions and drawing inferences from them. The speculations you suggest are highly interesting, and all who would understand the mind of man must enter upon them; but the science of Metaphysics, or of the Human Mind, has already taken them up, and, closely connected as Logic is with this science, it is *expedient* that they should divide the ground. Logic therefore presupposes a mind capable of, and actually receiving, impressions; though, perhaps, if there were no such science as Metaphysics, it would be necessary even in a logical work to give a preliminary account of the origin of all knowledge."

§ 11. *Pure Logic is a science of the form, or of the formal laws of thinking*, and not of the *matter*. The terms form and matter, in their philosophic use, will require some explanation.

A statue may be considered as consisting of two parts, the marble out of which it is hewn, which is its *matter* or *stuff*, and the *form* which the artist communicates. The latter is essential to the statue, but not the former, since the work might be the same, though the material were different; but if the form were wanting we could not even call the work a statue. This notion of a *material* susceptible of a certain *form*, the accession of which shall give it a new nature and name, may be analogically transferred to other natures. Space may be regarded as *matter*, and geometrical figures as the *form* impressed in it. The voice is the *matter* of speech, and articulation the *form*. But as it is the form which proximately and obviously makes the thing what it is (although there can be no form without matter), the word form came to be interchanged with *essence* and with *nature*. Already we have left the original sense at some distance.

§ 12. With thinkers to whom the metaphorical sense was not so prominent, the word is used in three distinct but cognate senses. It is, 1st, a law or an idea, which are the same thing seen from opposite points. "That which, contemplated *objectively* (that is, as existing externally to the mind) we call a Law; the same contemplated *subjectively* (that is, as existing in a subject or mind) is an Idea. Hence Plato often names Ideas, Laws; and Lord Bacon, the British Plato, describes the laws of the material universe as ideas in nature. *Quod in naturâ naturatâ lex, in naturâ naturante idea dicitur.*" * Lava, heated metal, boiling water, the rays of the sun, all rank under one common form (that is, law) of *heat*, namely: by which is meant that they, all and each, contain whatever is essential to heat. Lead, gold, vermilion, stones, and (in a greater or less degree) all bodies, possess weight; the law of weight then is their form—the law under which they all come, the condition with which they all comply. By virtue of this form they are, not bodies indeed, but *heavy* bodies; in other words, if we suppose that form or law to be expunged from the tables of the universe, their existence as to that nature or property would terminate; or if the *idea* of weight were removed from the mind, we could no longer know them as heavy bodies.

§ 13. Now how does every one of the given instances come under the forms heat and gravitation? By something contained within itself—by its embodying the law or definition; that which comes under the form of *weight* must possess weight, must

* *Coleridge's* Church and State, p. 12.

have in it all that the definition of weight demands. And here we may trace the second meaning of the word form: it is *that part of any object through which it ranks under a given law.* Every new object represented to the mind is referred to different laws, called forms, by virtue of various qualities in itself, each of which is termed metonymically, and with respect to the law under which it is the means of ranking the representation, its form. When we observe (say) a stone, the mind proceeds to class the representation of it, afforded by the senses, under the various forms of *colour*, *figure*, *size*, *weight*, *temperature*, &c.; and with reference to the *form* (law) of weight, the weight of the stone would be its form (essential part), with reference to the form of colour, the grayness of the stone would be its form. So that that, which in the object, when viewed in relation to one law or form, is its form (essential part), is not its form when it is viewed in relation to another. Now the *matter* of any representation is that part of it which with reference to any given law is non-formal.* Thus in our stone, the weight, size, temperature, are parts of the matter, as far as the law of colour is concerned, for they are all non-formal, and the colour of the stone alone is formal. The matter is that which, when added to the form (essential part), gives it extraneity—*outness*—objective † existence. Without something more than the

* Hence the same thing is alternately form and matter. See *Ritter's History,* III. p. 121 (Eng. trans.), for this point in Aristotle's doctrine.

† It will be well once for all to explain the modern use of the words *subject* and *object*—*subjective* and *objective.* The subject is the mind that thinks; the object is that which it thinks about. A subjective

mere form, there can be no *instance* of a law, an instance being the presence of the law in an object capable of containing it, and thus presupposing two things, the law and the capable object, whereof we term one the form and the other the matter. Ex. gr. *triangle* may be conceived by means of its own form or definition alone, but it must have a material part, it must become *a* triangle of stone, or wood, or ink on paper, as the condition of its external existence. When no separation, according to some law or other, of a representation into its formal and material part takes place, that is, where it is referred to no law or conception already in the mind, there must be total ignorance of the object represented; the representation must remain obscure, and can never amount to a cognition. The absolutely material part of a cognition would be that which remains unknown after it has been brought under as many forms as the mind can reduce it to; that which never becomes the condition of its ranking under a law. Forms have a triple mode of existence; they exist in the Divine Mind as ideas, and are the archetypes of creation;

impression is one which arises in and from the mind itself; an objective arises from observation of external things. A subjective tendency in a poet or thinker would be a preponderating inclination to represent the moods and states of his own mind; whilst the writer who dwells most upon external objects, and suffers us to know little more of his own mind than that it has the power to reproduce them with truth and spirit, exhibits an objective bias. As the mind, however, sometimes regards its own states, of feeling or sensation, as objects, it has been proposed to call them, when so employed, *subject-objects*, i. e. parts of the subject regarded as objects; whilst purely external things might be called *objects*. (*Krug's Phil. Lexicon*, under *Gegenstand*.) These words have undergone great changes of meaning, excellently traced out in *Sir W. Hamilton's Reid*, p. 806, in a note which only the Editor of that work could have written.

they exist as embodied in "instances" or examples, in which mode they are laws; they exist, lastly, in the human mind as ideas; thus they precede creation, they are in it, they succeed it.

§ 14. Writers of this school give yet a third sense to the word form; as it denotes the law, so by an easy transition it stands for the class of cases brought together and united by the law. Thus to speak of the form of animal might mean, first, the law or definition of animal in general; second, the part of any given animal by which it comes under the law, and is what it is; and last, the class of animals brought together under the law.

§ 15. The sense attached at the present day to the words form and matter is somewhat different from, though closely related to, these. The form is what the mind impresses upon its perceptions of things, which are the matter; form therefore means *mode of viewing* objects that are presented to the mind. When the attention is directed to any object, we do not see the object itself, but contemplate it in the light of our own prior conceptions. A rich man, for example, is regarded by the poor and ignorant under the form of a very fortunate person, able to purchase luxuries which are above their own reach; by the religious mind, under the form of a person with more than ordinary temptations to contend with; by the political economist, under that of an example of the unequal distribution of wealth; by the tradesman, under that of one whose patronage is valuable. Now the object is really the same to all these observers; the same "rich man" has been represented under all these different forms. And the reason that the observers are able so to find many in one, is that they connect him severally with their own prior conceptions. The form then in this view is mode of knowing; and the matter is the perception, or object we have to know.* Hence, when we call Logic a

* A few passages to illustrate these various meanings may be added here. *Plato* uses form in all the three senses, of law, distinctive or essential part, and species (which last word means *form*); as these places will show.

"Remember then, that I directed you not to teach me some one or two holy acts out of many, but that very form by which all holy acts are holy. . . . . Teach me, then, the nature of that form itself, that looking to it and using it for our example, I may declare any of the actions of yourself or any other, which partake of this nature, to be holy, and any not so partaking, not to be holy."—*Plat. Euthyp.* 6, D. E. "And of the just, the unjust, the good, the evil, of all the forms, in short, the same holds true, that each is one and simple, but because everywhere appearing by incorporation with actions, or matter, or other things, that each appears many."—*Resp.* 476, A. "For we have been accustomed to lay down one form for many particular cases, on which we impose the same name."—*Resp.* 596, A. "And according to the same form of justice, a just man will nowise differ from a just city, but will be like it."—*Resp.* 435, B. See also *Symp.* 205, D.; *Resp.* 581, E.; *Polit.* 258, E. Lord *Bacon* says, "The form of any nature is such that where it has place the given nature is also, as an infallible consequence. Therefore it is ever present where the given nature is so, it attests that nature's presence, and is in it all. The same form is such that upon its removal the given nature infallibly vanishes. Therefore it is invariably absent where that nature is so, it in those cases disavows that nature's presence, and is in it alone." *Nov. Org.* II. 4. "The examination of forms proceeds thus. Concerning the given nature we must first bring together before the intellect all the known instances, agreeing in that nature, though manifesting it in vehicles [*i. e.* in matter] the most dissimilar."—*Nov. Org.* II. 11. Again, "When we speak of forms, we understand nothing else than those laws and manifestations of the pure act, which order and constitute any simple nature, as heat, light, weight, in any sort of matter and subject that can contain them. Therefore, the form of heat or form of light, and the law of heat or light, is the same thing, nor do we ever abstract our thoughts from actualities and active manifestations."—*Nov. Org.* II. 17. Again, "For since the science of the formal laws, or the form, of thinking, we mean that the science is only concerned with that which is essential to, and distinctive of, the thinking process. Every act of thought is a thought *about* something; it has *matter* as well as *form*. Every common noun is a sign of the act of conception; thus crystal is a conception formed from comparing together many inorganic bodies which have spontaneously assumed certain regular forms: animal, a conception from comparing many live creatures. Here the form is the same, for both are

form of a thing is the very thing itself (*ipsissima res*), and the thing no otherwise differs from the form, than as the apparent differs from the existent, the outward from the inward, or that which is considered in relation to man from that which is considered in relation to the universe [*or* universal mind], it follows clearly that no nature can be taken for the true form, unless it ever decreases when the nature itself decreases, and in like manner is always increased when the nature is increased."—*Nov. Org.* II. 13.

Ritter in his History shows the analogy between form and difference, matter and genus respectively, in the writings of *Aristotle; Plotinus* indeed asserts their absolute identity. *Ennead.* II. iv. 4. For a collection of passages to illustrate *Aristotle's* doctrine, see *Waitz' Organon.* comm. on 94, a. 20. To our own great writers the philosophical senses of the word *form* were well known. *Taylor, Andrewes, Hooker, Berkeley, Butler, Sir Thomas Brown, Coleridge*—supply instances which are now before us. But the subject has already occupied our attention long enough. *Keckermann's* Logic affords materials for understanding the views of the old logicians.

The philosophic value of the terms matter and form is greatly reduced by the confusion which seems invariably to follow their extensive use. Whilst one writer explains form as "the mode of knowing" an object, another puts it for "distinctive part," which has to do with the being or nature of the thing rather than with our knowledge of it; where it means "shape" in one place, which is often a mere accident, in another it means "essence;" so that it may be brought to stand for nearly opposite things. I will add, that probably there is no idea which these terms represent that cannot be conveniently expressed by others, less open to confusion.

conceptions, and it is this quality which constitutes them thoughts; but the matter is different, for one is about certain inorganic solids, and the other about living creatures. Logic, not being concerned with the things that thoughts are formed from, ranks the two together; it is for Mineralogy and Zoology to distinguish between them, Logic only knows them for their formal or logical value. Are they conceptions? are they judgments, syllogisms, definitions, or genera? Occupied only with the bare laws of thinking, Logic must leave to other sciences the consideration of the various matters upon which these laws operate. In these thoughts—"life is short"—"Mirabeau was said to have been poisoned"—"the radii of a circle are equal," we have only one form or law of thinking, namely, Judgment, exhibited in connection with various things or matter.

§ 16. Logic is said, in the language of the old writers, to be concerned only with second notions or intentions. The distinction between first and second intentions is connected with that which has been drawn between matter and form. Notions are of two kinds; they either have regard to *things as they are*, as horse, ship, tree, and are called first notions; or to things as they are *understood*, as notions of genus, species, attribute, subject, and in this respect are called second notions, which, however, are based upon the first, and cannot be conceived without them. The first intentions precede in order of time, for, as Boethius explains, men *first intended* to give names to things, before they intended to find names for their mode of viewing them. Now Logic is not so much employed upon first notions of things, as upon second; that is, as we have said, it is not occupied so much with things as they exist in nature, but with the way in which the mind conceives them. A logician has nothing to do with ascertaining whether a horse, or a ship, or a tree exists, but whether one of these things can be regarded as a genus or species, whether it can be called a subject or an attribute, whether from the conjunction of many second notions a proposition, a definition, or a syllogism can be formed. The first intention of every word is its real meaning; the second intention, its logical value, according to the function of thought to which it belongs.*

* Vox articulata est signum conceptus, qui est in animo: duplex autem est ejusmodi vox, alia namque significat conceptum rei, ut homo, animal; alia vero conceptum conceptus, ut genus, species, nomen, verbum, enunciatio, ratiocinatio, et aliæ hujusmodi; propterea hæ vocantur secundæ notiones; illæ autem primæ. *Zabarella de Nat. Log.* i. x.

Prima notio est conceptus rei quatenus est, ut animalis, hominis, secunda notio est conceptus rei quatenus intelligitur, ut subjectum et attributum. *Pacius. Anal. Comm.* p. 3, A.

See also *Buhle* (*Aristotle*, i. p. 432); *Crackanthorp* (Logic. Prooem.); and *Sir W. Hamilton* in *Ed. Rev.*, No. 115, p. 210. There is no authority whatever for *Aldrich's* view, which makes second intention mean apparently "a term defined for scientific use;" though with the tenacious vitality of error it still lingers in some quarters, after wounds that should have been mortal.

OUTLINE

OF THE

LAWS OF THOUGHT.

LANGUAGE.

"'Εστὶ μὲν οὖν τὰ ἐν τῇ φωνῇ τῶν ἐν τῇ ψύχῃ παθημάτων σύμβολα."
Arist. de Int.

§ 17.

HITHERTO we have assumed that the adequate object matter of Logic is *thought*, rather than language; that having explained the laws of thinking, it is not bound to examine under what conditions these manifest themselves in speech. But logicians do not invariably follow this course; those who regard it as an act of reasoning, seeing that reasoning is not conducted but by language, and that many of the chief impediments to the correct performance of the process, lie in the defects of expression, make speech, and not thought, the matter with which they are primarily concerned. The name of Logic itself would not be inconsistent with this view; since *logos* may mean the outer or the inner word—

the *sermo internus* or the *sermo externus*—the articulate expression or the thought itself. Here then the relation between thought and language must be ascertained.

§ 18. Language, in its most general acceptation, might be described as a mode of expressing our thoughts by means of motions of the organs of the body; it would thus include spoken words, cries and involuntary gestures that indicate the feelings, even painting and sculpture, together with those contrivances which replace speech in situations where it cannot be employed,—the telegraph, the trumpet-call, the emblem, the hieroglyphic.* For the present, however, we may limit it to its most obvious signification; it is a system of articulate words adopted by convention to represent outwardly the internal proofs of thinking.

§ 19. But language, besides being an interpreter of thought, exercises a powerful influence on the thinking process. The logician is bound to notice it in four functions:—(i.) as it enables him to analyze complex impressions, (ii.) as it preserves or records the result of the analysis for future use, (iii.) as it abbreviates thinking by enabling him to substitute a short word for a highly complex notion, and the like, and (iv.) as it is a means of communication.

* Language is thus divided by M. *Duval-Jouve*, Logique, p. 201.

Languages are	Natural	Absolute—*Cries* and *Gestures*.
		Conventional—*Speech*.
	Artificial	Absolute—*Painting* and *Sculpture*.
		Conventional—*Emblems*, *Telegraphic Signs* *Hieroglyphics*, *Writing*.

§ 20. (i.) The language of words never records an impression, whether internal or external, without some analysis of it into its parts. Besides the objects which we observe, and their qualities, we can reproduce in speech the mutual relations of objects, the relations of our thoughts to objects, and, lastly, the order and relation of our thoughts themselves. Now as the mind does not receive impressions passively, but reflects upon them, decomposes them into their elements, and compares them with notions already stored up, language, the close-fitting dress of our thoughts, is always analytical,—it does not body forth a mere picture of facts, but displays the working of the mind upon the facts submitted to it, with the order in which it regards them. This analysis has place even in the simplest descriptions. "The bird is flying" is an account of one object which we behold, and in its present condition. But the object was single, whilst our description calls up two notions—"bird" and "flying,"—and it is plain that this difference is the result of an analysis which the mind has performed, separating, in thought, the bird from its present action of flying, and then mentioning them together.* In painting and sculpture, on the contrary, we have languages that do not employ analysis; and a picture or statue would be called by some a *synthetic*, or compositive, sign, from the notion that in it all the elements and qualities of the object which would have been mentioned separately in a description, are *thrown together* and represented at one view. The statue of the Dying Gladiator gives at one glance all the principal qualities so finely

* See Mr. *Smart's* Sematology, ch. I. § 3.

analyzed by the following description, which, however, includes also the poet's reflections upon and inferences from the qualities he observes; the *objective* impression is described, but with a development of the *subjective* condition into which it throws the narrator.*

"I see before me the Gladiator lie:
He leans upon his hand—his manly brow
Consents to death but conquers agony,
And his drooped head sinks gradually low—
And through his side the last drops, ebbing slow
From the red gash, fall heavy, one by one,
Like the first of a thunder-shower; and now
The arena swims around him—he is gone,
Ere ceased the inhuman shout which hailed the wretch who won

"He heard it, but he heeded not—his eyes
Were with his heart, and that was far away;
He recked not of the life he lost, nor prize,
But where his rude hut by the Danube lay:
There were his young barbarians all at play,
There was their Dacian mother—he, their sire,
Butchered to make a Roman holiday!
All this rushed with his blood—shall he expire
And unavenged? Arise! ye Goths, and glut your ire!"

BYRON.

Here the analysis of the impression is carried to its farthest; and in the second stanza the object becomes quite subordinate to the inferences and fancies of the subject. But it is all the more striking as an illustration of the principle, that language presents to us the analysis, as painting and sculpture the imitations, of a sensible impression.

§ 21. But different languages are more or less analytic, and the same language becomes more analytic

* P. 25, note.

as literature and refinement increase.* This property indicates, as we should expect, corresponding changes in the state of thinking in different nations or in the same at different times. With increasing cultivation, finer distinctions are seen between the relations of objects, and corresponding expressions are sought for, to denote them; because ambiguity and confusion would result from allowing the same word or form of words to continue as the expression of two different things or facts. Many ambiguous phrases, however, are suffered to remain, although the inconvenience of them must have been perceived from the first; thus in Greek, the words ἡδοναὶ τέκνων bear the two opposite senses of "pleasures which children feel" and "pleasures derived from one's children," and in Latin *metus hostium* may mean either "the fear we have of our enemies," or "the fear our enemies have of us." In the Bible, words as important as "the love of God" express the pious regard we have towards our Father or his benignity towards his creatures. Prepositions are our interpreters to clear away this confusion. Again, where the powers of a particular case of a substantive were once sufficient to denote the person whose action the verb described, whilst the pronoun was only used as an additional mark when great emphasis was required, more modern habits, exalting the notion of personality, always assign a distinct word to the person. Thus the Greeks were able to express "I have a pain in my head" by three words, Ἀλγῶ τὴν κεφαλήν: they needed no word to distinguish the person, and

* See *Donaldson,* New Cratylus, B. I. ch. 3; *Duval-Jouve,* Logique, p. 203; *Damiron,* Logique, p. 207.

merely qualified the verb by "the head," to express the seat of the pain. Our expression analyzes the verb into three distinct notions, "I," the person, "pain," the thing I suffer, and "have," the relation; and shows more explicitly by the preposition "in" that the head is the seat of the pain. As a language acquires more of this character, and multiplies pronouns, prepositions, and conjunctions, it begins to forget its inflections, because it can express all their powers by circumlocution with these new expletives. As syntax becomes more complex, inflections grow simpler. Our own language has almost lost the terminations of cases and persons; and French writers attribute part of the clearness of their own tongue to the same cause, and to the consequent necessity of determining the relations of words clearly by proper connectives. The Greek has preserved its inflections, although it has also acquired a full and complicated syntax; which is owing probably to the fact that the Homeric poems moulded and set the former before the necessity for the latter had arisen. Perhaps the Greek of Homer shows more than its original complexity of syntax, from the touch of later editorial hands, like that of Peisistratus. Here then is a further use of language, and a proof of its intimate adaptation to thought. As the distinctions between the relations of objects grow more numerous, involved, and subtle, it becomes more analytic, to be able to express them; and, inversely, those who are born to be the heirs of a highly analytic language must needs learn to *think up* to it, to observe and distinguish all the relations of objects, for which they find the expressions already formed, so that we have an instructor for the thinking powers in that speech which we are apt to deem no more than their handmaid and minister.

§ 22. The superiority of spoken language over the language of painting and sculpture, has been the frequent subject of remark. One reason for it is that whilst the artist can only effect with certainty an impression upon the eye, and must depend upon the sensibility, often imperfect, of the spectators for the reproduction in their minds of the emotions that suggested his subject and guided his hand, the poet by his description can himself call up the appropriate feelings. Upon the forehead of the Dying Gladiator what chisel could inscribe plainly that which the poet bids us read there?

—"his manly brow
Consents to death but conquers agony."

In the picture of the Crucifixion at Antwerp, by Rubens, one of the most powerful specimens of "the brute-force of his genius," the action and purpose of more than one of the figures have been variously understood, and therefore by one party or another misunderstood. It is a disputed question whether the mounted soldier is looking with reverence at the chief Figure, or with cruel calmness at the agonies of one of the thieves; and whether the soldier on the ladder has broken the legs of the thief, or is preparing to do so. Art finds few to understand its sweet inarticulate language; but the plainer and fuller utterances of poetry cannot be misunderstood. Another reason of its superiority may be found in the greater power of words to *suggest associations* that knit up our present impression with others gained from the past, or, better still, bring our emotions and moral feelings into connection with our present impression. What painting of a house can ever convey so much to a feeling heart as the short description—"This is the home in which I spent my childhood?" The sculptor raises a tomb, and covers it with the ensigns of piety and death, but his art tells us less after all than the brief inscription, "He died for his country," or, "he looks for immortality."* The painter cannot dip his pencil in the hues of the spirit; the sculptor's drill and chisel cannot fix in matter the shapes which the mind assumes. The artist's thought remains unexplained, or depends upon the casual advent of congenial interpreters. In the comments upon our famous pictures and statues we have so many acknowledgments of the inferiority of the language of art to that of speech. Art would need no commentators, if it were thoroughly competent to tell its own story.

§ 23. (ii.) The *second* function we ascribed to language was that of preserving and recording our thoughts for future use; *nomina sunt notionum notæ.* A discovery can hardly be said to be secured, until it has been marked by a name which shall serve to recall it to those who have once mastered its nature, and to challenge the attention of those to whom it is still strange. Such words as inertia, affinity, polarization, gravitation, are summaries of so many laws of nature, and are so far happily chosen for their purpose, that, except perhaps the third, each of them

* Compare *Cousin,* Philosophie du Vrai, &c. leçon 27; and *Burke,* on the Sublime, § vii. 5.

guides us by its etymology towards the nature of the law it stands to indicate. When Gay-Lussac and Mitscherlich discovered that some chemical substances either crystallize in the same form, or may be substituted for one another in compounds without change in the form which the compounds assume, they were not content with a statement of this beautiful and instructive law, but they invented the name of *isomorphism* (tendency to equal forms) to be an index and summary of the law and the experiments that illustrated it. When two opposite theories of medicine are termed Homœopathy and Allopathy, these two compound words contain in fact an account of the opposing theories. A recent popular and instructive book* has reminded us that it is possible to exhume from under the words that are their monuments, many a buried and forgotten theory. Thus we speak of a jovial, a saturnine or a mercurial temper, without remembering that this implies an ascription of its qualities to the planet Jove or Saturn or Mercury. Physiologists now ignore the systems from which such terms as animal spirits, good humour, vapours, proceed. But if words often serve as tombstones, and remain when the theory has mouldered away, they are as often the keys by which we unlock the casket of the living and precious discovery, to exhibit it to the world. On the other hand, our eminent anatomist, Professor Owen, complains of the embarrassments produced in his science, by having to use a description where a name would serve; for instance, a particular bone is called by Soemmering

* *Trench* on the Study of Words, Parker, 1851. A logical student will find both amusement and profit in the little volume.

"pars occipitalis stricte sic dicta partis occipitalis ossis spheno-occipitalis,"* a description so clumsy that we may be certain the bone will not be mentioned more frequently than absolute need requires. In many cases, the privilege of giving the name which all the world shall employ, is conceded to the man or the nation who first clearly perceives the attributes, sees that they make one notion, and determines how it shall be designated. We are indebted to the finer observation of the French for the names *ennui*, *naïveté*, and *finesse*, for which we have given our own *comfortable* † in exchange; and an Englishman may notice with a smile of satisfaction that *das gentlemanlike* makes its appearance in a German author.

§ 24. But it is not only in the higher laws of science, or the more subtle qualities which social refinement develops in men and in society, that the power of naming is the power of fixing the fleeting colours of thought. So long as we are content with the bare reception of visual impressions, we can in a measure dispense with words, because our remembrance of the image of each object will serve instead of its name to ourselves, and a picture of it may represent it, though by a cumbrous and difficult process, to the minds of others. But thought never stops with the mere inspection of objects. In the simplest case, we proceed to *decompose* the sensitive impression into its parts. The tree which our eyes

* See *Owen* on the vertebrate skeleton in Report of British Association for 1846.

† "Mot Anglais," says *M. Philarete-Chasles* (ix. p. 16), "né d'un vieux mot Français." But *confortare* is found in the Latin of the Vulgate.

behold is found, upon reflection, to be tall or stunted, blooming or withered, old or young, straight or gnarled, waving in the wind or still; and these properties have no independent existence, but are parts of the visible object; they are *entia rationis*, and exist separately in the mind alone. Whence then, is our power of recalling them with such marvellous precision and facility? How is it that we can keep them safely apart in the mind, instead of being obliged to look for them mingled and confused, in the objects from which we first disentangled them by reflection? By virtue of the name we have attached to each of them; which, like the labels upon the chemist's jars or the gardener's flower-pots, enable us at once to identify and secure the property we seek. Names then are the means of fixing and recording the result of trains of thought, which without them must be repeated frequently, with all the pain of the first effort.*

§ 25. (iii.) Leibnitz was the first, so far as I know, to call attention to the fact that words are sometimes more than signs of thought; that they may become thoughts. His distinction between *symbolical* and *intuitive* [*notative*] conceptions † conducts us to the third function of language, that it abbreviates the processes of thought. Where our notion of any object or objects consists of a clear insight into all the attributes, or at least the essential ones, he would call it intuitive. But where the notion is complex, and its properties numerous, we do not commonly

* Upon this, consult *Damiron*, Logique, p. 200, seq. and *Duval Jouve*, Logique, p. 199, seq.; *Mill* on the Human Mind, vol. i. p. 86.

† *Erdmann's* Ed. p. 79. Acta Erudit. an. 1684.

realize all that it conveys; the process of thinking would be needlessly retarded by such a review. We make use of the name commonly given to the notion as a symbol, even for ourselves, of all the properties it possesses. A name then, employed in thought, is called a *symbolical cognition;* and the names we employ in speech are not always symbols to another of what is explicitly understood by us, but quite as often are symbols both to speaker and hearer, the full and exact meaning of which neither of them stop to unfold, any more than they regularly reflect that every sovereign which passes through their hands is equivalent to 240 pence. Such words as the state, happiness, liberty, creation, are too pregnant with meaning for us to suppose that we realize their full sense every time we read or pronounce them. If we attend to the working of our minds we shall find that each word may be used, and in its proper place and sense, though perhaps few or none of its attributes are present to us at the moment. A very simple notion is always intuitive; we cannot make our notion of brown or red simpler than it is, by any symbol. On the other hand a highly complex notion, like those named above, is seldom fully realized—seldom other than symbolical. Here then is a farther use of names; they serve to abbreviate the process of thought, as we have seen that they are useful in recording its results. And it may be noticed here that this distinction of cognitions throws a new light on the nature of definitions, or explanatory propositions, which are not, as they are often regarded, mere explanations to others of a meaning which we ourselves duly apprehend, but are real acts of thought, which by unfolding before us some marks of our conception, partially or wholly unseen by us, have all the power of new truths even for ourselves.

§ 26. (iv.) That language hath a fourth use, the most obvious of all, as the medium of communication between mind and mind, needs no explanation. We might dispense with articulate speech for certain purposes, and might make gestures and changes of the countenance, which are the language of action, supply its place. But actions and the play of features, whilst they serve to express love or hatred for some present object, need of food or rest, joy or sorrow, can but express a very small and confined list of thoughts if we would indicate our feelings towards some absent person, or our wish for something at a distance, or direct attention to some inward state or sentiment; we cannot guide the thoughts of the spectator to the object present to our own mind, with any precision and certainty. Hence, it is necessary to appropriate to every object a signal, always available, which all men by a tacit convention accept as a substitute for the object, and which therefore recalls the object to the fancy whenever it is employed; and such a signal is a noun or name, defined by Aristotle to be "a sound which by convention is significant, but does not determine time."* The

* *῎Ονομα μὲν οὖν ἐστὶ φωνὴ σημαντικὴ κατὰ συνθήκην ἄνευ χρόνου, ἧς μηδὲν μέρος ἐστὶ σημαντικὸν κεχωρισμένον.—On Enouncement, ch.* 2. (The last words express that it divides into syllables only, and not words, otherwise it would be a sentence.) *Ῥῆμα* (verb) *δέ ἐστι τὸ προς σημαῖνον χρόνον.—Ch.* 3. *J. C. Scaliger* traced the distinction between the noun and the verb to a difference of time, for the noun represented a permanent thing, the verb a temporary and transitory state.

convention or agreement by which a whole nation confines a noun to one object or class of objects, is of course merely tacit; whatever theory of the origin of language we adopt, we cannot suppose that a nation ever formally met and agreed upon the several names that should thenceforward express their various notions. Language is based upon general agreement, if we give our assent to its use every day by hearing and answering it, just as truly as if the view of Maupertuis were correct, that language was originally formed by a session of learned societies. Names however are representatives of things; and the different states of things must find an expression likewise; hence the need of adjectives and verbs. The verb has the power of assigning to the thing at a particular time the condition of being, doing, or undergoing something; but as every verb may be resolved into an adjective-notion, and one particular word simply expressive of past or present or future state, as, for example, "he loved" is explained by "he was—loving," "he hopes" by "he is—hoping," we are justified in regarding all verbs as fundamentally one, the verb *to be*, with its three times or tenses of *is*, *was*, *shall be*, and their variety as arising from the incorporation of various adjective-notions with this simple verbal element. When two or more names come together, it is frequently necessary to express the mutual relation in which they stand; a thing may be to, from, by, in, near, above, or below another, and prepositions are invented to determine this. Here then are the four principal parts of speech, substantives, or names to express substances, adjectives to stand for attributes, prepositions to denote relations, and a single verb to assign attributes or relations to substantives at a determinate time.*

§ 26. Aristotle's mode of arranging the classes of words admits of a brief, and (it may be hoped) intelligible statement. Words are conventional signs of what takes place in the mind; natural signs, as a scream to express terror, a scowl for hatred, a laugh for pleasant surprise, are not to be ranked among them. The question whether some sounds are not naturally more suitable to certain ideas, for examples, the sound of *st* to express strength and solidity, in stand, stout, sturdy, stick, stop, stubborn, or the sound of *wr* to express turning with an effort, as in wring, writhe, wrest, wrestle, wrist, is passed over; and it is evident that even if the sounds are suitable to the ideas they express, there was no necessity for adopting them, and they are, like the rest, subject to a tacit convention. Now some words, or rather vocal sounds, are simple, and consist of parts which, taken separately, have no meaning, or at least are not intended to have any in their present position; such are the single sounds which we call words, as weapon, free, hardship, master, in which the components—ship and mast—have lost their proper meaning on entering into their several words. Some again are more complex, and are not only significant themselves, but consist of significant parts; these are what we call propositions or sentences, as The sun

* See *Condillac, Grammaire,* ch. viii. The more advanced student will not fail to notice that as the ten Categories of Aristotle answer to the parts of speech, so the simpler division of categories adopted by many later writers, into substance, attribute and relation, answers to three parts of speech. See below, the Section on Categories.

has set. Following first the simple words, we find that some of them express a state or action at a given time, and are known as verbs; others again are irrespective of time, and are called nouns. Of nouns, some have a sense independent of any auxiliary words, and therefore can be employed alone as terms in a proposition, as city, wilderness, revenue; others require the aid of other words to complete and determine their meaning, as—of a city, good, to Greece, which prompt the questions, *what part* of a city? Good *what?* What happened to Greece? and therefore are not complete in themselves. The former, properly speaking, are perfect nouns or names, but the latter, which include all cases of nouns except the nominative, are only parts of compound names, and require an addition to complete them. If a verb is added to one of the imperfect names, there will not be an intelligible sentence. Perfect names again might be either definite or indefinite, though the latter, which are nothing more than nouns with a negative prefix, as non-philosopher, are hardly worthy to be called names, both because they represent too large a number of objects, and because we explain them by saying what they do *not* mean. Turning now from simple words to propositions, we notice that some sentences are declaratory, as All must die; others are only precatory or exclamatory, as "Oh that this too too solid flesh would melt!" Truth and falsehood, with the investigation of which Logic is concerned, belong only to the declaratory propositions, and indeed these only can truly be called propositions.

DIVISION OF WORDS.

(See *Aristotle on En.* Ch. i.—iii.)

- Words
  - Whose parts have no meaning—simple words.
    - Verbs
    - Nouns
      - Perfect
      - Imperfect
    - (Verbs and Nouns:) Definite / Indefinite
  - Whose parts have meaning—sentences.
    - Declaratory—true or false propositions.
    - Not declaratory, as a prayer or wish.

§ 27. It is the province of Universal Grammar to examine the means of oral and written communication, and their laws; and the hints here offered are rather intended to suggest than to supersede a further study of that science; to which alone belong the details of the doctrine of the Parts of Speech and their construction. Our business has been to point out the principal uses of language in aiding the process of thought. But great as these services are, it must not be supposed that an examination of the rules of language would answer every purpose of a logical system. As we are now constituted, our thoughts are invariably clothed in speech; we use words even if we do not utter them. But if articulate speech were withdrawn from man, it cannot be supposed that thought would for ever cease. On the contrary, wherever personal defects or external circumstances deprive the mind of this means of communication, it succeeds in providing an efficient substitute, and attains by practice much the same facility in the use of it as we enjoy in the exercise of the powers of speaking. Those among the deaf and dumb who have been taught by the pains of an enlightened humanity to converse and to think, must use, instead of the remembered words which we employ, the remembered images of hands in the various combinations of finger-speech, as the symbols of their thoughts. The deaf and blind, taught the names of objects from raised letters, must think, not by associations of sound, but of touch. The telegraph, and the signals on railroads, are new modes of speech; and though an inexpert practitioner may have at first to translate such signs into common language, the skill which comes from practice soon prompts him to omit this needless intermediate step. The engine driver shuts off the steam at the warning sign, without thinking of the words to which it is equivalent; a particular signal becomes associated with a particular act, and the interposition of words become superfluous. Dr. Hooke, the inventor of the telegraph, called it "a method of discoursing at a distance, not by sound but by sight;" and it is conceivable that we might learn to think by the telegraphic signals, so that "red flag over blue," seen with the eye or recalled by the memory, might be our *word* for happiness. Leibnitz,* suggests the possibility of employing various tones instead of articulate words to convey our notions; and mentions that the Chinese, having a slender vocabulary, use the aid of tone and accent to vary and augment it. The *Ranz-des-vaches* that rends asunder the heart of the Swiss exile, to him is but a *word* for "country and home;"

* Nouv. Ess. iii. 1

and the signet of the king sent to his servant, or the broken *astragalus*, by which the "guest-friend" reminded his fellow of his plighted hospitality, are signs which plainly and certainly suggest thoughts, and therefore they are words also. Without thought, language would cease; but we can conceive the language we use might be denied to us, and yet thought still proceed with the assistance of some other class of signs. And it is scarcely philosophical to found an analysis of the reasoning powers upon that which, however useful to the reason, may be conceived to be universally, as it is now in isolated cases, separated from it, without destroying its action. Granting that the processes of thought may be traced to a great extent in the signs which it employs, they are still but signs, and if the process beneath them can be examined in itself—as we need not fear to maintain that it can—then to view it only in the instruments it uses is to leave our survey shallow and incomplete. Logic should expound the laws of thinking, and universal Grammar the laws of speech, apart from their special modifications in any given language. These two sciences would mutually illustrate each other; whilst a clear separation between them would probably have the effect of elevating the latter into an importance not hitherto assigned it. But no confusion can result from introducing principles of language into Logic, as has been often done, so long as thinking is made the adequate object matter of the science, and language comes in only as the minister of thought.

§ 28. The question we have just considered—whether thinking could proceed without articulate words as its signs—must be distinguished from the more difficult one—whether thinking could dispense with *all* signs. The latter we do not pretend to answer here; but it may be hinted that thinking and science are not identical, that even if trains of systematic reasoning are quite beyond the reach of any but a speaking, "word-dividing" being, the simpler acts of thought may perhaps be within his reach. Without language, all the mighty triumphs of man over nature which science has achieved would have been impossible. But this does not prove that man might not, without speech, observe objects, gather them into groups in his mind, judge of their properties, and even deduce something from his judgment. Weak and incomplete the process of thought would be; but we dare hardly say that one could not think at all. But in no subject is it more necessary to distinguish between the actual, and the merely conceivable. Language and thought have never been put asunder, but in a few exceptional cases. With some nations they have the same name; with all, the rules of the one are readily applied to the other.

§ 29. The opinions about the origin of language may be divided into three classes, as follows.

a. The belief that man at his creation was endowed with a full, perfect, and copious language, and that as his faculties were called forth by observation and experience, this language supplied him at every step with names for the various objects he encountered. In this view, which has found many able advocates, speech is separated from, and precedes, thought; for as there must have been a variety of phenomena both outward and in his mind, to which the first man was a stranger, until long experience gradually unfolded them, their names must have been entrusted to him long before the thoughts or images which they were destined ultimately to represent, were excited in his mind.

b. The belief that the different families of men, impelled by necessity, invented and settled by agreement the names that should represent the ideas they possessed. In this view language is a human invention, grounded on convenience. But "to say that man has invented language, would be no better than to assert that he has invented law. To make laws, there must be a law obliging all to keep them; to form a compact to observe certain institutes, there must be already a government protecting this compact. To invent language, presupposes language already, for how could men agree to name different objects without communicating by words their designs?" In proof of this opinion, appeal is made to the great diversity of languages. Here it is supposed again that thought and language were separate, and that the former had made some progress before the latter was annexed to it.

c. The third view is, that as the Divine Being did not give man at his creation actual knowledge, but the power to learn and to know, so He did not confer a language but the power to name and describe. The gift of reason, once conveyed to man, was the common root from which both thought and speech proceeded, like the pith and the rind of the tree, to be developed in inseparable union. With the first inspection of each natural object, the first imposition of a name took place: "Out of the ground the Lord God formed every beast of the field, and every fowl of the air; and brought them unto Adam to see what he would call them; and whatsoever Adam called every living creature, that was the name thereof." (Gen. ii. 19.) In the fullest sense, language is a divine gift, but the power and not the results of its exercise, the germ and not the tree, was imparted. A man can teach names to another man, but nothing less than divine power can plant in another's mind the far higher gift, the faculty of naming. From the first we have reason to believe that the functions of thought and language went together. A conception received a name; a name recalled a conception; and every accession to the knowledge of things expanded the treasures of expression. And we are entangled in absurdities by any theory which assumes that either element existed in a separate state, antecedently to the other.

§ 30. It is impossible to trace the growth of language with certainty; but it is most probable that many of the *roots* of the primitive language were originally imitations of the various sounds emitted by things in the natural world. A bird or animal perhaps received a name derived from, and resembling, its own peculiar utterance. The cry or exclamation that man emitted instinctively under the pressure of some strong feeling, would be consciously reproduced to represent or recall the feeling on another occasion; and it then became a word, or vicarious sign. Where natural sounds failed, analogy would take the place of imitation; words harsh and difficult to pronounce would be preferred to stand for unpleasing objects, over those of a more bland

and facile character, which would be appropriated to pleasant things and conceptions. Mere agreement among those who used the language, would be sufficient to stamp a vocal sound as the name of a certain object, where neither imitation nor analogy suggested one. But these original roots, the simplest form of substantives, would gradually become less and less discernible as the language grew richer and more intricate. Wherever new arts are practised, we may easily find opportunities of watching the growth of new names for its instruments and processes, guided by these three principles, imitation, analogy, and mere convention.

§ 31. The various parts of speech took their origin from the noun and verb, or possibly from the noun alone.* Many instances can be found of adverbs and prepositions which are distinctly substantives, and of conjunctions which are but parts of verbs. Then the close connection between the verb and noun is indicated by the number of words which, in our own language, are both verb and noun, and only distinguished by mode of pronunciation. Inflexions perhaps originated in the addition of one word to another, so that the terminations of nouns and verbs are in reality distinct words incorporated with them. These are but slender hints of the direction in which profound and acute researches have been made. And I do not think that such attempts to dissect and analyze language, pursued with proper caution, tend at all to lower our esti-

* "Omnes Hebreæ voces, exceptis tantum interjectionibus et conjunctionibus, et una aut altera particula, vim et proprietates nominis habent."—*Spinosa, Gram. Heb* 5.

mate of the importance of the gift of speech, or of its marvellous nature. It is not more wonderful surely that the Giver of Good has endowed man with a complete language, than that He has endowed him with faculties which out of the shrieks of birds in the forest, the roar of beasts, the murmur of rushing waters, the sighing of the wind, and his own impulsive ejaculations, have constructed the great instrument that Demosthenes and Shakspeare and Massillon wielded, the instrument by which the laws of the universe are unfolded and the subtle workings of the human heart brought to light. But in no line of inquiry is caution more necessary, are deductions more likely to be fallacious. It does not follow that a word as we use it now bears a gross, narrow or material sense, because the root to which we can refer it had a limited meaning, and was connected with matter. If *truth* according to its etymology means that which we *trow* or think, according to long usage it means that which is certain whether we think it or not; if spirit meant originally no more than breath, it has so far left that sense behind, that when the breath is exhaled the spirit remains immortal.*

* On the origin and growth of Language, see *Herder Ursprung des Spraches* (a prize Essay); *Rauch's Psychology*, New York, 1840; *Tooke's Diversions of Purley; Harris's Hermes; Donaldson's New Cratylus; Mansel's Prolegomena*, p. 17; *Cousin, Frag. Philos.* on *Maine du Biran; Duval-Jouve, Logique*, §§ 189, seq.; *Plato's Cratylus.*

OUTLINE

OF THE

LAWS OF THOUGHT.

INTRODUCTION.

CONCLUDED.

"Hujus disciplinæ studium atque cognitio in principiis quidem tetra et aspernabilis insuavisque esse et inutilis videri solet: sed ubi aliquantum processeris, tum denique et emolumentum ejus in animo tuo dilucebit, et sequetur quædam discendi voluptas insatiabilis."—AULUS GELLIUS.

§ 32.

LOGIC *has been called an* a priori *science.* The distinction between truths *a priori* and truths *a posteriori*, as observed universally by modern writers, may be drawn as follows. If there are any truths which the mind possesses, whether consciously or unconsciously, before and independent of experience, they may be called *a priori* truths, as belonging to it *prior* to all that it acquires from the world around. On the other hand, truths which are acquired by observation and experience, are called *a posteriori* truths, because they come to the mind *after* it has become acquainted with external facts. How far *a priori* truths or ideas are possible, is the great *campus philosophorum*, the great controverted question of mental philosophy. In entering into it, and that only so far as our present purpose requires, we must remove from it one great cause of misunderstanding. No one at present maintains that the mind can know any thing at a point of time before its observation of external things began; a mind in that condition would be full of thick darkness. However independent of experience any process may appear to be now, as for instance that by which geometrical truths are proved, we may be sure that we made much use of observation before we educed the very laws which place it in our minds far above all need of confirmatory evidence from observation. A mind which never observed, would not be a mind. But the question is whether even the facts which we observe do not furnish evidence that something has been in the mind before it was directed to the facts; just as we know by looking at something that we have eyes, and must have had them before we looked, although without putting them to their proper use we could never have known that we had them at all.* Now without going into the dispute as to how much of our knowledge is *a priori*, we may be able to show that at least the conditions of all knowledge are so, —that the mind does not simply reflect the images of things without, but impresses characters of her own upon them,—that our knowledge of things is not the exact counterpart of the things, but of the things and the mind operating together. When we

* *Coleridge, Lit. Rem.* i. 326; and *Friend,* i 307, note.

see our image in a mirror (to use Bacon's similitude), we know that our shape is the cause of it on the one side and the power of reflection in the mirror on the other; if we were to see it multiplied, or increased, or diminished, or changed in hue, we should infer that the mirror had several angular faces, or was concave, or convex, or made of tinted glass. Each of these properties would be inherent in the mirror *prior* to our presenting ourselves before it; they are its *a priori* laws; although we could only ascertain them *a posteriori*, by a trial. When an image is received upon the mirror of the mind, we see that the latter also has its laws and properties. Our remark upon one object of common occurrence is "the bird is flying against the wind." Have we here no more than the single object which the eye presents? There are three distinct notions, of a bird, of its being in the act of flying, of the direction of its flight; so that the mind has decomposed the one object into three impressions; and there is besides an act of deciding upon the agreement of these impressions, expressed by the word "is." And as the object does not resolve *itself* into three parts, but is to all intents and purposes one, and as there can be nothing in the object to correspond to the act of judging expressed by the word "is," we conclude that the power of analysis of the simple impression into three, together with that of judging upon it, belong to the mind itself. Further, as we have no reason to think that this object created the two powers, or did more than call them into action, we conclude that they were present *a priori*, that is, prior to the impression from without. And again, for the same reason that they are not found in this object of sense,—that is, because they decompose it into many parts and judge upon its parts, which no object can do for itself—we conclude that they were not learnt from any object we may have seen before; and therefore they are absolutely *a priori*, they are independent of all experience.*

§ 33. Hence we may understand the importance which attaches to Leibnitz's well-known comment on the maxim of the school of Locke †; to the *nihil est in intellectu, quod non fuerit in sensu*, he adds — *nisi intellectus ipse.* The mind does not simply receive the impressions of the senses, like the passive surface of a mirror; it groups them, judges about them, separates their qualities from each other, and draws inferences about the qualities which like objects, hitherto unknown, may be expected to have. But qualities, classes, inferences, are not objects of sense, however they may reside in or be drawn from those objects. They have no separate existence out of the mind; whilst, within it, they are perfectly distinct. This transmutation of objects of sense into their elements must therefore be the work of the mind alone. It is

* The various modes of expressing the antithesis between thoughts and things are here exhibited in a tabular form :—

Man, .	as opposed to	Nature
Thoughts,	„ „	Things
Theories,	„ „	Facts
Reflection,	„ „	Sensation
Subject,	„ „	Object
Form,	„ „	Matter.

Whewell's Phil. of Ind. Sci. vol. I. B. i.

† *Leibnitz, Nouveaux Essais,* ii. I. p. 223, *Erdmann's Ed. Locke* himself admits "ideas of reflection," gained by observing the mind's own actions, besides "ideas of sensation." *On Hum. Under.* II. v. 1.

a law of the intellect itself, and never was nor can have been in the sensuous impressions we have received.

§ 34. Pure Logic treats only of those laws or conditions to which objects of sense are subjected in the mind; and hence it is called an *à priori* science. It unfolds the laws of the *intellectus ipse*, and gives no account of the representations of the senses as such. It will enumerate, for instance, all the different kinds of judgments which can be formed, but will not pretend to decide upon the truth of any one judgment respecting something which is now before the eyes. As the laws of the understanding are few and invariable, whilst the phenomena in the world around us appear, from our imperfect knowledge of their complicated laws, very uncertain, Logic is far less liable to error than those sciences which have to do with external facts. Thus the truth that "if A is B and B is C, then A must be C," cannot be denied, whatever we suppose these letters to represent. The formula is universal and necessary; it was so in the days of Aristotle, and will be as long as there remains upon the face of the world one mind to think. But an *a posteriori* science—a science of external facts—like Astronomy, though using demonstration, depends upon observation, and the accuracy of its calculations is in a direct ratio to our opportunities of observing all the circumstances which may affect them. It can never be a necessary truth that after each interval of two hundred and twenty-three lunations the sun will be eclipsed: grounded only upon facts, whenever some convulsion shall be prepared by the Creator to disturb them, its prediction will fail. Calculations of the period of the return of comets have sometimes failed, because of our defective means of observation; thus the return of the comet of 1770 was promised in five years and a half; it falsified the prediction, and never returned at all.

This view of Logic as an *a priori* science, it is hoped, will meet with a pretty general assent; and we purposely abstain from touching the great question of Metaphysics — how much of our knowledge is from the mind itself and how much from experience. The conflicting opinions upon this matter will never be reconciled, and perhaps the best service which philosophy could receive would be rendered by marking out the region which must be mutually ceded by the opposite schools.*

§ 35. By explaining some of the various names bestowed on Logic by those who have treated it, we shall have a clear view of the position they intended it to occupy. (a.) It has been called the Architectonic Art, by which is meant that it occupies the same position with regard to the sciences and arts in general, that Architecture does to the labors of the carpenter, the mason, the paviour, the plumber and

* Before leaving the subject, it must be noticed that the term *a priori* has undergone important changes of meaning. In *Aristotle's* philosophy the general truth is "naturally prior" (πρότερον τῇ φύσει) to the particular, and the cause to the effect; but since *we* know the particular before the universal, and the effect before we seek the cause, the particular and the effect are each "prior in respect to us" (πρότερον πρὸς ἡμᾶς). *Anal. Post.* I. ii; *Top.* VI. iv.; *Metaphys.* V. (Δ) xi. p. 1018. *Ed. Berol.* Following this, the Schoolmen call the argument which proceeds from cause to effect, *a priori* demonstration. But with *Hume* (*Skeptical Doubts*) *a priori* has the sense given in the text, which *Kant* has fixed in the language of philosophy. See *Trendelenburg's* Excerpta, p. 81, Ed. III.; *Sir W. Hamilton's Reid*, p. 762.

the glazier; arranging and directing them indeed so as to contribute to one common end, but not necessarily knowing the details of their business, nor putting its hand to their toil. Used by Plato as an illustration (*Polit.* 259, *E.*) the word Architectonic was adopted by Aristotle as a general name for all arts which kept other arts subservient to them (*Eth. Nic.* I. i.). And as the rules of Logic must be obeyed not by one art or the other but by every one, other writers were naturally led to apply the name Architectonic to it especially. The same supremacy is vindicated to Logic in another of its names; by the followers of Aristotle it was called (b.) the Instrument (or Organon) and the Instrument of Instruments. Aristotle himself did not affix the name of Organon to that collection of logical treatises that now bears the name; but he speaks of our possessing in ourselves two instruments (ὄργανα) by which we can employ external instruments, the hand for the body *and reason for the soul;* and adds that science is the instrument of reason;* and it is probable that Alexander and John Philoponus were led by these and similar expressions to apply to the laws of reasoning, as displayed in the two "Analytics" of their master, the name of the "Instrument," or Organon. Once affixed to these treatises, it was soon extended so as to embrace all the works that are now included under it. Elsewhere Aristotle calls the hand of man "an instrument before instruments" and "an instrument of instruments," and again compares the mind to the hand, so that to transfer this

* *Arist. Probl.* Λ. 5, (955, b.) *De An.* Γ. 8, (432, a. I.) *Polit.* A. 8, (1253, b.)

compound title also to Logic is just as agreeable to the master's mode of expression. Because the rules of Logic are employed in every scientific inquiry, Logic may well be called emphatically the instrument of the mind, just as the hand is the instrument employed before all others in every act with which the body is concerned. Further, just as a hand wielding a spade may be considered an instrument with an instrument, so may Logic when directing the procedure of another science (and where is the science it does not direct?) be regarded as an instrument with an instrument. By its title of Architectonic we recognized Logic as the chief or master-science; by the title Instrument of Instruments we assert that it is the science next and nearest to the mind itself, by which it handles, as it were, the other sciences. Some logicians of eminence indeed refuse to give Logic any other title; thus Zabarella (*de Nat. Log.* I. x.) denies that it is either an Art or a Science or a Faculty in the proper sense, and affirms that the name of Organon is alone applicable to it. Other names which establish the preëminence of Logic over the real sciences will not require any explanation; such are (c.) the Art of Arts (*ars artium*), (d.) the System of Systems (*disciplina disciplinarum*), (e.) the Key of Wisdom, (f.) the Head and Crown of Philosophy (*caput et apex philosophiæ*). But these swelling titles must not lead us to forget that if Logic is the highest science of all, it is also the servant of all; if it is the widest in its scope, it is also by itself the most bare and fruitless; it gives no knowledge of things, for it is an instrumental and not a real science, and only when working in conjunction with sciences of humbler style and pretensions can it further the interests of philosophy or add to the stock of useful knowledge.— As it offers rules for seeking after truth it has been called (g.) Zetetic or the Art of Seeking; as these rules are not given in vain, we may regard it also as (h.) Heuristic or the Art of Discovering Truth. As it cures the mind of prejudices and errors, it is called (i.) *Medicina Mentis*, and (k.) the Cathartic of the Mind. Logic, upon a lower view of its pretensions, as teaching the right use of the faculties in the discussion of any question, with or without the purpose of attaining truth, is called (l.) Dialectic.* The name of (m.) Canon was given by Epicurus to the Logic of his school, though, if we may trust Diogenes and Cicero, it was a very different system from, and much more free from technical details than, the Logic in general use. But in the sense of a rule by which thoughts are to be gauged and measured, to secure their truth and correctness, it may be applied to any view of logical science.

§ 36. *Uses and pretensions of Logic.* The acts of the mind are so quick, so numerous, so complex, that they are not easy to note and describe, although we

* With *Aristotle,* Analytic teaches the formal laws of thought, which philosophy applies to the discovery of truth; Dialectic (as taught in the "Topics") is a popular application of these laws to discussion and the defence of a proposition, rather than to the attainment of truth, although it makes attempts in that direction; Rhetoric closely resembles Dialectic, in using popular forms of argument and in postponing truth to some lower aim, only that the aim of the former is to work conviction in the intellect, that of the latter to persuade, through the intellect and the moral nature combined; Sophistic is like Dialectic, except that it seeks to mislead under pretence of convincing us of a truth, and so implies a wrong moral bias; and Eristic is the art of disputing cleverly so as to put an adversary to silence.

paily perform them, and that without serious mistake. Logicians have generally erred on the side of underrating the number both of the mental processes themselves, and of the particular acts which go to the attainment of any judgment or conception. As the act of standing erect, so simple apparently, calls into operation a numerous array of muscles, by means of which the body perpetually sways and adjusts itself, without conscious effort, so we may believe that the mind goes through acts, which from long practice scarcely awaken her own attention, much less the sense of pain and effort, yet which involve a great number of subordinate acts, depending on distinct principles. And as it takes the physiologist many pages of explanation to analyze a posture which a three-years' child assumes and retains without difficulty, so the logician seems to spend too many words upon the rules of thinking, since all men, from the statesman to the clown, are able to think, whether they have learnt rules or not. To show that the complexity we speak of, really belongs to thoughts apparently very simple, we may examine an example. When Captain Head was travelling across the Pampas of South America, "his guide one day suddenly stopped him, and, pointing high into the air, cried out 'A lion!' Surprised at such an exclamation, accompanied with such an act, he turned up his eyes, and with difficulty perceived, at an immeasurable height, a flight of condors soaring in circles in a particular spot. Beneath this spot, far out of sight of himself or guide, lay the carcass of a horse, and over that carcass stood, as the guide well knew, a lion, whom the condors were eyeing with envy from their airy height. The signal of the birds was to him what the sight of the lion alone would have been to the traveller, a full assurance of its existence."* Here was an act of thought which cost the thinker no trouble, which was as easy to him as to cast his eyes upward, yet which from us, unaccustomed to the subject, would require many steps and some labour. The sight of the condors convinced him that there was some carcass or other; but as they kept wheeling far above it instead of swooping down to their feast, he guessed that some beast had anticipated them. Was it a dog or a jackal? No; the condors would not fear to drive away, or share with, either; it must be some large beast; and as lions abounded, or had been seen in the neighbourhood, he concluded that one was here. These steps of thought at least, and probably many more, rushed through his mind with the proverbial swiftness of thought, but they were summed up in the words "A lion." Daily and hourly we run through similar or more complicated trains of thinking, with no more consciousness of the several links than the organ-player has of each note he strikes in a rapid passage of full harmony. As the logician professes to give an account of the thinking process, he must try to follow all these out, and show the laws on which they severally depend. He may incur the charge of tediousness in showing (for instance) that our notion of "house" is formed by the successive steps of Comparison, Reflection, Abstraction, and Generalization, for every one has been forming such general notions all his life without knowing one of these hard names; or that "he will

* *Sir J. Herschel's Prelim. Discourse*, p 84.

come, for he said he would," contains three terms and three propositions, joined together by a sign of inference, which constitutes them a syllogism; for we can all manage our inferences without these formalities. But still he must not shorten his explanation at the expense of truth; these are laws of thought, and it is his business to ascertain them, just as the physiologist thinks himself bound to examine all the laws of the bodily motions and positions so unconsciously assumed. But is there any gain to mankind from this analysis? Would not natural logic suffice, without a number of technical rules, uninviting to learn, hard to remember, and seldom applied? What is the *use* of Logic?—I answer, that knowledge itself is a use, and that all legitimate inquiry rewards itself with its own pleasures. The appetite for finding out laws from facts, causes from effects, necessary truth from fleeting occurrences of the day, puts in its claim to gratification, which is as legitimate, if less imperious, as that of the animal nature for food and sleep. The studies which enwrapt the soul of Archimedes in the siege, of Aquinas at the royal feast, of Joseph Scaliger during the massacre of Saint Bartholomew's, must have been a source of pleasure, pure and high, from which they had a right to draw. If the question, what "fruit" does it bring?—which the Baconian philosophy puts so often—be understood, as it certainly ought not, to refer only to the *material* wants and comforts of humanity, it is a base, sordid, and stupid question, against which every better mind indignantly protests. Science was never brought to its present height by hopes of wealth, plenty, and comfort alone, but chiefly by those *mirabiles amores* with which she can inspire her followers. He who loves to see the processes of his mind reduced to their laws and causes, to him are logical studies a pleasure—to him they bring fruit.

§ 37. But whilst even the coldest followers of Bacon * admit that the value of science must not be estimated by what she can actually perform, no doubt it must be granted that even the highest sciences do condescend to help our lowest wants. Astronomy, Chemistry, Geology, and Mechanics not only furnish delightful contemplations to the student, but they put food into the mouths of the vulgar; they clothe them, and fill their purses, they put houses over their heads, and adorn them with objects of beauty and convenience. Logic has its use also in improving the condition of men; it teaches, or perhaps I may only say, may be made to teach, them to think. This is often denied, and partly on account of the extravagant claims put forward by logicians, who assume that the acquisition of a few logical rules will enable men to think correctly, just as the possession of a watch enables them to ascertain the hour. No science can make such pretensions. The active intellect has two parts, one of which originates our thoughts, and may be called the suggestive, whilst the other checks and judges thoughts as they arise, and may be called the critical, power. Thoughts are continually suggested without the consent of the will. One would think indeed, were it not for the obvious similarity these spontaneous visitors bear to

* See *M. Comte, Philosophie*, iii. p. 280, as against the brilliant but (I think) mistaken view of Bacon and the old philosophers, in *Macaulay's Misc. Essays. " Bacon."*

the matter of former study, that they were in no sense our own, that an independent being, over whom one had absolutely no control, was whispering within us. In the poetical temperament, where the power of suggestion strongly predominates, the thoughts which arise are less like any thing one remembers, than in ordinary minds; and hence poets have maintained, perhaps in full sincerity, that an unseen spiritual power, higher than themselves, used them as the channel of its teaching,—that they were inspired.* The suggestive power may be educated as certainly as, though more gradually than, the critical. The discovery which we call a flash of genius, a happy thought, really depends as much upon previous acquirements, as the power of stating a case or applying a rule does. These bright suggestions never occur to the ignorant; † they have the facts before them, but their imaginations are not trained to leap to the proper inference from them. All discipline of the suggestive must proceed from the critical power; it is by a long, careful, patient analysis of the reasonings by which others have attained their results, that we learn to think more correctly ourselves. He who reads over a work upon Logic

* *Plato* again and again mentions this claim of poets. See *Ion*, 533; *D. Apol. Soc.* 22; *B. C. Legg.* 719; *C. Meno*, 99; *B. C. Phædrus* 245. *A. Stallbaum* (*Preface to Ion*) does not think that *Plato* would deny to the poet a modifying power over the dictating principle. But the truth is, *Plato* still allows them all they claim, in order that the want of independence (*αὐτοπραγία*) may be seen and despised. Compare *Ovid* (*Fasti*, vi. 5.); *Cicero* (*de Div.* i. 37.); *Morgenstern* (*de Rep.* p. 296.). Dictation and inspiration are distinguished. *Coleridge's Table Talk*, ii. 30.

† See this beautifully illustrated in *Whewell, Phil. Ind. Sci.* B. xi. § 5. And below, the section on Anticipation.

probably thinks no better when he rises up than when he sat down; but if any of the principles there unfolded cleave to his memory, and he afterwards, perhaps unconsciously, shapes and corrects his thoughts by them, no doubt his whole powers of reasoning gradually receive benefit. Perhaps the principal advantage which science has received from Bacon's great work has arisen from his denouncement of hasty generalization,* which being easily remembered, and applicable to all subjects, has much influenced the practice of all scientific students. In a word, every art, from Reasoning down to Riding and Rowing, is learnt by assiduous practice, and if principles do any good, it is proportioned to the readiness with which they can be converted into rules, and the patient constancy with which they are applied in all our attempts to excel.

§ 38. No one will pretend to say that Logic has been fairly treated in this respect. Our view of the elements of Logic has indeed been very imperfect, and would be quite insufficient for scientific analysis; but no attempt has been made to widen and improve it, because we have not tried to put it to use, and so found out its inadequacy. In some popular treatises, of latest date, both English and French, the rules of syllogism are passed lightly over, as rusty weapons that have no place in the armory of science—"You will find them somewhere—in Aristotle, in the Schoolmen, or in Manuals;—we admit their exist-

* *Nov. Organ.* I. 19, 20, 22. Not that *Bacon* first discovered this abuse of the law of Anticipation. *Plato* knew it well enough (*Philebus*, 16, E. οἱ δὲ νῦν κ. τ. λ.), and has stated it almost in the same way.

ence, but to teach them is beside our purpose ;—we present you only with a small specimen or two for curiosity's sake." This course is to us unintelligible. The rules in question claim to be those which regulate the act of reasoning; if a system professes to teach reasoning, it should either give us the rules complete, or prove that they are false or defective. A large book on Logic that refers us to another book for the rules of the great logical act, does not fulfil its duty; and suggests a suspicion that these rules have not been made use of as the instrument of scientific research—that proper trouble has not been taken to ascertain how far they are really applicable to such a purpose, and how far absurd and useless. I believe that if a set of rules, as free from technicalities of form and expression as is consistent with complete accuracy, be sedulously applied to the examination of the books we read, more especially to the history and theory of some particular science, the mind will receive great and signal benefit, and the creative powers will be increased as well as the judgment strengthened. In past days it was worth while to learn the scholastic terminology, because it ran through all scientific practice; the theology and metaphysics of Aquinas and Occham vindicate their right to spend time upon the barbarisms of their Logic. Let us get by degrees a Logic which is to our philosophy what that of the Schoolmen was to theirs, and no one will complain that some of its expressions are technical and its rules hard to understand. Technicalities are only wearisome, where we have no hope of their after-fruits to lure us through them.

On these grounds, we try to make the analysis of thinking as complete as possible, and beg the student to master a few new names, expecting that the trouble so bestowed will not be grudged as a preparation for that habitual examination of thoughts and arguments which is the great means of teaching us to reason. For, the rules of Logic, those of syllogism, for example, do not teach a new trick of argument, nor furnish an instrument by the possession of which we are at once enabled to speak or dispute. There is neither trick nor magic in them; they are principles which we call into use every hour of our lives. They do not impart any new faculty, but lay bare before us the nature of that reasoning which has been from childhood our delight and our prerogative. Who shall say that this is a frivolous or unworthy study?

§ 39. But it is thought advisable that young men who are not inclined to examine with habitual patience their own thoughts or the procedure in any of the real sciences, should acquire some slight knowledge of Logic. In this case, we cannot expect the same diligence in learning technical terms and rules, as they will not be required hereafter. But what is the course adopted? We attenuate the science, where we ought to simplify it; we reduce the size of our manuals, in the vain hope of lessening their difficulty; and there remains little more than a catalogue of hard terms with harder explanations—little else than a reliquary of the dry bones of that system of knowledge which five hundred years ago was alive and breathing. No wonder that untrained minds are repelled. Instead of explanation and illustration of common things, they find the plainest and simplest veiled behind the terms of a forgotten metaphysical system; they are commanded to master all the rules required for an extensive practice of logic, though they never mean to enter upon such a course, and are not encouraged to do so now, except by the most puerile examples. It is not worth their while to learn the language of a region of philosophy in which they are never to travel. Surely it would be possible to give them some sound and accurate instruction in the nature of their thoughts and minds, making use only of the language of common life. There are not wanting to our literature popular works on mental science, and on the intellectual processes involved in the physical sciences, out of which a general yet not inexact knowledge of the laws of mind may be easily acquired.

§ 40. In the division of the subject, I see no cause to deviate materially from the ordinary distribution into three parts, the first treating of Conception, or the power of forming general notions; the second of Judgment, or the power of deciding whether two notions agree or not; and the third of Syllogism, or the power of drawing one judgment from another.* To these a fourth part, in which Method, or the power of using the other three functions in the discovery of truth, is explained, has been usually added; which answers to the applied Logic of the present work. But it is proper to notice one or two objections to this division.

* Another division has been adopted from *Porphyry* (*Isag.* I. 1.) by some logicians, who consider Logic as the science of defining, dividing, and arguing.

§ 41. In beginning with conceptions, we are charged with putting the last first. Men cannot get a clear conception without passing a judgment about it; nor can they always pass a judgment without certain reasonings, or syllogisms; so that we go to the third part of Logic to establish what belongs to the second, in order that from that we may more clearly understand something which relates to the first. Why not *begin* then with the third?

Whilst this regressive order is certainly natural, and whilst a Logic might be written which set out from the sentence or the syllogism, and analyzed it into judgments, and these again into conceptions, the contrary procedure, from the simplest element of reasoning, the conception, to the syllogism which is its complete act, will be found in our opinion easier to follow. The analysis has long since been performed, and we find it convenient to proceed by synthesis, in this as in many other sciences. But the objection is valuable, as bringing out the contrast between the natural course of reasoning and its technical explanation. Why do we reason? To find whether some judgment, which has suggested itself to our minds, be true or not. Why do we seek to make this judgment? To add something to the clearness of the notion that is its subject. Copernicus reasoned to prove that the globe revolved round the sun; and he established this judgment that when men thought of "the globe" in future they might know it as "the revolving globe." All the reasonings in Aristotle's Ethics are to give a more adequate notion of happiness,—of Plato's

Republic, to improve our notion of justice,—of Bacon's Organon, to afford a more accurate conception of Method.

§ 42. Another objection against the division is that it distinguishes parts which are really confused;* that, for example, when we divide such a conception as that of "gases" into inflammable and non-inflammable, we really pass a judgment, though we explain division in the first part of Logic, which treats of Conception.

The answer to this may be suggested by that to the preceding one. We do not deny that the processes of the mind run into one another, that a man judges when he forms conceptions, and so on; we only ask for leave to *describe* each process separately. Our arrangement is confessedly artificial.

§ 43. Some logicians indeed argue that properly speaking Judgment is no distinct act of thought, but rather a part and condition of every act. Every notion seems to imply a judgment; when I think of the Queen, gravitation, or virtue, I mean that the Queen—gravitation—virtue *exists;* so that we have one common attribute which we affirm of every thing, that of existence. But it is one thing to say that a judgment *may* be, and another that it *is*, made. Before the component parts of any complex notion could be brought together in the mind, many judgments must have been passed; but when the notion recurs, we do not surely pass the judgment over again. My notion of freedom implies that it is the state of being able to do as I will, having respect however to the rights of others, and that this is a state possible for

* *Damiron,* Logique, p. 4.

men; but I do not formally *affirm* either that it contains these attributes or that it is possible, and therefore my mentioning freedom involves no judgment, although I may if I please form judgments about it. We must carefully distinguish between a possible and an actual judgment—between a notion which is and one which may be the subject of a judgment.

§ 44. Method, which is usually described as the fourth part of Logic, is rather a complete practical Logic. Whilst the other three parts describe each a distinct and complete product of thought, the Conception, the Judgment, and the Syllogism, no such whole is treated of in the doctrine of Method; which may be used for making a whole science, or a whole speech, a system or a sentence. Method is rather a power or spirit of the intellect, pervading all that it does, than its tangible product.* Hence we put in the place of rules for Method as a *part* of Logic, an Applied Logic, which shows under what conditions in the several regions of inquiry the three acts of thought may be safely performed, and how far rules can avail to direct the mind in the use of them to profitable or beautiful results.

§ 45. The attempt to apply the rules of Logic will both raise and lower the opinion which obtains concerning the worth of the science. Those who condemn it altogether, as arbitrary and artificial, as a set of rules for arguing, put together in an age when truth was less the object of desire than argument, may find to their surprise that it is only a searching and systematic account of processes which they daily perform, whether in thought, or in argument, in the

* See the fragment on Method in *Coleridge's* Friend, vol. iii.

pursuit of a science or in the transactions of the street and market. Those on the other hand who expect that Logic will be to them a golden key to unlock the treasure-house of the knowledge of the universe, will find that it neither gives them nor pretends to give, any new power; that it only refines and strengthens powers they already possess; that out of a dunce it never yet made a philosopher. Whilst its rules apply to every science, and it may therefore lay some claim to its ancient titles,—the Art of Arts, the Instrument of Instruments,—it only assists us in the study of the sciences, not stands in their stead. We must fight our own way over every inch of ground in the field; but Logic will often prevent our throwing away our blows. She can do no more. Sophists of Greece may offer to teach us "a trick worth a hundred minæ," which is to be the secret of all wisdom; or Lully and Bruno may pretend so to arrange in tables the results of human research that a child may know where to put his hand on the most recondite secrets, and employ them at pleasure. But these are wild dreams of the infants of science, which thinkers in their sober, waking moments hardly mention but with a smile. We only affirm, that when men think, these are the rules according to which their thoughts run, that the knowledge of laws and principles, independent of ulterior profit, is always gratifying to active minds, and that, inasmuch as the clear understanding of what is right is always useful for the avoidance of what is wrong, Logic is an useful instrument in thinking. But it gives us the forms of knowledge, not the matter. It will not lay bare the hidden springs of moral action; nor explain the mystery of life, of sleep, of fancy, of memory; nor display the future destination of man and the world. Still less will it be to us instead of eyes, if, turning away from this ball of earth on which we stand, we try to look off to the Infinite—the Absolute—the Eternal, whose nature will not take the mould of our intellectual forms, who comprehends us, when we vainly think that we comprehend Him.

OUTLINE

OF THE

LAWS OF THOUGHT.

PART I.

CONCEPTIONS.

"Non obstant hæ disciplinæ per eas euntibus, sed circa illas hærentibus."

QUINCTILIAN.

CONCEPTIONS.

§ 46. *Cognitions in General.*

THE impression which any object makes upon the mind may be called a Presentation. Some Presentations are admitted into the mind without being noticed, as is the case with the words spoken to a dreamy or absent man, or with a house or tree which, forming part of a great landscape, escapes the special notice of the beholder. The mind is unconscious of them; it sees or hears, but does not know that it sees or hears, so that the impression is not clear. And yet it is a real impression, because, when attention is directed to it, we know that it must have been there before. A man stares his friend in the face without recognizing him; when his friend awakens his attention, the recognition takes place. But he knows that it is not the impression upon his eye which begins at that point of time, but his attention to the impression. Presentations then are divided into Clear and Obscure, and the former, with which alone Logic is concerned, may be called Notions or Cognitions.

Clear Presentations, or Cognitions, are subdivided

into confused and distinct. Where the marks or attributes which make up the Presentation cannot be distinguished, it is confused; where they can be distinguished and enumerated, it is distinct. For example, we have a clear notion of the colour red; but we cannot tell by what marks we identify it; we could not describe it intelligibly to another; and hence our cognition of it is confused: again we have a clear notion of house; but we can declare its various marks, namely, that it is an enclosed and covered building fit for habitation; and therefore our notion is distinct.

We subdivide the class of distinct notions twice, according to two principles of division; and first, into adequate and inadequate notions. Adequate notions are those in which, besides enumerating the marks, we can explain them; that is, can enumerate the marks of the marks of the distinct notion, and again the marks of those marks. As this kind of analysis is almost interminable, we call a notion adequate, not when the enumeration of subordinate marks has been carried to the farthest, but when they have been enumerated sufficiently for our present purpose, in whatever subject we are employed. Our notion of happiness, for instance (according to Aristotle), is adequate, when we not only know that it is "an energy of the soul according to the best virtue, in a complete life," but can explain what we mean by an energy of the soul, the best virtue, and a complete life. So we have an adequate notion of what Hobbes means by Right, when we not only know that it is "unresistible might in a state of nature," but can explain what unresistible might and state of nature are. The same two notions would be inadequate, if we had the respective definitions of them but could not explain them.

The other division of distinct notions is into symbolical and notative; it has been already explained.*

TABLE OF NOTIONS.

- Presentations
  - Clear (=Cognitions)
    - Confused.
    - Distinct
      - Adequate
      - Inadequate
      - Symbolical
      - Notative.
  - Obscure.

§ 47. *Intuitions and Conceptions.*

The notions formed in the mind from things offered to it, are either of single objects, as of "this pain, that man, Westminster Abbey;" or of many objects gathered into one, as "pain, man, abbey." Notions of single objects are called Intuitions, as being such as the mind receives when it simply attends to or

* P. 45, seq. Throughout this section we have followed *Leibnitz*, with some slight alterations. See *Erdmann's Leibnitz*, p. 79. *Acta Erudit. an.* 1684. Some useful distinctions in the various names of notions are given by *S. T. Coleridge.*

"The most general term (*genus summum*) belonging to the speculative intellect, as distinguished from acts of the will, is Representation, or (still better) Presentation.

"A conscious Presentation, if it refers exclusively to the subject, as a modification of his own state of being, is=Sensation.

"The same, if it refers to an object, is=Perception.

"A Perception immediate and individual, is=an Intuition.

"The same Mediate, and by means of a character or mark common to several things, is=a Conception.

"A Conception, extrinsic and sensuous, is=a Fact or a Cognition.

"The same purely mental and abstracted from the forms of the understanding itself is=a Notion."—*Church ar d State*, p. 301.

inspects (*intuetur*) the object. They are also called Singular Representations. Notions formed from several objects are called Conceptions, as being produced by the power which the mind possesses of taking several things together (*concipere*, i. e. *capere hoc cum illo*) according to the principle to be explained presently. They are also called General Notions or Representations.

§ 48. *Formation of Conceptions.*

On a first inspection of an object of an entirely novel kind, we are unable to distinguish between its essential and accidental properties, between what it must always exhibit and what it might dispense with. A person who had lived all his life on the shore of the Atlantic, would believe, unless otherwise informed, that every other sea resembled this in all particulars, in its tidal movement, though the Mediterranean is almost tideless, in its degree of saltness, though the taste of the Dead Sea is much more bitter and its composition different, and so on. In travelling, or in reading a book of travels, he is made acquainted with another sea with properties not quite identical indeed, but still so far similar that he cannot help regarding the new specimen as of the same kind as the old. This he sees at once upon making the comparison of the two objects; and he then proceeds to reflect upon the properties of each, with a view to discover the points in which they agree, as well as those in which they are at variance. Having ascertained what they are, he sees that a separation must be made between the dispensable and the indispensable properties, because the latter will belong to each and every specimen of this kind, whilst the former, as he now sees, need not be present to constitute a sea what it is. He proceeds then to abstract, or draw off (*abstrahere*), the points in which seas are to agree from those in which they may differ; and the properties so drawn off and kept apart, are called the Notes or Marks or Attributes of a sea, and form when taken together a Universal or Common Nature (*Universale*). But he cannot think of a common nature without implying a class of things, be the number large or small, in each of which this set of attributes is to be found, and each of which must exhibit them as its credentials for admission into the class; in taking this further step he generalizes, or forms a Genus or Class. Lastly, as he cannot be sure of remembering the class, nor hope to recall it to the minds of others who have gone through, or who at least take for granted, the same steps of thought, without a name to represent it, he either invents a new name, or applies that by which he once designated a single thing, to the whole class; which is an act of Denomination.

There are here no less than five steps, which must have been taken by every one who fully and fairly realizes a general notion, and some of which must have been made even by those who have a less distinct apprehension of what they mean when they speak of classes. i. Comparison is the act of putting together two or more single objects with a view to ascertain how far they resemble each other. ii. Reflection is ascertainment of their points of resemblance and their points of difference. iii. Abstraction is the separation of the points of agreement from those of difference, that they may constitute a new nature, different from, yet including, the single objects. iv. Generalization is the recognition of a class of things, each of which is found to possess the abstracted marks. v. Denomination is the imposition of a name that shall serve to recall equally the Genus or Class, and the Common Nature.

The process thus analyzed into five acts is often described generally by the principal of them, as Abstraction; and for convenience' sake that word shall be reckoned sufficient here.

§ 49. *Higher and Lower Conceptions.*

The functions of Abstraction do not cease, as soon as we have compared several intuitions, to form one conception. We may proceed to form a larger conception from several narrower ones; and this too is done by Abstraction. By observing John, Thomas, and Peter, and abstracting from their accidents the essential marks, we get the notion of man; but again, by comparing the conception man with other conceptions, cow, sheep, wolf, whale, and observing the mark common to all, that they suckle their young, we form the wider conception Mammalia,—wider, because it concludes man and many other conceptions. We may carry the process farther still; and, with writers on Natural History, compare the Mammalia, with Aves, Amphibia, Pisces, Insectæ, and Vermes, when we shall discover that all these, however different, agree in having life and sensation, from which marks we gain the new conception animal, wider than any of the former, as including them all, —higher, as requiring a second step in the abstractive process to reach it.

§ 50. *Genus, Species, Individual.*

In this scale, composed of more or fewer steps, the lowest is always the intuition or Individual. The next is called the Lowest Species (*infima species*), which can only contain single objects, not subordinate kinds or classes. All the higher rounds of the ladder, except the highest, are called Subaltern (*subalterna*) Genera, which are alternately genera and species, genera to the lower, and species to the higher and wider conceptions. The widest class, with which Abstraction ceases, is called the Highest (*summum*) Genus, because in this hierarchy of conceptions it is not brought under any other genus as its species, but is itself the genus to each conception in the series. Thus the

Individual is neither genus nor species.

Infima Species is never a genus.

Summum Genus is never a species.

Subalterna Genera are genera to those below them, and species to those above.*

A series of this kind, in which the same individuals are found throughout, is called a system of cognate genera. Thus, in the series Socrates, Philosopher, Man, Animal, the same individual, Socrates, is found

* With the Greek Logicians the Summum Genus is *γένος γενικώτατον*, the Infima Species, *εἶδος εἰδικώτατον*, the subaltern genus, *εἶδος μέσον καὶ ὑπάλληλον*.

in each of the three conceptions, and might have the name of it applied to him.

It must be remarked that the Summum Genus and the Infima Species are fixed somewhat arbitrarily. There can only be one absolute summum genus, and we may go on abstracting until we come to some wide notion, be it "thing" or "substance" or "essence" or "object," that comprehends all that we can think about. If we stop short of this, as the Naturalist does when he makes Animal his highest genus, the name can only be used in a qualified sense, and our genus is only the highest because we will make it so. Then, we can scarcely ever ascertain the *infima species*, or that kind that is too narrow to be divided into other kinds, because even in a handful of individuals we cannot say with certainty that there are no distinctions upon which a further subdivision into classes might be founded.

The genus next above a given species is called proximate; those that are still higher are called remote. A number of species that have the same proximate genus are said to be coördinate.

§ 51. *Marks or Attributes.*

Those properties by which we recognize any object, and assign it a place under some appropriate conception, are called its marks. If these are invariably found in the objects of a given sort, they are called essential; if only a portion of the class possesses them, they are accidental. The whole of the essential marks of a species make up its specific character, or its essence. Two marks which are in the very mode of expressing them opposed to each other, as wise and unwise, mortal and immortal, are called contradictory, because it is impossible to assign them to the same object without a contradiction in terms; and this is certain *a priori*, because the one is the mere negation of the other, so that their opposition does not depend on an examination into the nature of these marks. If they were represented as A and not-A, we should be as sure that they were diametrically opposed, as if A was a word of well-known meaning, instead of an arbitrary symbol. Marks which are opposed to each other, but not as a positive and negative, so that we know their contrariety *a posteriori*, from experience, as sweet and sour, hard and fluid, are termed repugnant marks. Those which may meet in the same object, as sweet and fluid, sour and hard, we may call compatible.

§ 52. *Extension and Intension.*

When we compare a vague and general conception with a narrower and more definite one, we find that the former contains far more objects in it than the latter. Comparing plant with geranium, for example, we see that plant includes ten thousand times more objects, since the oak, and fir, and lichen, and rose, and countless others, including geranium itself, are implied in it. This capacity of a conception we call its extension. The extension of *plant* is greater than that of *geranium*, because it includes more objects.*

* Mr. *Mill*, Logic, I. vii. 1, thinks it only "accidental" that "gen eral names" should be the names of classes. But his own language contradicts him; if they are *general* they belong to *genera*; it cannot be accidental that a class-name should be the name of a class.

Scheme of CONCEPTIONS *in the three wholes of* EXTENSION, INTENSION, *and* DENOMINATION.

		A. Name.	B. Intension, i. e. the *marks* which compose the Conception.	C. Extension, i. e. the *objects* which the Conception stands for.
(Process of		Denomination.	Abstraction.	Generalization.)
Genus	Summum	*Body*	Body	Stone, Plant, Brute, Man, &c.
Genus	Subalternum	*Living body*	Body with life	Plant, Brute, Man.
Genus	Subalternum	*Animal*	Body with life and sensation	Brute, Man.
Species	Infima	*Man*	Body with life, sensation, and reason	Man.

In the Summum Genus the Intension is least, the Extension greatest. In the Infima Species the Intension is greatest, the Extension least.

But conceptions have another capacity. Whilst plant has more objects under it than geranium, it has fewer marks in it. I can describe the leaves, petals, stamina, and pistils of geranium; but of plant no such description is possible. I cannot say that every plant has a stem, for there are the lichens to contradict me; nor a flower, for ferns have none, and so on. I can say little more about plant, than that all plants have growth and vegetable life. The logical expression of this defect is, that its intension is very limited.

The greater the extension, the less the intension; the more objects a conception embraces, the more slender the knowledge which it conveys of any of those objects; and *vice versâ*.*

With the help of the important distinction between extension and intension, or, as others express it, the sphere and matter of the conception, *magnitudo et vis conceptûs*, we can understand the meaning of the saying—that the subject of a judgment is in the predicate, and the predicate in the subject. "Man is an animal;" this conveys two notions, that man is contained in animal, as a species in a genus; and that whatever makes up our notion of animal

* The various modes of expressing the double capacity of conceptions are as follows:—

A conception viewed as a

Logical whole	Metaphysical whole
has	has
Extension	Intension or Comprehension
Breadth	Depth
Sphere	Matter
Objects	Marks
Power to denote	Power to connote.

—all the marks of animal—are contained in (ὑπάρχει*) man. So they are mutually contained.

§ 53. *Determination.*

The reverse of the abstractive process, that of descending from higher conceptions to lower, by resuming the marks laid aside, is called determination. Thus from the broad class of diseases, we determine or mark out the class of fevers, by the peculiar symptoms of heat, rapid pulse, &c. which are their marks; and from fevers we descend further to intermittent fevers, by bringing in the fresh mark of time.

As abstraction augments the extension by diminishing the marks, so determination augments the intension by increasing them. Notions of individuals, and they only, are said to be fully determined, because to them there are no more marks to add. The use of the word determination in its logical sense is already sanctioned by our older writers.

§ 54. *The three powers of a Conception.*

That all simple cognitions have three powers or a threefold value, in that they consist of marks, and include objects, and are summed up in names, has been stated already. To these three functions as many processes correspond; Division of a Conception enumerates all the objects or classes that are included under it, and so deals with the extent of

* *Aristotle* (Anal. Pri. I. i., and many other places) adopts in preference this mode of putting the proposition. Instead of "Man is an animal," he has "Animal inheres in man."

the notion; Definition expounds all the marks implied in the notion, and so represents to us the nature or specific character of it; and Denomination, and Explanation of Names, affix the verbal sign to a conception, and interpret given verbal signs already in use, so that they may be referred to the notions they really represent, and to no others. The nature of these processes must be explained more in detail.

§ 55. *Logical Division.*

Division is the enumeration of the various co-ordinate species of which a proximate genus is composed. The rules for conducting this process correctly are

i. The constituent species, called the dividing members (*membra dividentia*), must exclude one another.

ii. The constituent species must be equal, together, to the genus divided (*divisum*).

iii. The division must be made according to one principle or ground (*fundamentum divisionis*).

The reason of these rules, and of the terms of the explanation of Division, will be apparent when the uses to which the process was intended to minister are fairly considered, and these, although they belong rather to applied Logic, may be introduced here. The treatment of a subject is greatly facilitated by an orderly arrangement of its several parts. If Natural History, for example, were to go no further than its name seems to require, if it were a mere collection of curious information about natural products, without order and completeness, no memory would be able to master its details. Omissions would detract from its value; and repetitions would disgust the student. But it maps out the kingdom of nature into great districts, and subdivides these into smaller portions, so as to secure us from serious omissions, to preclude confusion, and to assist the memory; and so becomes worthy of the name of a science. The first rule then, as given above, is to secure that the classes and subclasses shall be distinct from each other, that they shall not overlap each other, or be what Leibnitz calls *communicant* species. Exceptions to this rule are often unavoidable, especially in subjects that do not belong to strict science; thus, in enumerating the species of imaginative writers, one would probably mention poets, dramatists, and writers of tales; yet some poets are dramatists, and some tales are poems. The second rule provides that no class shall be omitted, and secures completeness. The principle of division mentioned in the third rule is some new conception, for the marks of which we seek in the conception to be divided. Thus man may be divided into European, African, Asiatic, American, and Australian; and again into Christian, Mohammedan, Jew, and Pagan, and again into just and unjust; and in the first division locality, in the second religion, and in the third behaviour, is the principle of division.* Now as it is impossible to divide without

* Where we divide a conception upon several principles, the whole number of the dividing members will be the product of the numbers under the several principles multiplied together. In the example in the text, the principle of locality gives 5 species, religion 4, and behaviour 2; then the whole number will be $5 \times 4 \times 2 = 40$. For Europeans may be subdivided into 4 classes according to their relig-

seeking for marks of difference, and as the enumeration of marks is the explanation of the nature of an object possessing them, it is plain that no Division can take place without unfolding some of the properties of the conception divided. It is true that trifling and useless divisions, like those in the Sophist of Plato (which perhaps were not intended to be regarded seriously) have brought the process into some contempt; but in many sciences a natural division, or one which is based upon natural properties, and not upon fancies or trifling resemblances, is of great use both in arrangement and in securing a full and complete knowledge of a subject. Thus in that branch of medicine called *Materia Medica*, where the mode of treatment is purely divisive, it will be found that almost all the various schemes by which drugs are classified involve so many distinct theories of medicine.

But as we descend from a high genus to a species, we must avoid a sudden leap over any of the subaltern genera in the series (*divisio non faciat saltum*), because their distinctive properties may be overlooked at the same time; and hence division was described above as the enumeration of the species of the *proximate* genus. Subdivision is the process of dividing some species of a genus already subjected to that operation; and it may be repeated

ion, and so may each of the rest; then each of the subdivisions may be again divided according to uprightness of conduct; so that we have European-Jews who are just—Asiatic-Jews who are just, and so on, up to 40 combinations. This logical subtlety is of little practical importance, because, amongst other reasons, many of the subdivisions will commonly be entirely vacant. See *Drobisch. Logik*, § 119.

until we reach the lowest species, which we cannot properly divide, though the individuals contained under it may be enumerated. A division where the species are not coördinate, although correct in other respects, would offer a bad arrangement for purposes of science; thus, Sciences should not be divided by a reader of Aristotle into "Theoretical and practical, together with Poetry, Rhetoric, and Dialectic," because the first two are divisions, and the last three are subdivisions of a genus that has been omitted, namely, the Poetic Sciences.

Logicians test every division by the possibility of reducing the constituents to two, a positive and a privative conception. If A is a genus divisible into the species x, y, and z, we may represent the dividing members as x and not-x, the latter being really equivalent to y and z. This division into two members (*divisio debet esse bimembris*) called dichotomy (διχοτομία) is alone purely logical, because we know *a priori*, and without any researches into the particular case, that it must be complete. But on the other hand it is comparatively useless,* because, of one of our constituents, and that the larger, we know nothing but that it wants the marks of the other. "Insincerity," so long as it remains in our mind as a merely privative conception, implies nothing, except that it has not the mark or marks that sincerity has. The mind, however, does not allow conceptions to

* Compare the mode of stating this objection in *Plato*, Politicus, 262, C. D. τοίονδε οἷον . . . τῶν σχισθέντων. If, as *Rassow* and *Waitz* suppose, *Aristotle* had *Plato* in his mind in censuring the divisive method, as useless in the discovery of truth (see An. Post. II. ch. 5, and An. Pri. I. ch. 31), we believe that *Plato* saw its defects perfectly.

retain their merely privative character; such words as infinite, intolerant, undying, become substantial conceptions, as much so as those with which they are contrasted by the form of their expression.

§ 56. *Partition.*

The separation of the parts of any individual object, as of a sword into blade and hilt, is termed partition. An individual (ἄτομον) is that which cannot be divided without ceasing to be what it is; its parts cannot have the name of the whole. When a genus is divided, every part of it remains unchanged, and may have the name of the genus. The trunk and limbs of a man cannot be severally called the man; but a European is a man, and so is an Asiatic and an American.

§ 57. *Definition of a Conception.*

As Division ascertains the various classes of objects united under one Conception, so does Definition ascertain those common marks which all the objects possess, or that common nature represented by the conception. Division therefore answers to Generalization (§ 48), and Definition to Abstraction; the former viewing the conception only as a class, the latter only as an abstract nature or set of properties. The attributes of this nature may none of them be peculiar to it when taken singly, provided that the whole of them do not concur in any other conception. Hence every definition will recount the marks of the genera above the conception it has to unfold, together with some other mark called the Difference, by which this species is distinguished from every other. But this difference may only be a distinctive mark when brought into its present connection; apart from which it may be an attribute of some high and wide genus.

As Definition and Division are but two sides from which the same conception is viewed, they might be expected to lend each other assistance. (§ 52.) In dividing successively a set of cognate conceptions, from the highest to the lowest, we do in fact bring in one by one the marks that compose the definition, and hence the fullest and most complete definition would be formed after such a process of division had been gone through, provided, of course, that essential marks, and not mere accidental ones, had been brought in to divide by. Definition in turn, by enumerating the essential marks of a conception, furnishes a guide to its genus, and its coördinate species; thus if "animal" were defined "an organized being with life and sensation," its proximate genus would appear to be that of "organized living beings," divisible into those which had and those which were destitute of sensation.

The rules of Definition may be stated here, as a help to understanding the process itself, although they belong more properly to applied Logic.

1. A definition must recount the essential attributes of the thing defined (*Definitio fiat per notas rei essentiales*). Thus, in defining "words" as "the articulate signs of thoughts," we are not to introduce such a superfluous mark as "Words are the articulate signs *by which an orator* expresses his thoughts,"

for whilst this is true, it is not necessarily found in the conception in our mind, and consequently has no place in the act of analyzing it.

2. The definition must not contain the name of the thing defined; as this is precisely the word we are bound to explain. Thus if "life" is defined to be "the sum of the vital functions," we have not logically defined "life," as the word "vital," which implies life, stands unexplained in the definition. This fault is called *circulus in definiendo* (also διάλληλος τρόπος), because vital is given to explain life, and life would be used probably to explain vital, so that we should travel "in a circle" back to our old difficulty.

3. A definition must be precisely adequate to the species defined (*Definitio sit adæquata, neque latior neque angustior suo definito*). If it explains a species below, it is said to be too narrow, as when triangle is defined "a rectilinear figure with three *equal* sides and angles." If it is applicable to the genus above, it is too wide, as when we define words as "the signs of thoughts," whereas there are other signs also.

4. A definition must not be expressed in obscure or figurative or ambiguous language. Oken's definition of Philosophy cannot avail much; it is "the recognition of mathematical ideas as constituting the world." The Divine Nature has been represented as "a circle whose centre is everywhere, and whose circumference is nowhere;" but this bold figure cannot for a moment be accounted a definition.

5. A definition must not be negative, where it can be affirmative. "Evil is that which is not good. A

point is that which has no parts and no magnitude." These definitions are to be judged according to our view of the possibility of finding others of the affirmative form. Some conceptions are in their nature negative, as indivisibility, blindness, and must be defined negatively.

The position which definition holds in the construction of a science need not be discussed here; it belongs to the application of Logic.

§ 58. *Third power of Conceptions. Denomination.*

A Conception is not complete until it has received a name, to preserve and represent it for the future (p. 52). The principal divisions of nouns or names are the following.

a. Nouns are either Proper, Singular, or Common. A proper name represents a single object, apart from that connection with others, which is effected in abstraction (p. 95), as Socrates, Rome, Sirius. A common noun applies to a class of objects, and their common marks or attributes, ascertained by abstraction, as man, city, star; and it applies to each and every one of the objects in that class. A singular noun applies to only one object, like a proper name, but then it is only singular in its present application, as, a song, this world, my horse, the King of Prussia; it is evident that song, world, horse, king, are common nouns, and their singular meaning is obtained by adding some word of limitation.

b. Distributive and Collective Nouns are to be distinguished. The former are common nouns, the latter nouns of multitude; the former are applicable to each and every one of the objects they denote, the latter, though denoting many objects, can only be applied to them when combined, as army, senate. Sometimes it is important to distinguish between the distributive and collective uses of words that may assume either form; thus, "All that glitters is not gold," means "all taken together," not "each and every thing;" and "the Greeks conquered the Persians," means "the Greeks as a body," whereas "the Greeks loved philosophy," means "each Greek."

c. Nouns are either Substantives, Attributives, or Relatives. Substantives are names of things, which have either in fact or in thought an independent existence, as Charlemagne, botany, wisdom. Attributives are nouns which assign a mark to a substantive, as great, good, docile. Relatives are pairs of nouns, each of which implies the existence of the other, as father and son, debtor and creditor, king and subjects. The properties of relative conceptions must be further explained below.

d. Nouns are either Positive, which stand for certain definite marks and an ascertainable class of objects, or Privative, which only imply the absence of certain marks, and consequently belong to a vague and indeterminate class. Of the former, mortal, sincere, honest, are examples; of the latter, immortal, insincere, dishonest. This is a distinction of some importance in Logic, as will appear hereafter.

e. Nouns are either Univocal, Equivocal, or Analogous, in their signification. Univocal nouns have one meaning only, in which they are applicable to the objects they stand for. Equivocal have several meanings, and are in fact several words, with a casual resemblance in form, as gall, for a wound and a bitter substance; ball, for a dance and an orb; light, for the contrary of darkness and that of heavy. In analogous nouns, one meaning is extended to new sets of objects from some proportion or resemblance between them, as foot, extended from a part of an animal to the lowest part of a tree, a mountain, and the like. Where equivocal or analogous words are to be employed in Logic, it is requisite to give them the power of univocals, by adding words to specify the exact application we mean to make of them. Analogous words pass into equivocals as soon as we lose sight of the analogy that connects them; this has occurred in post, and in file as applied to a string of papers and a line of soldiers.

§ 59. *Privative Conceptions.*

Besides conceptions which arise from marks, there are others formed from the privation or absence of marks. Our notion of kindness arises from some properties which a kind person always exhibits; but whence our notion of its opposite, unkindness? From the want of the marks, whatever they may be, of kindness. So, too, in marking by a name any class of objects, as animal or stone, we necessarily imply that there are corresponding classes which are not animals and not stones; about which, it is true, we know very little, as we can only say what they are not. Any pair of conceptions, a positive and a privative, must, speaking absolutely, divide the whole universe. Either in man or in not-man, all objects must be found,—star, flower, form of government, moral quality, and any other things the most unlike. But practically we limit this absolute division; though unkind does include every thing except the beings that show kindness, it would be absurd to apply it to the whole of these. It is more convenient to think of such a pair of conceptions as kind and unkind, as dividing between them, not the whole universe, but some proximate genus, say man or moral being; so that we mean to include in our notion of unkind not every *thing* that is unkind, but every *man* that is so. Such a larger conception, which a positive and a privative divide between them, may be called the second sphere of the positive.*

Privative conceptions not only afford the means of varying the forms of thinking, by furnishing for every affirmative judgment, equivalent negatives, and for every negative, affirmatives, but they enter into and assist the higher processes of the reason in all that it can know of the absolute and the infinite. To attribute the properties of one or many individuals to every other of the same class is within the reach of the mere understanding, and the brute creation enjoy some share of it; but from the seen to realize an unseen world, not by extending to the latter the properties of the former, but by assigning it attributes entirely opposite, is a prerogative of reason alone.

* The δευτέρα οὐσία of *Aristotle* (Cat. Ch. v.) may justify the term *second sphere*. Professor *De Morgan* proposes to call it the *universe* of the positive conception. The privative has been called by some the contradictory, by others the contrary, of the positive; but either expression tends to confound conceptions with judgments.

§ 60. *Relative Conceptions.*

There is a class of conceptions which have the peculiarity that none of them can even be thought of alone, that the existence of each implies and depends on some other; thus *a father* implies *offspring*, *a king* implies *subjects*, *a debtor a creditor*, and so on. Some of these are of distinct things or beings, like the examples just given; and are expressed by nouns substantive; but other relatives are only attributes, expressed by adjectives; thus *larger* implies *less*, *akin* implies a relationship to some one, *near*, *high*, *heavy*, have reference to some standard of distance, stature, or weight.

A Relation is either simple or complex; simple where it subsists between two correlates, as between debtor and creditor, complex where it is a relation of *relations*, i. e., where it binds two or more pairs of relatives together. Thus the word *family* implies not merely a set of simple relationships, between father and son, brothers and sisters, but the action of these relationships upon each other. The word *state* in like manner implies not only the aggregate of the relations between the several classes, but the mode in which these simple relations act on and modify one another.

The relative conceptions that appear as adjectives, as *great*, *distant*, require no separate treatment. Conceptions have two kinds of marks, namely, attributes, which belong to the conception in itself, and relations, which belong to it when viewed in connection with other conceptions. To say that man is mortal is an act of attribution, for mortality is a quality residing in himself, without any reference to other beings; to say that man is long-lived, is to bring him into *relation* or comparison with other creatures whose days are shorter than his own. Relative adjectives then express a particular kind of marks of conceptions.

Simple relations expressed by substantives, are not more difficult to dispose of. These relatives always appear in pairs,—father and son, ruler and subject; and that which is the more prominent in thought at a given time is called the relative, and the other its correlative. This order however can always be inverted; if it is the property of a ruler that he has a subject, then inversely he is a subject that has a ruler. But what is it that thus connects them? A certain act or state of facts, called the ground of relation (*fundamentum relationis*); for *relatio non est ens per se reale, sed per suum fundamentum*. In one of our examples the ground of relation would be procreation of offspring, in the other civil government. Now if a pair of relatives, with the ground of their relation, are to be resolved into substance and attribute, as other conceptions are, this will be possible in three different ways, the facts of course remaining the same, and the order of thought alone varying. The relative may be viewed as substance, and the correlative may become its attribute, or this may be inverted; or thirdly, the ground of relation may become the substance of which both the correlatives are attributes; thus, we attribute to the ruler that he has subjects, or to the subjects that they must have a ruler, or to civil government that it implies a ruler and subjects. Nor is it necessary to break the sym metry of the doctrine of conceptions in order to find a place for what may at first appear to demand it by their peculiarity of form.

§ 61. *Abstract and Concrete Representations.*

Abstract and concrete are relative terms; when a higher conception is seen to exist in a lower, or in an intuition, as we see the marks of animal in the conception horse or a horse, we are said to see the abstract in the concrete. So of two cognate conceptions, the more abstract bears the name of *the abstract*, the more fully determined we call *the concrete.*

The received explanation among logicians in this country is that an abstract term is the name of a quality considered apart from the subject in which we should look to find it, as prudence, strength; and that a concrete term is a name expressing the quality as residing in some subject, as prudent, strong. There is an analogy between this narrow sense, and that assigned by us; we say that the abstract is to the concrete as universal to particular, and they, that it is as the general quality to particular cases of it.*

§ 62. *On the nature of general Notions.*

There is a pretty general agreement at present as to the mode of the *existence* of general notions; the

* See the excellent note in *Trendelenburg.* Excerpta: on § 36. Also *Waitz* on Organon. Comm. on 81, 6, 3; *Trendelenburg* on Ar. de Anima, 478.

differences of opinion referring chiefly to the use that shall be made of them. Formed in the mind, they are not entirely dependent upon its mere arbitrary decision; because in most cases there are properties in the objects around us which compel us to generalize in a particular way. Every nation, for example, would without any express convention put men into one class and horses into another, because the common properties of men are so marked and striking, that they seem as it were to cry aloud to be classed together. No one would be absurd enough to neglect such similarities; and to put some men and some horses invariably into one class, because they were white, and some other men and some other horses into one class because they were black! General notions exist in the mind alone; but they are founded on common properties which exist without the mind, not in a separate state, but as inherent in the objects of intuition. Further, these common properties were given to the various objects by design. For example, when the same vertebral column is found in a hundred species of animals, sometimes joined to large and powerful limbs, sometimes to small, rudimental ones, now to wings, now to fins, and now to arms, sometimes carried vertically, sometimes horizontally; and when, amidst all the specific variations, many of them modifying its own structure, the vertebral column is easily recognized as fundamentally unchanged, it is natural to infer that the possession of this part of the frame was preordained to be the link of connection of these species, and that in forming a class of "Vertebrate Animals" we are seeking after a form or idea which was in the Divine Mind when animals were created. So that general notions exist without the mind of man, in as far as they are in another mind. The Divine Mind stamps them on material things; the human reads them there.

With the controversies upon this question, and with the various opinions indicated by the names, Realism, Nominalism, and Conceptualism, we need not concern ourselves much in this place; they must be studied historically, in their connection with Theology and in the order of their development, before we can hope to understand them. Still, a few remarks may be of use in guiding those who have time to pursue the study.

The question concerns Universals (*universalia*), or those general properties which many things share alike, and which are acquired by the mind only by abstracting from the things that exhibit them (§ 48). These Universals have names of their own, just as much as the most tangible things; whiteness, humanity, animal, may serve as examples. Now the question, broadly stated, to the neglect of many nice subtleties and shades of opinion brought out in the history of the controversy, is this—Are these Universals real existences, apart from the mind that has formed them by abstraction, and independently of the things in which alone they appear to us,—or are they mere modes of intellectual representation, that have no real existence, except in our thoughts? Those who adopted the former alternative were called Realists; those who adhered to the latter might fitly be designated by a name of later origin, as Conceptualists, if we should object to the name of Moderate Nominalists, which indeed would imply that they held these Universals to be mere *names*. To each of these more moderate opinions belongs a cognate exaggeration; so that there are four principal answers to the question—what are Universals.

1. That of the Ultra-realists. Universals, or the Ideas of things, are real existences, nay, inasmuch as visible things change, grow, decay, and perish, the Universals or Ideas are the only real existences, for they are subject to none of these conditions. Wise men perish; but the idea of wisdom, of which they partake, after which they have their name, perishes not, does not change,—is the same in the Seven Sages as in the philosophers now living. In conformity to these ideas the world was created; and thus they even governed and guided the creating mind itself. This form of Realism has been attributed to Plato; but it is probable that he stopped short of believing that the Divine Mind was subject to the ideas. What general notions are to our minds —he probably held—ideas are to the supreme reason (νοῦς βασιλεύς); they are the eternal *thoughts* of the divine Intellect, and we attain truth when our thoughts conform with His—when our general notions are in conformity with the ideas. It is, however, very remarkable that Plato has left his opinions upon this important point open to a reasonable doubt.*

2. That of the Realists. Universals exist independent of things and of our conceptions of them, in the Divine Intellect. Under various forms this doctrine—of *universalia ante rem*—was the doctrine

* *Stalbaum, Prol. to Plat. Parm.* p. 269.

of the Schools before Roscelin, and of the Realist Schoolmen after him.

3. That of the Moderate Nominalists. Universals exist as a product of the mind only; they are formal representations of things, constructed by the mind through the assistance of language. Occham founded his Nominalism (so called) upon the position *Nullum universale est aliqua substantia extra animum existens.** Many shades of opinion, however, are to be detected among the Moderate Nominalists; and that of the Conceptualists, represented by Abelard, should be particularly studied.

4. That of the Ultra-Nominalists. Universals are mere names; and the only realities are individual things, which we group together by the aid of names alone. The name of Roscelin is usually connected with this opinion; but in what sense he held that Universals were only *flatus vocis*, we cannot decide from the scanty and adverse accounts in our possession.

Before we indicate some of the principal sources of the history of Nominalism and Realism, one remark is to be made, which, if it will not remove the difficulties of the subject, will perhaps define the common ground upon which the more moderate of both the adverse parties may be brought together. Making allowance for much confusion of statement in the scholastic writers, and for extreme assertions, which, there is reason to think, their authors understood in a modified sense, we have two views of the nature of general notions; that of the Realist, who maintained that they exist in the mind and also with-

* *Logica*, I. 15.

out it—in the Divine Mind; and that of the moderate Nominalist, who held that they exist only in the mind as notions, and that we use names to fix and recall them. Now I venture to think that the interminable contest between Platonist and Aristotelian, Realist and Nominalist, is at bottom, not so much a question of what universals are, as of how they shall be treated; not so much a question of Metaphysics, as of Method. Upon the *nature* of general notions there is a large amount of agreement between the parties: the Realist believes, with the Nominalist, that they are in the human mind, whilst, if the Nominalist believes at all that the world was created by design, he can scarcely escape from recognizing the Realist's position, that such ideas as animal, right, motion, must have had their existence from the beginning in the creative mind. Whence then the controversy? The burden of Aristotle's objections to the Platonic scheme of ideas is, that it teaches what cannot be known, and gives out as certain truth what lies far beyond the reach of our powers of investigation. "Instead of being content," he would say to the Platonist, "with classifying particular objects so as to form general notions, which we could always compare with the objects, as being inseparable from them, you jump to certain ideas, separate from the objects, though they cause and determine the manner of their existence, fixed whilst these are changeable, eternal whilst these pass away. Be it so; you offer these transcendent ideas to our understanding—you must remove the difficulties which the understanding meets in receiving them. How do you know that they exist? For we must not, in order to explain the world which we see, devise another world, of ideas, which no eye has seen.* Again, how they are connected with the things to which they belong? The man, for instance, with the idea of humanity? To say that things 'participate' in, or 'are copies' of, the ideas, is to avoid the difficulty by vague metaphorical language. Must there be an idea for every sensible object? If so, before Socrates could be born, there must have been an eternal idea of Socrates; which would lead us to a multiplication of ideas too great even for the imagination. In a word, you cannot explain the properties of these ideas without vagueness and self-contradiction; and, therefore, should not assume them to exist and found a system upon them."†

If this view be correct, Aristotle does not so much intend to deny the existence of ideas, as to maintain that the evidence for them is insufficient, and that no system can stand secure upon so weak a foundation. And looking to the paradoxical and seemingly inconsistent statements of Plato on the one hand,‡ and the evident misapprehensions of Aristotle upon

* So *Occham*—"*Entia non sunt multiplicanda præter necessitatem.*"

† Compare Metaphys. XIII. (M.) 4, p. 1078, b. ed. Berol.; ibid. 5, p. 1079, b. 36; ibid. I. (A.) 6, p. 987; ibid. 9, p. 990, b.; *Ravaisson*, Metaphysique d'Aristote, III. ii. 2; *Renouvier*, Histoire, II. p. 42. To avoid misunderstanding, let me remark that the resemblance between Aristotle and the Nominalist lies only in his denying a *separate* existence to universals. "Different philosophers have maintained that Aristotle was a Realist, a Conceptualist, and a Nominalist, in the strictest sense."—*Sir W. Hamilton.*

‡ For he speaks of the ideas, now as if they were merely mental conceptions, now as independent existences. *Stalbaum's* Parm. Prol. p. 273. And he does not clearly explain *where* the ideas exist, and whether they depend on the Divine Mind, or It upon them. Ibid. p. 272.

the other, I can conceive it possible that a sage mediation might have reconciled these two great spirits; and Aristotle might have owned that the universal notions in his mind might answer to certain ideas in the Divine, whilst his illustrious master might have confessed that, putting revelation out of the question, there is no way to the absolute—to knowledge of the idea—except a careful observation of and reasoning from the facts we possess, in our own mind and in the world around us. Plato indeed was an inductive reasoner, not inferior to Bacon himself; though the one confined himself too exclusively to the facts of the human mind, and the other to those of the external world. The question then between Plato and Aristotle, as any one may satisfy himself who will refer to the original places in the works of the latter, chiefly concerned Method, and did not turn so much upon a belief in the existence of ideas as upon the right to assume them as the ground of teaching.

It is impossible here to follow out this hint through the scholastic controversies, where the nature of universals was discussed in connection with religion, as it had been in its bearings on science; but its importance will be felt in that region also. We must distinguish between the opinions, that universals cannot possibly exist, and that the attempt to explain them as independent natures involves us in logical difficulties and contradictions.

Thus divested of one element of confusion, the question will assume a less repulsive form; but its difficulties do not disappear, nor is its importance lessened. Indeed, at the present day the great division between scientific men has assumed this form. "We cannot attain truth," say the more bigoted followers of Bacon, "except by confining ourselves simply to the facts of nature, and their arrangement. We must not view them in any theological connection; we must not call in any metaphysical idea to assist us in grouping them. We have simply to arrange them, using names and language for that purpose." Here again the question is regarded as pertaining to method; in other words the existence of the Deity, the existence and nature of Ideas, are not denied, they are only declined or put aside, whilst it is denied strenuously that they can be brought in to aid man in the investigation of truth. The opinions of such writers as Auguste Comte are but the latest exhibition of pure Nominalism, under its logical as opposed to its metaphysical form. "We must regard individual things as the only realities *for us*, and language as the means of discovering and preserving their connection." *

§ 65. *Questions about Conceptions.*

When a conception is recalled to the mind, under what form does it appear? Under that of a bare word, or of all the marks which we abstracted to

* Upon the history of Nominalism and Realism may be consulted —*Brucker*, vols. iii. and vi.; *Tennemann's* Manual; the brilliant Preface by *Cousin* to "Ouvrages inédits d'Abelard," Paris, 1836; also *Cousin*, Leçons, 1829, Leç. 9.; *Hauréau*, Philosophie Scolastique, 1850; *Hegel*, Geschichte, iii. 180. In *Degerando*, Histoire, i. p. 235, there is a good account of the shades of opinion in the two parties. Sir *W. Hamilton's Reid*, p. 405; *Dugald Stewart*, Phil. of Human Mind, vol. i. ch. 4, § 2; *Brown's* Lectures; Bishop *Hampden's* Bampton Lectures, Lecture ii. and Notes.

form it, or of some single object used as the representative of all the others of the same class? We have seen already (§ 25,) that the word, or the array of marks, may be employed to recall the conception. In any proposition which conveys a definition, we have examples of both forms. In such a sentence as "honesty is uprightness in all dealings which respect property," the former of the two conceptions is used as a counter (*notionis tessera*) to represent the marks, which the latter explicitly conveys; in the phraseology adopted above, "honesty" is a symbolical, and "uprightness in dealings which respect property" a notative conception. As to the third opinion, the understanding, which, for convenience' sake, puts symbols for true conceptions, does on the same account put examples of a conception instead of the conception itself, the singular instead of the general. For the notion animal, I think of a particular horse or cow; for honesty, of some honest man; for justice, of some Brutus or Aristides; for city, of London or Paris; but always with a conscious reservation that there are many points about this particular case which are not general, and do not belong to the conception. But it will hardly be questioned by any, that the understanding can, by a somewhat severer self-control, throw aside the particular case, and retain only the common marks which belong to the whole conception. For we must admit the power of abstracting some marks from the rest, as the *having life*, which is the mark of *animal*, is abstracted from the thousand different circumstances of size, shape, colour, food, temper, which distinguish animals from each other; else how are conceptions formed? And if we can abstract the marks from the accidents, surely we can retain them in our grasp when abstracted.

ii. Are representations of the imagination—the notion we have of a landscape from some poetical description, for example—to be considered as intuitions or conceptions? If the description could be so complete, and the reader's apprehension so accurate, that every portion of the landscape were distinctly seen, and we could distinguish that scene from every other, even from one that resembled it most closely, then it would be in accordance with the definition we have given (§ 47,) to call it an intuition. But this, I suppose, is never the case. The poet can describe a lake-scene with distinctness enough to prevent our having an impression from it of any other *kind* of landscape, as a plain with a distant city, or the cliffs of the sea-shore. But still the description must be far too obscure to prevent our mistaking this lake-scene for one closely resembling it, or even our recalling some lake we remember, to supply the deficiencies of his delineation, although we know that we are adopting one scene whilst he drew another. He can limit our general notion of landscape to some particular species, but not to this individual landscape—can reduce our "all" to "some," but not to "this." Therefore, such an image is a conception, used *particularly*, i. e. only some *part* of it is called up. It is a representation of some landscapes, but not of *one*, to the exclusion of the possibility of confounding it with others.

iii. Can there be abstraction without generalization, as Archbishop Whately maintains? "Suppose we are speaking of the King of France," says he; "he must actually be either at Paris or elsewhere; sitting, standing, or in some other posture; and in such and such a dress, &c. Yet many of these circumstances (which are *separable* accidents, and consequently) which are regarded as *non-essential to the individual*, are quite disregarded by us; and we abstract from them what we consider as essential; thus forming an *abstract* notion of the Individual. Yet there is here no generalization." A great error lies hid in this passage—that of not perceiving that the power of separating circumstances called essential to the individual from those which are not so, results from former generalizations. How do we know that "sitting" or "standing" is not essential to a king? How do we know that a crown and a robe of state are separable from the King of France? By prior generalization; by the help of the conception we have formed of a king already. If we had never known of other kings, or the same king at other times, we should have looked on the accidents and essentials of the King of France as alike essential. We know that "sitting" is not essential, because we know that kings sometimes do not sit. There is no abstraction without generalization; and in the case before us, we abstract, to refer to a former general notion or conception.

§ 66. *Summary.*

The first part of Logic explains that power of the mind which groups single objects into classes, so that the classes have names and attributes of their own.

Its principles are these: 1. The nature of every higher notion is found in the lower; consequently 2. The name of the higher may always be applied to the lower. Thus man may be called an animal, because the marks of life and sensation which distinguish animals are found in him. 3. The higher notion (*genus*) includes the lower notion (*species*) with other species, and is therefore of wider extension than it. But the species implies more *marks*—has a fuller definition—than the genus; and is said, therefore, to be of deeper intension than it. 4. That set of marks which distinguishes any species from the other species in the same genus is called its Specific Difference. 5. The whole nature of a species is ascertained, and its definition given, when the properties of the genus and those which make the specific difference are brought together. 6. We ascend from lower conceptions to higher by throwing away specific differences, *i. e.* by abstraction. We descend to lower ones by resuming the marks we have thrown away, *i. e.* by determination. 7. In a system of subordinate genera each must contain the individuals included in the lowest. 8. Coördinate species cannot contain the same individuals. 9. The conception of an object consists of the aggregate of its marks, with the notion of existence superadded. 10. Singular objects are invariably referred to and viewed through general conceptions. 11. A conception is complete and adequate, when it can be resolved at pleasure into its implied marks by definition, and into its contained species by division. 12. Two marks which stand to each other as positive and privative, like *wise* and *unwise*, are called contradictory, because it would be a contradiction in terms to assign them at the same time to the same object. Two marks are called contrary, when it is known *a posteriori* by experience, and not *a priori* by the very form of expression, that they cannot belong to the same object, as *wise* and *wicked*, *warm* and *frozen*.

OUTLINE

OF THE

LAWS OF THOUGHT.

PART II.

JUDGMENT.

Οὐδεμίαν γὰρ οὔτε οὕτως οὔτ' ἐκείνως πρᾶξιν οὐδ' ἀπραξίαν δηλοῖ τὰ φωνηθέντα, πρὶν ἄν τις τοῖς ὀνόμασι τὰ ῥήματα κεράσῃ.—PLATO.

JUDGMENT.

§ 67. *Judgment defined.*

EVERY act of judgment is an attempt to reduce to unity two cognitions. When one decides that "Socrates is wise," it is that hereafter one may, by combining the two notions, think of "the wise Socrates." Again, when one decides that "the world is not eternal," it is that hereafter one may refrain from combining the two notions as "the eternal world."

A Judgment then is an expression that two notions can or cannot be reconciled—that the marks of the one may or may not be henceforward assigned to the other.* A proposition is the expression of a judgment in words.

* This definition is rejected by Mr. *Mill*, Logic, vol. i. p. 116, seq. on the ground that a judgment expresses the agreement of *things* rather than of *notions*. But the notions are controlled by the things, otherwise assent and dissent would be arbitrary. I am *forced* to say "the day is fine" when the sky is cloudless, because my perceptions must correspond with the facts. This correspondence then the definition in the text is considered to imply; and it is retained because it is believed to be the only one that includes and describes every kind of judgment. But the weight allowed to Mr. *Mill's* objection will depend on the theory of Perception we adopt, and that

Though the truth or falsehood of a judgment, and consequently its value, depend upon its correctly representing things without us, rather than thoughts within us, it is primarily concerned with those representations in the mind by means of which alone things are brought into the arena of thought, whether as single objects or as the ground of abstract and general notions.

Every judgment has three parts: the subject or notion about which the judgment is; the predicate, or notion with which the subject is compared; and the copula or nexus, which expresses the mode of connection between them. The subject and predicate are called the terms of the judgment, i. e. the extremes or boundaries (*termini*) which it brings together.

§ 68. *Doctrine of Relation in Judgments.*

When we examine such a judgment as "Man is a rational animal" (which, trite as it is, will serve for our present purpose), we find that the subject and predicate are exactly coextensive; in other words, no object comes into the class of rational animals which is not also in man, and conversely no object comes under man which is not also under rational animal. The two conceptions, the one symbolical the other notative,* are derived from and represent the very same class of beings. This equality of subject and predicate is an important property

great metaphysical question we cannot here discuss. See, however, *Reid*, Int. Powers, Essay VI. 3; *Hamilton's Reid*, Appendix C. and D.*; *Cousin*, Histoire de la Phil. Leçon, 24; Edinburgh Review, vol. lii. Art. "Reid and Brown."

* P. 52.

of the judgment, for it conveys the power to substitute the one conception for the other, at pleasure.

Other judgments want this property. To say that "trees are plants," is to say indeed that no object is a tree which is not also a plant; but then there are plants which are not trees; so that plant and tree are not conceptions of equal extent.

It is true that the copula—the "is" or "are" which couples the conceptions—does not express the great difference we have noticed; being used in common language for either relation of the two terms. But as the correctness of some trains of reasoning depends entirely upon observing the relation of coincidence between subject and predicate, it is usual to alter the copula in some way, to express it, as by saying "is defined to be—is divided into—is coextensive with." In the present book, instead of the copula "is" or "are," the mathematical sign of equality (=) will be employed in affirmative judgments in which the predicate is *distributed*, or taken entire.

Every affirmative judgment indeed may be regarded as an *equation* of subject and predicate, as every negative is a decision that an equation cannot be established. By "All men are mortal" I mean that all men *are equal* to some mortal creatures; and by "Sŏme plants are poisonous" I mean that a part of my conception of plants coincides with a part of the conception of poisonous things.*

* Sir *William Hamilton*.

§ 69. *The Two Predicable-Classes.*

Logicians have always formed a classification of predicates according to the relation in which they stand to their respective subjects. We propose to give the simplest form to this scheme of Predicable-Classes, or classes of conceptions which can stand as predicates, taking Aristotle's doctrine as the basis.

Every judgment, according to Aristotle, declares either a genus, or the property, or the definition, or an accident* (*γένος—ἴδιον—ὅρος—συμβεβηκός*) of its subject.

The genus is that mark or attribute, which, whilst it never fails to accompany the subject, belongs to other subjects equally; as in "Envy is a passion." The property is that mark or attribute which belongs to the subject invariably, and to no other, without being the mark that would be used if we had to explain the nature of the subject; as "Man has the faculty of speech." Definition is the mark, or aggregate of marks, that would explain the very nature of the subject; as "A state is a community governed by its own laws." Lastly, the accident is an attribute that happens to attach to the subject, but is separable from it; as "Life is sweet."

The difference, or that mark or marks by which the species is distinguished from the rest of its

* *Top.* A. ch. iv. Of the names which A. adopts for the classes, *γένος*, and perhaps *ὅρος*, seems to express rather the extension, the others the intension; but he uses them as having both powers. The common division of Predicable-classes is that of *Porphyry*, into Genus, Difference, Species, Property, and Accident.

genus, does not occupy a distinct position in Aristotle's list, but is said to belong naturally to genus (ὡς οὖσαν γενικήν.)* The species may be regarded as composed, not of the marks of the genus and the difference, so well as of those of two concurrent or communicant genera; for the difference is but a genus which from its overlapping part of another is used as a distinctive mark of that part which it overlaps. If (for an easy example) in analyzing our notion of "the red-flowering currant" (*Ribes sanguineum*) we regard "currant" as the genus and "red-flowering" as the difference, we may also regard "red-flowering" as a wide genus, wider in fact than "currant," and therefore we may say that our notion of the plant is formed from the concurrence of two genera.†

This we suppose to be Aristotle's meaning in considering difference as having the nature of genus. But we are now to notice that he examines and arranges his four Predicable-classes according to this test—Can each of them, without logical fault, change

* Like the genus, the difference can be predicated of many things differing in species. But the genus is predicated ἐν τῷ τί ἐστι, the difference, ἐν τῷ ποῖόν τι. *Alex. Aphrod.* in Berlin ed. of *Arist.*; Top. A. ch. IV.

† Let A be the class of "red-flowering" things, B the class "currant;" then x, the part of each which is in the other, will be our notion of "red-flowering currant."

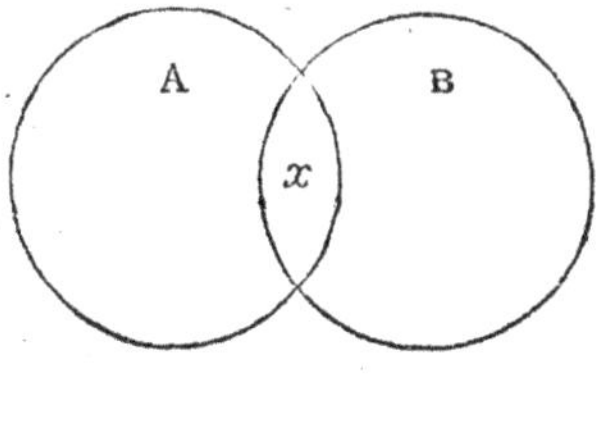

places with its subject? In other words, is each of them coextensive with its subject or not? The results of the test will be apparent from an account of each of the classes.

Definition* is a description which manifests completely the nature of the thing defined. Such a description would of course enable us to identify the subject, and to distinguish it from all other notions. And therefore it must be applicable only to the subject, otherwise it manifests, not the peculiar nature of the thing defined, but its *common* nature, the qualities which it shares with other things. As being applicable to the subject and to no other notion, it is coextensive with it, and therefore may change places with it in the judgment. It is just as true to say that "every rational animal is man" as that "every man is a rational animal." But if we said that "man is a warm-blooded animal," or that "man is a civilized animal," neither of them would be a definition, nor could the predicate in either become the subject, without some limitation. The former is a description that applies to more than man, the latter to a part only of man; and of course neither of them would enable us to apprehend exactly what man's nature was.

Property† is not easily distinguished from definition. Indeed, Aristotle confesses that property (ἴδιον) *i. e.* something *peculiar* to the subject, and essentially its own, is a name which would naturally include definition, and would mean some attribute which belongs to all the subject and to it only; but he adds

* Top. A. ch. v. More fully treated of in Top. Z. *passim.*

† Top. A. ch. iv. and v.

the special limitation "without declaring the essence or nature of the subject." Every quality then which belongs to all the subject, and to no other, is a property, provided it be not used in the definition. It is coextensive with the subject, and can therefore change places with it in the judgment without logical fault. Thus, "Man is capable of learning to write and speak correctly," might become "Every being capable of learning to write and speak correctly is a man."

But this subtle metaphysical distinction between the definition and the property is as difficult to maintain as it is unnecessary for the purposes of pure logic. How can we rely on being able to separate our notion of the nature or essence of a thing from the properties which accompany that nature? Let it be the definition of man that he is "a rational animal," and the property, that he is "capable of speaking correctly;" and how can we say that the latter is not in the essence, yet necessarily follows from the essence of man? It is *a part* of the essence, for "rational" implies it. In like manner, all the properties seem to be implicitly contained in every perfect definition. No criterion can be given for distinguishing between the essence and the inseparable accompaniment of the essence; and a larger acquaintance with the nature of things makes it evident that what one science regards as a property another must consider as essential, and that there is no one paramount quality which is absolutely essential and can never be degraded to the rank of a property.

The predicable Genus is a class of which the subject is a contained part. It declares, though not completely, the nature of the subject. A subject may be included in many different genera by different sets of marks; a man may be good, brave, rational, mortal, fallible, sick, learned, and so on. But some of these qualities, as wholly separable from the nature of man, are to be considered not as genera, but as accidents. Genus, as being of the very nature of the subject, is inseparable from it. As including the subject in common with other species, it is not coextensive with it. Hence the transposition of the subject and predicate in a judgment which predicates the genus, cannot take place; "all roses are plants" cannot become "all plants are roses."

Accident is a quality which belongs indeed to a subject, but can be taken away from it without destroying its nature or essence. We predicate accident when we say that "a man is speaking." Accident cannot change places with its subject, because it does not apply to the whole of that subject and to it alone. But a criterion is wanting to distinguish between accident and genus or species. It is an accident to the people of this country that they were born in it; because we might conceive them to have been born elsewhere; but then it has modified their nature or essence, and we understand by Englishman not merely one who was born within the four seas, but a man of particular feelings, views, and privileges, which are parts of his very nature. Here accident and genus or property seem to become confused. It is an accident too that this nail is rusty and that guinea bright, but then it shows that the gold has a *property*—of resisting oxidation—which the iron wants, and might serve to place them in two distinct species of metals. Aristotle actually speaks of man as an accident of the genus animal, although it is commonly represented as one of its species; * no doubt because we might conceive that species annihilated without the destruction of the genus. It does not appear then that the predicable accident can at all times be distinguished from the others, which would be a valid objection against retaining the doctrine in which it holds a place.

We propose to abandon, as at least unnecessary for logical purposes, the distinction between property and definition, genus and accident; and to form, as Aristotle has also done, two classes of predicables; one of predicables taken distributively, and capable of becoming subjects in their respective judgments without limitation, the other of such as have a different extension. In the former, the predicable has the same objects as its subject, but different marks or a different way of representing the marks. In the latter there is a difference both in the marks and the objects. The former may be called Definition, or Substitute; the latter, Attribute.†

* Cat. vii. 14. In quoting the passage *Crackanthorp* says: "Omnia inferiora accidentia sunt respectu suorum superiorum." See too Cat. vii. 13; Pacius, marginal note.

† *Aristotle's* arrangement is :—

Predicables	Capable of becoming subjects—convertible.	Definition. Property.
	Incapable of becoming subjects entire—Inconvertible.	Genus. Accident.

§ 70. *Definition explained.*

Every predicate which denotes exactly the same class of things as the subject, may be called a definition. Whether it unfolds the genus and difference, or the property, or only substitutes one symbolical conception for another, it is useful to *mark out* for us more clearly the limits of the subject defined, and is therefore capable of being employed as a definition for some thinker or other. Logicians have always allowed that in our definitions we are bound to consider, not merely what is *absolutely* the explanation of the subject, but what our hearers can adopt as an explanation. They would not allow that a definition which was conveyed in a metaphor, nor one of which the words were strange or obsolete, was properly a definition, because it would not be clear * to the hearer. They believed that there was an absolute definition; but this was to be conveyed with due regard to the hearer's needs and attainments. Now our reason for enlarging the limits of definition, is that any of the predicates we propose to include, though not the *absolute* definition, not the genus and difference, may be employed as a definition by some particular person, and may to him fulfil the purpose of the best logical definition which can be given; and therefore ought, if possible, to be comprehended under the same head. Thus, if I wish to define "honesty," I may say that it is uprightness in transactions relating to property, that it is probity, that it is the best policy; and any one of these concep-

* Aristotle, Top. Z. (vi.) ch. ii. *πᾶν γὰρ ἀσαφὲς τὸ κατὰ μεταφορὰν λεγόμενον . . . . . πᾶν γὰρ ἀσαφὲς τὸ μὴ εἰωθός.*

tions would enable some of my hearers to identify honesty, even though that word had not before occurred in my speech, or been suggested to their thoughts. If there were any one paramount conception, which would be to the minds of all a sufficient definition of honesty, I should employ that, and place it in a class by itself. But this is not the case. To many a humble thinker, "honesty is the best policy," would convey an idea, not adequate indeed, but still distinct, when "honesty is uprightness in respect to transactions connected with property," would be but a string of confused words. Let us then consider definition as any conception which, from having precisely the same sphere as another conception, may be used to ascertain its nature and mark out its limits. And the judgment in which definition is predicated, we call a substitutive judgment, because it furnishes a predicate identical with the subject as to sphere or extension, and therefore capable of being substituted for it. The subject of a substitutive judgment is called also the definitum, or conception defined.

§ 71. *Sources of Definition.*

As the subject and predicate of every substitutive judgment are coextensive, they may change places in the judgment, so that the definitum may become in its turn a definition. We may define a conception, by exhibiting in our definition its extension, or by unfolding its intension, or by the substitution of one symbol for another, or one set of marks for another. It will be found from these principles that there are six sources from which definitions may arise. i. From Resolution, when the marks of the definitum are made its definition; as in "a pension is an allowance for past services." It is not necessary that the marks should be completely enumerated—that the conception should be strictly adequate—but only that the marks should suffice for the identification of the subject, as belonging to it all and to it alone; so that Aristotle's Property would be included in it. ii. From Composition, the reverse of the last method, in which the definitum, a conception of which the component marks are enumerated, stands subject to a definition implicitly containing those marks; as, "those who encroach upon the property of others are dishonest." iii. From Division, where we define the subject by enumerating its dividing members; as, "Britons are those who dwell in England, Scotland, or Wales." All the judgments called disjunctives are under this head. iv. From Colligation, the exact reverse of the last; where the dividing members of a conception are enumerated in the subject, and the divided conception itself added to define them; as, "historical, philosophical, and mathematical sciences are the sum (i. e. *are all*, or *equal*) of human knowledge." This is the form which Inductive Judgments naturally assume. v. From change of Symbol, where both subject and predicate are symbolic conceptions, the latter being given as a substitute for the former on a principle of expedience only; as, "probity is honesty." This is the nominal definition of some logic-books. vi. From Casual Substitution, where one representation is put for another on a principle of expedience only, as serving to recall the marks, which both possess in common, more readily to the hearer's mind; as, "the science of politics is the best road to success in life; pleasure is the opposite of pain."

TABLE OF DEFINITION.

A Conception is defined	By its Intension (or Marks)	being unfolded,	= i.	Resolution, or Definition proper.
		being reunited,	= ii.	Composition.
	By its Extension (or Sphere)	being divided,	= iii.	Division.
		being reunited,	= iv.	Colligation.
	By Accidental Coincidence	of a Symbol,	= v.	Nominal Definition.
		of Notation,	= vi.	Accidental Definition.

§ 72. *Attribute.*

A predicate, the exact limits of which are not determined, cannot be used to define and determine a subject. It may be called an attribute; and conveys not the whole nature of the subject, but some one quality belonging to it. "Metals are heavy," "Some snakes are venomous," are judgments in which this kind of predicable occurs.

§ 73. *The Common Division of Judgments as to Relation.*

The relation in which the subject stands to the predicate in a judgment, whether as coincident or not coincident with it, we call *the doctrine of Rela-*

tion; as to which we find that predicates are of two kinds, substitutes or definitions, and attributes. The common account of Relation, which we are bound to consider, is somewhat different.

Judgments are divided, according to it, into three classes, the Categorical, the Hypothetical, and the Disjunctive Judgment.

The Categorical Judgment is one in which one conception is affirmed to belong or not to belong to another; as, "Men are endowed with conscience," "An enslaved people cannot be happy."

The Hypothetical expresses seemingly a relation between two judgments, as cause and effect, as condition and conditioned; for example, "If the autumn is very dry, the turnip crop is scanty," "If the heart is right, so will the actions be."

The Disjunctive Judgment expresses the relation (apparently) of two or more judgments which cannot be true together, and one or other of which must be true; as, "Either the Bible is false, or holiness ought to be followed;" or the proverb — "A man is either a fool or a physician at forty."

Categorical Judgments are easily referred to the two classes of substitutives and attributives, according as their predicates are or are not equal in extension to the subjects. This kind of judgment presents little difficulty, after the explanations already given.

Perhaps our readers may be slow to admit that for all logical purposes the hypothetical judgment may be treated as a categorical. Yet this is the view to which we must adhere, in common with the best logicians. In the hypothetical, there are not two judgments, but one. In the example, "If the heart is right, the actions will be so," we neither say that any one's heart *is* right, nor that his actions will be; we do not pass a judgment about either absolutely, but we say that *if* the one is, *then* the other will be. So that what we really decide is that there is a connection between the two facts; and the logical copula, though not expressed there, has its proper place between the two clauses, thus [" the case, fact, or notion of the heart's being right] is [a case, fact, or notion of the actions being so."] But there are several kinds of hypothetical judgments, which have different properties.

The hypothetical judgment appears, as we have said, as two judgments, the former of them, containing the condition, being called the antecedent, and the latter, containing the effect of the condition, being called the consequent. In each of these there are two terms, which would give four in all, if one of the terms of the antecedent did not sometimes reappear in the consequent, when the number of distinct terms is of course but three. Now only five arrangements of these terms are possible; in four of which there are but three terms, and in the fifth, four.

They are—

1. If A is B, A is C.
2. If A is B, B is C.
3. If A is B, C is A.
4. If A is B, C is B.
5. If A is B, C is D.

The following are examples of these formulæ :—

1. If one of the angles of a triangle is a right angle, it must be opposite to the greatest side.
2. If this be poetry, poetry is worthless.
3. If animals are creatures with a digestive cavity, polyps are animals.
4. If virtue is voluntary, vice is voluntary.
5. If the moon exerts her attractive force in the same line as the sun, the tides are at the highest.

The obvious difference between the first four examples and the fifth is, that the fifth alone expresses two separate facts, brought together as cause and effect, whilst in all the rest, from the recurrence of a term in both clauses, it is impossible to separate entirely the two things stated. This leads to the observation of a real difference in their nature. Without attempting to examine the origin of our idea of cause and effect, we may state, as a thing generally admitted, that all men are accustomed to regard some one fact as the necessary result of another, which they have observed invariably to precede or accompany it; and that they may learn, however different in nature the two facts may appear, to identify them so far as invariably to expect the effect where they have observed the cause. The vibration of a tense wire, and the hearing of a musical note, are two distinct facts, yet the one causes the other. The drawing of a trigger is a very different fact from the sudden death of a healthy man; yet every one knows that under certain circumstances the one will infallibly cause the other. The revolution of the moon has so little apparent connection with the spring and neap tides, that it would be long before men observed what is really the case, that the position of the moon influences the tide's fluctuations. Experience observes that events happen together, or in a close succession, and the mind, after adequate observations, connects them by its idea of cause. Whether this idea be also a part of the experience, or one of the primitive constituents of the mind itself, even as the eye is a constituent part of the body, is a question much debated; but it need not occupy us. We have to remark that two facts, which do not resemble one another, between which perhaps we once saw no connection, may be inseparably linked together in our minds, as a cause and an effect. And when the connection between them is stated, in a hypothetical (that is, a conditional) judgment, the truth of the statement will entirely depend upon the correctness of our observation, since there can be nothing in the statement itself to serve as a criterion of its truth. In "If A is B, C is D," we have no test but the application of our idea of cause and effect to the facts for which these letters stand. But in "If A is B, A is C," we appeal, not to the idea of cause, but to a categorical judgment of which we have the materials before us. "If A is B, A is C" will be true provided "All B is C" be true. "If this is an equilateral triangle, it is also an equiangular" must be tried by the rule, "All equilateral triangles are equiangular." Here is no notion of cause; but a statement of a rule, with the supposition that some one case comes under it. It really means, not that one event is caused by another, but that a conception has certain marks, which is the function of the categorical judgment.

All judgments apparently hypothetical, but having three terms only, may be reduced to categoricals by leaving out the term that is repeated, and using the other two for subject and predicate. Thus, "If this be poetry, poetry is worthless," becomes, "This (poetry) is worthless;" and "If virtue is voluntary, vice is voluntary," means that "Virtue (in so far as pertains to the control of the will) is the same as vice." But as they have the conditional form, they may also be reduced to categoricals in the mode already described;—"The case of virtue being voluntary is a case of vice being voluntary." The conditional particle *if* means, in judgments of this kind, "if it should prove that—or, be granted that," since the facts exist already, and the supposition refers to our knowledge of them. But in the true conditional the "if" signifies "if it occurs that," since the fact must come about to necessitate the occurrence of another fact.

But whilst conditional judgments differ essentially from categoricals, the former affirming the casual connection between two distinct facts, and the latter declaring that a thing or class of things has some property, there is also a sufficient similarity to admit of their being identified, for logical purposes. Both alike affirm the invariable connection of their two terms. By "All the tissues of the body continually decay and are reproduced," is meant that wherever one of the tissues of the human body exists, decay and reproduction are going on, and cannot be absent; and in like manner, by "If the moon's attraction acts against that of the sun, the tides are low," is meant that whenever these two heavenly bodies are found in the supposed position, we find a particular state of the tides. In both cases one thing is affirmed to be an accompaniment of another. In the categorical, a thing has the mark expressed by the predicate; and in the conditional, a fact has another fact for its mark. In the example given of the former kind of judgment, we affirm that without the notion of decay and reproduction, our notion of the tissues of the body would be wrong and incomplete; in the other example that our notion of that position of the heavenly bodies would be incomplete, if we did not take into view its influence on the tides. Logic, willing to simplify her formulæ, and to leave the examination of the idea of cause and effect to Metaphysics, reduces the conditional to the same rules as the categorical. The formula, "The case, fact, or notion of *this* existing, is, a case, fact, or notion of *that* existing," is sufficient for the reduction of *any* conditional to a categorical. For true conditionals, i. e. those where the supposition relates to the occurrence of facts, not to our knowledge of facts, we shall generally say, "The *fact* of his being," &c.; for the other kinds, "The *notion*," &c. But some variations are admissible. Thus, recurring to our examples, we may say,—

1. The case of one angle of a triangle being a rectangle—is—a case of its being opposite to the greatest side.
2. The admission that this is poetry—would be an admission that poetry is worthless.
3. The statement that animals are creatures with a digestive cavity —implies—that polyps are animals.
4. The notion that virtue is voluntary—implies—the notion that vice is voluntary.
5. The fact that the moon exerts her attractive force in the same line as the sun—implies—the fact that the tides are at the highest.

But let it be noticed that the four first examples contain the materials not so much of a judgment, as of a perfect argument, of which one of the judgments is *supposed* to be true.

1. Every right angle of a triangle is opposite the greatest side,
   This angle is a right angle;
   Therefore it is opposite to the greatest side.
2. This poetry is worthless,
   This poetry is *all* poetry (i. e. is a fair sample of every kind);
   Therefore all poetry is worthless.
3. Animals=creatures with a digestive cavity,
   Polyps have this;
   Therefore they are animals.
4. Virtue is voluntary,
   Vice (as far as the will goes) is the same as virtue;
   Therefore vice is voluntary.

Conditionals may appear either as substitutive or attributive judgments. If they set forth some cause which not only produces a given effect, but is the only cause that does so, they belong to the former class. "If the moon comes between the sun and the earth, the sun will be eclipsed"—is a judgment of this kind, for there is no other cause which produces that effect; and therefore we may either say, "All cases of the moon's coming between the sun and the earth—are—cases of the sun's being eclipsed," or the simple converse, "All cases of the sun's being eclipsed—are—cases of the moon's coming between the sun and the earth." But where the cause stated is only one of several which might have produced the effect—as in "If it rains, the flower-beds will be wet," where the same effect would be produced by the falling of dew, or the use of the watering-pot,—we cannot employ the simple converse, for the predicate is wider than the subject. We may say, "All cases of its having rained are cases of the flower-beds being wet," but obviously not "All cases of the flower-beds being wet are cases of its having rained." These are attributives.

Disjunctive judgments may all be referred to the head of substitutives; for the sphere of the predicate is just equal to that of the subject, the latter being a conception, and the former the same conception logically divided (§ 55.). In "Either Shakspeare is wrong, or Richard III. was a monster," our meaning may be expressed thus—"The possible cases in this matter are that Shakspeare is wrong, and that Richard III. was a monster;" which is a substitutive judgment. The real premiss in a disjunctive *argument* is not the disjunctive judgment itself, but, as will be shown, a certain immediate consequence from it.

§ 74. *Doctrine of Quantity, or of the extension of the subject in a judgment.*

A judgment is either about the whole of a conception, as, "All stars shine," and this we call a universal judgment; or about part of a conception, as, "Some lakes have an outlet," and this is a particular judgment; or about an intuition, as, "Northumberland House is near Charing Cross," and this is a singular judgment.

For logical purposes we may regard all singulars as universals, because they agree in bringing in the whole, and not a part, of their subject. So that as to Quantity, judgments are either universal or particular.*

* See *Wallis's* Logic, *Thesis* I. Further distinctions of judgments

§ 75. *Doctrine of Quality, or the agreement or disagreement of subject and predicate.*

Where a judgment expresses that its two terms agree, it is called Affirmative; as, "All planets move in an elliptic orbit;" where it expresses their disagreement, it is termed negative; as, "No human knowledge is perfect." This part of the judgment is its Quality. Although the negative particle is not always connected with the copula, but may appear in other parts of the sentence, in every real negative judgment it belongs only to the copula. The two terms are given, and the question always

as to Quantity have been brought in by the acuteness of logicians, which for philosophical purposes are not very important. The judgment—"Most men are prejudiced," cannot, it is argued, be considered as particular, for it implies not only that *some* men, but *more than the half* of mankind are prejudiced. These are termed *plurative* judgments; and will be mentioned again in examining the syllogism. To Professor *De Morgan* belongs the merit of recalling attention to them; and in his elaborate and acute "Formal Logic," p. 325, he inserts Sir *W. Hamilton's* remark upon the use of them, that "all that is out of classification—all that has no reference to genus and species, is out of Logic, indeed out of Philosophy;" that Philosophy seeks to know whether *all* or *some* or *none* of a subject comes into a predicate, but not whether much or little, for "Philosophy tends always to the universal and necessary," to which this distinction does not seem to belong. At the same time the plurative judgment deserves attention, as being a possible mode, and as one more proof of the incompleteness of the doctrine of the syllogism as commonly taught.

In the same work (p. 142), another class of propositions is mentioned, called the "numerically definite proposition," where the number of objects both of the subject and predicate is known and specified. The same objection and defence would apply to them as to the plurative judgments; only that their practical use seems even less, and it is difficult even to invent an example likely to occur is whether *is* or *is not* shall be the connecting link between them.

But by removing the negative sign from the copula and attaching it to the predicate, we may turn the judgment into an affirmative of a peculiar kind, sometimes called an indefinite,* which is equivalent in signification to the negative. Instead of, No human knowledge is perfect, we may say with equal truth, All human knowledge is *non*-perfect, or *im*-perfect. This license is founded on the law that it amounts to the same thing whether we say that our subject is shut out from some positive conception or included in the cognate privative, for any given subject whatever must be found in one of the two. (p. 153.) But for logical purposes these indefinite judgments may, without inconvenience, be considered as affirmatives.

To distinguish between negative judgments and such as are so only in appearance, we must consider whether the sign of negation, *not*, is meant to affect the copula, or whether it really belongs to one of the terms. In, "Not to submit would be madness," there is no negation, though the sign of it is expressed.

§ 76. *Doctrine of Modality.*

The degree of certainty with which a judgment is made and maintained, is called its modality; as being the *mode*, or measure, in which we hold it to be true. We affirm with very different degrees of assurance, the two judgments, that "An equilateral triangle is equiangular," and that "Zeno of Elea

* By Wolff, *Phil. Rat.* § 209, and Kant, *Logik*, § 22.

was the inventor of dialectic;" since we can prove the former to demonstration, whilst doubts may be entertained as to the evidence on which the latter rests. Opinions differ as to the place which this doctrine ought to hold in Logic. Not without hesitation, it is here excluded from pure, to be discussed in applied Logic, on the ground that the modality of a judgment is not part of itself, and does not belong to the copula,—as seems to be shown by the fact that the degree of certainty about the same judgment fluctuates in the mind of the same person at different times, and, still more, in different persons, the mode of expression remaining unaltered.

§ 77. *Distribution of Terms in Judgments.*

Universal judgments distribute, *i. e.* introduce the whole of, their subject; particulars do not. In "All the fixed stars twinkle" and "No man is wise at all times," it is obvious that we are speaking of the whole of the fixed stars, and of men, respectively; and therefore each term is distributed.

Negative judgments distribute the predicate. If "No minerals are nutritious for animals" is asserted, it means that nothing which is nutritious for animals can have the properties of minerals; and so the term "nutritious for animals" is distributed; and if we suppose that only *some* nutritious things are asserted not to agree with minerals, it would follow that *some other* nutritious things might agree with, *i. e.* might be, minerals, so that we might say at the same time —"No minerals are nutritious for animals" and "Some minerals are nutritious for animals;" whereas we know that we meant by the former judgment to exclude the possibility of our receiving the latter. If the predicate of a negative is not distributed, it can have no real negative power; for if the subject is only excluded from one part of the predicate, it may be included in some other part.

Substitutive judgments distribute the predicate. Since the predicate in them is used to define the subject, or in other words to mark its exact limits, it must itself be definite, and therefore the whole of it must be given, otherwise the uncertainty as to what *part* was meant, would make it useless for definition.

We may here remark that an ambiguity attaches to some particles which have important duties in Logic. The copula *is* means always *exists*,* but when used in a proposition, it expresses an existence modified or limited by the predicate; when employed alone, it expresses *absolute* existence, *i. e.* that the subject is among the class of really existing things. Upon this variation a well-known fallacy † was founded; that of arguing that because "Ptolemy is dead" (*i. e.* only exists to us in the way that a dead person can, by a remembered or traditionary notion) therefore "Ptolemy *is*" (*i. e.* has an actual existence among other living persons,) which is a very different statement.

Again, the word *all* in its proper logical sense means "each and every;" but it stands sometimes for "all taken together—" "All these claims upon

* See however *Waitz*, on Organ. 16, a. 12, for the sense of the copula in Aristotle.

† *Aristotle*, de Soph. Elench. ch. v. iii. Tauchnitz.

my time overpower me." Hence may arise in ambiguity; instead of the *all* in its logical use, we may put *every;* but to exercise the same liberty with the other sense of it would be absurd. The example given could not mean, "Every single claim upon my time overpowers me."

The word *some* is likewise the cause of confusion, in its logical use. In what sense is the "some" of a particular proposition to be understood? Does it mean, "Some, we know not how many," or, "A certain number, which we may have in our thoughts?" Suppose that historical reading leads to the conviction that "Some democratic governments have ended in a tyranny," it may be doubtful whether this result includes precisely those democracies which we have found in our researches were consummated by despotism, and no others, in which case the conception in our minds is definite and precise, though conveyed in an indefinite expression, or only expresses that this has occasionally happened to democracies, possibly to others besides those which we have studied, in which case the conception "some democracies" would be purely indefinite. The word appears to be employed in the two senses of "Some or other," and "Some certain," in common language; and it becomes a question in which sense it is to be regarded in Logic.

Now the different steps in attaining knowledge are marked by the acquirement of new laws or rules, that is to say, of universal judgments, expressing that to the whole of a given class of things or facts, some mark or property belongs. And wherever a definite number of things is ascertained to possess a mark, it is the tendency of the mind to set them apart from other things that most resemble them, by some name which may stand for them both in thought and speech, for the sake of making the statement universal. If by "Some democracies have ended in despotism," we mean simply to assert that in three or four countries, with the history of which we are familiar, and which we could name, this result has occurred, the statement is really universal, because our subject is only a species arbitrarily formed of the genus "democracies;" and we ought to say, "The democracies (three or four) whose history we have traced." But as our having studied them is not of importance enough to found a distinction upon, a universal assertion of this kind would have no philosophical value; and by "Some democracies end in despotism" we should mean to declare that in trying to find the agreement between these two terms, we had not succeeded in establishing the rule, the universal judgment, but that a partial agreement had appeared, the extent of which, though it was discovered from some particular cases, was not, so far as we knew, limited to them, but remained thoroughly indefinite. Every term then which, though indefinitely expressed, refers to a definite class of things, should be rendered definite. Wherever the things denoted by the subject are really definite, as having some marks that group them in a smaller class by themselves, science requires that instead of appearing as part of a larger class, they should have their own name and position.

Summary of the Analysis of Judgments.

The Nature or Form of Judgments consists in their having a certain

- Quantity — as to which they are either
  - Universal — where the whole subject is joined to the predicate,
  - or Particular—where part of the subject is joined to the predicate,
- Quality — as to which they are either
  - Affirmative — where the predicate is decided to agree with the subject,
  - or Negative — where the predicate is decided not to agree with the subject,
- Relation — as to which; *affirmative* judgments are either
  - Attributive—where an indefinite (i. e. undistributed) predicate is assigned to the subject,
  - or Substitutive—where a definite (i. e. distributed) predicate is assigned to the subject, which may be substituted for it, and serve as its definition.

§ 78. *Table of all the Judgments.*

The following table contains examples of the six kinds of judgments, with their Quantity, Quality, and Relation expressed, and the vowels which may conveniently be used as symbols of them.

SIGN.	EXAMPLE.	QUANT.	QUAL.	REL.
A.	All plants grow.	Univ.	Affirm.	Attrib.
E.	No right action is inexpedient.	Univ.	Neg.	
I.	Some muscles act without our volition.	Part.	Affirm.	Attrib.
O.	Some plants do not grow in the tropics.	Part.	Neg.	
U.	Common salt is chloride of sodium.	Univ.	Affirm.	Substi.
Y.	Some stars are all the planets.	Part.	Affirm.	Substi.

An inspection of the table will show that of the six judgments there are three of universal and three of particular quantity; that there are four of affirmative and two of negative quality; that there are two of attributive and two of substitutive relation, whilst the two negatives, as denying that either relation subsists between the subject and predicate, are undetermined as to relation. The vowels in the first column are very useful in abbreviating the processes of Logic; for instead of saying that a given judgment is a universal affirmative judgment, it is sufficient to say that it is an A, which conveys, to one conversant with Logic, the same meaning. The last example, of Y, is given in the words best adapted to show the distribution of its terms; but in practice it would probably occur as, "Stars *include* the planets," which has precisely the same import. But this form of judgment is seldom used,* because, the subject being the principal notion in every judgment, it is unnatural to put an indefinite (i. e. undistributed) conception in the principal place, and a definite (i. e. distributed) conception in the place of second importance. That notion of which we had the whole be

The old logicians would have called it, probably, an "*inordinata propositio*," or unnatural proposition—*Keckermanni*, Log. B. II. § i. cap. I., not quite upon the same grounds. Comp. *Arist.* An. Post. I. xxii. 3; and *Zabarella* upon it, p. 909.

fore us, would naturally occur first; and this, it seems, is the psychological principle on which "All planets are stars" is a more obvious and natural judgment than its converse, "Some stars are all planets." Nor is the predicate of Y strictly definitive, since it only serves that purpose for *a part* of the subject.

§ 79. *Table of Judgments according to Sir W. Hamilton.*

To the six judgments just given, a very distinguished logician adds two. Extending the doctrine of distribution, he says that in negative judgments as well as in affirmative, we may speak of—the whole of both terms—part of both terms—the whole of the subject and part of the predicate—part of the subject and the whole of the predicate; so that there are four kinds of affirmatives and four of negatives. Putting X and Y to stand for any subject and predicate, we may exhibit them thus:—

Sign.	Affirmatives.	Negatives.	Sign.
U.	All X is all Y.	No X is Y.	E.
I.	Some X is some Y.	Some X is not some Y.	ω.
A.	All X is some Y.	No X is some Y.	η.
Y.	Some X is all Y.	Some X is no Y.	O.

On comparing this table with that given in the last section, it will be found that with the exception of the two negatives marked η and ω, each judgment here has a counterpart there. Why have we ventured, in accordance with the practice, it is believed, of all logicians, to exclude these two?

The answer is, that whilst Sir William Hamilton

gives a table of all *conceivable* cases of negative predication, other logicians have only admitted *actual* cases. It is not inconceivable that a man should say, "No birds are *some* animals," (the η of the Table,) and yet such a judgment is never actually made, because it has the semblance only, and not the power, of a denial. True though it is, it does not prevent our making another judgment of the affirmative kind, from the same terms; and "All birds are animals" is also true. Though such a negative judgment is conceivable, it is useless; and feeling this, men in their daily conversation, as well as logicians in their treatises, have proscribed it.—But the fruitlessness of a negative judgment where both terms are particular is even more manifest; for "Some X is not some Y" is true, whatever terms X and Y stand for,* and therefore the judgment, as presupposed in every case, is not worth the trouble of forming in any particular one. Thus if I define the composition of common salt by saying "Common salt is chloride of sodium," I cannot prevent another saying that "*Some* common salt is not *some* chloride of sodium," because he may mean that the common salt in *this* salt-cellar is not the chloride of sodium in *that*. A judgment of this kind is spurious upon two grounds; it denies nothing, because it does not prevent any of the modes of affirmation; it decides nothing, inasmuch as its truth

* Except of course they represent individuals; and all that could be inferred from such a judgment would be, that its terms were general, not individual—conceptions, not intuitions. Even this, however, is provided for, as we know from their being particular, that they must be capable of division, and therefore general. "Some Nicias" could only be said with propriety if there were several men bearing that name.

is presupposed with reference to any pair of conceptions whatever. In a list of *conceivable* modes of predication, these two are entitled to a place.*

* To my objection, that the two weaker negatives have never occurred in the examination of logical examples, Sir *William Hamilton* replies in the *Athenæum* (in a letter dated February 25, 1851) as follows: "The thorough-going quantification of the predicate (on demand) in its appliance to negative propositions, is not only allowable, is not only systematic, is not only useful,—it is even indispensable. For to speak of its very weakest form, that which I call parti-partial negation, "*some—is not some;*"—this (besides its own uses) is the form which we naturally employ in dividing a whole of any kind into parts: "*Some A is not some A.*" And is this form—that too inconsistently—to be excluded from logic?—But again (to prove *both* the obnoxious propositions summarily and at once)—what objection, apart from the arbitrary laws of our present logical system, can be taken to the following syllogism?—

'*All man is some animal,*
Any man is not (*no man is*) *some animal;*
Therefore some animal is not some animal.'

Vary this syllogism of the third figure to any other; it will always be legitimate by nature, if illegitimate to unnatural art. Taking it, however, as it is:—the negative minor premise, with its particular predicate, offends logical prejudice. But it is a proposition irrecusable; both as true in itself, and as even practically necessary. Its converse, again, is technically allowed; and no proposition can be right of which the converse is wrong. For to say (as has been said from Aristotle downwards) that a particular negative proposition is inconvertible,—this is merely to confess that the rules of logicians are inadequate to the truth of logic and the realities of nature. But this inadequacy is relieved by an unexclusive quantification of the predicate. A toto-partial negative cannot, therefore, be refused.—But if the premises are correct, so likewise must be the conclusion. This, however, is the doubly obnoxious form of a parti-partial negative:—

'*Some animal* (man) *is not some animal* (say, brute).'

"Nothing, it may be observed, is more easy than to misapply a form; nothing more easy than to use a weaker, when we are entitled to use a stronger proposition. But from the special and factitious absurdity thus emerging, to infer the general and natural absurdity

§ 80. *Import of Judgments. Extension and Intension. Naming.*

Upon the examination of any judgment which appears to express a simple relation between two terms, we shall find it really complex, and capable of more than one interpretation. "All stones are hard,"—means in the first place that the mark, hardness, is found among the marks or attributes of all stones; and in this sense of the judgment, the predicate may be said to be contained in the subject, for a complete notion of stones contains the notion of hardness and something more. This is to read the judgment as to the intension (or comprehension) of its terms (p. 105). Where it is a mere judgment of explanation, it will mean, "the marks of the predicate are among *what I know to be* among the marks of the subject;" but where it is the expression of a new step in our investigation, of an accession of knowledge, it must mean, "the marks of the predicate are among *what I now find* to be the marks of the subject."

Both subject and predicate however not only imply certain marks, but represent certain sets of objects. When we think of "all stones," we bring before us not only the set of marks — as hardness, solidity, inorganic structure, and certain general forms — by which we know a thing to be what we call a stone,

of the propositional form itself,—this is, certainly, not a logical procedure."

This also occurs, with a few verbal alterations, in *Hamilton's Discussions in Philosophy, &c.* p. 163.

but also the class of things which have the marks, the stones themselves. And we might interpret the judgment, "All stones are hard," to mean that "The class of stones is contained in the class of hard things." This brings in only the extension of the two terms; according to which, in the example before us, the subject is said to be contained in the predicate. Every judgment may be interpreted from either point of view; and a right understanding of this doctrine is of great importance. Let it be noticed against a mistake which has been reintroduced into logic, that all conceptions, being *general*, represent a class, and that to speak of a "general name" which is not the name of a class, is a contradiction in terms. But this is very different from asserting that a class of things corresponding to the conception actually exists in the world without us. The conceptions of giant, centaur, and siren are all of classes; but every one knows, who realizes them, that the only region in which the classes really exist, is that of poetry and fiction. The mode of existence of the things which a conception denotes is a mark of the conception itself; and would be expressed in any adequate definition of it. It would be insufficient to define "Centaurs" as a set of monsters, half men and half horses, who fought with the Lapithæ, so long as we left it doubtful whether they *actually* lived and fought, or only were feigned to have done so; and by some phrase, such as "according to Ovid," or "in the Mythology," we should probably express that their actual existence was not part of our conception of them.

The judgment selected as our example contains

yet a third statement. We observe marks; by them we set apart a class; and lastly, we give the class a name or symbol, to save the trouble of reviewing all the marks every time we would recall the conception. "All stones are hard," means that the name hard may be given to every thing to which we apply the name stones.

All judgments then may be interpreted according to their Intension, their Extension, and their application of names or descriptions; as the following examples may help to show.

A. "All the metals are conductors of electricity" means

Intension. The attribute of conducting electricity belongs to all metals.

Extension. The metals are in the class of conductors of electricity.

Denomination. The name of conductors of electricity may be applied to the metals (among other things).*

E. "None of the planets move in a circle" means

Intension. The attribute of moving in a circle does not belong to any planet.

Extension. None of the planets are in the class (be it real, or only conceivable) of things that move in a circle.

Denomination. The description of things that move in a circle cannot be applied to the planets.

I. "Some metals are highly ductile" means

Intension. The mark of great ductility is a mark of some metals.

Extension. Some metals are in the class of highly ductile things.

Denomination. The name of highly ductile things may be applied to some metals.

O. "Some lawful actions are not expedient" means

Intension. The attribute of expediency does not belong to some lawful actions.

* "Among other things." This qualification is required by the rules of distribution, for metals are only *some* conductors.

Extension. Some lawful actions do not come into the class of expedient things.

Denomination. The name of expedient cannot be given to some lawful actions.

U. "Rhetoric is the art of persuasive speaking" means

Intension. The attributes of the art of persuasive speaking, and of Rhetoric, are the same.

Extension. Rhetoric is coextensive with the art of speaking persuasively.

Denomination. "The art of persuasive speaking" is an expression which may be substituted for Rhetoric.

Y. "The class of animals includes the polyps" means

Intension. The attributes of all the polyps belong to some animals.

Extension. The class of animals includes the polyps.

Denomination. The name of polyps belongs to some animals.

§ 81. *Explicative and Ampliative Judgments.*

Some judgments * are merely explanatory of their subject, having for their predicate a conception which it fairly implies, to all who know and can define its nature. They are called explicative (or analytic) judgments, because they *unfold* the meaning of the subject, without determining any thing new concerning it. Though they cannot be said to augment our knowledge of the subject, the habit of thinking of things without realizing all their marks, is so common, that judgments in which the marks are predicated anew are useful to revive our remembrance of them; whilst they are indispensable in explaining to others the nature of our subject, of which they may not have an adequate notion. If we say that "all triangles have three sides," the judgment is explica-

* *Kant*, Logik, § 36, and Prolegomena, § 2. Also, for the names here adopted, Sir *W. Hamilton* in *Reid's* Works.

tive; because "having three sides" is always implied in a right notion of a triangle.*

Judgments of another class attribute to the subject something not directly implied in it, and have been called ampliative, because they enlarge or increase our knowledge. They are also called synthetic, from *placing together* two notions not hitherto associated. For example—"All bodies possess power of attraction" is an ampliative judgment; because we can think of bodies without thinking of attraction as one of their immediate primary attributes. But if our knowledge of any object were complete, we should conceive it invested with *all* its attributes, and no ampliative judgments would be required.

We must distinguish between explicative and tautologous judgments. Whilst the explicative display the meaning of the subject, and put the same *matter* in a new *form*, the tautologous only repeat the subject, and give us the same matter in the same form, as "Whatever is, is." "A spirit is a spirit." Whether in thinking or in teaching, the tautologous judgments are useless.†

* Such judgments, as declaring the nature or essence of the subject, have been called "essential propositions." *Mill's* Logic, B. I. ch. VI. It is, however, a misnomer to call them all "identical propositions." "Every man is a living creature" would not be an identical proposition unless "living creature" denoted the same as "man;" whereas it is far more extensive. *Locke* understands by identical propositions only such as are tautologous — "by identical propositions, I mean only such wherein the same term, importing the same idea, is affirmed of itself." (Hum. Under. IV. viii. 3). But he condemns the use of what we have called analytic judgments likewise (Hum. Under. IV. viii. 4), as adding nothing to real knowledge; he would probably admit them as *explanatory* propositions.

† *Kant*, Logik, § 37; *Locke*, Hum. Under. IV. viii. 2.—They may accidentally, and by a particular emphasis, become the vehicles of

emotion or rebuke. The "Sensation is sensation," of Dr. *Johnson*, means, "One cannot help feeling." So too the obvious analytic judgments, "A negro has a soul, please your honour," of *Sterne's* Corporal, and "He has no wife," of the agonized Macduff, convey a pathos from their accidental use, and from the train of judgments they suggest, but disdain to express, which their mere logical import does not account for.

OUTLINE

OF THE

LAWS OF THOUGHT.

—◆—

PART III.

SYLLOGISM. REASONING.

Ο μὲν γὰρ συλλογισμὸς ἐκ τινῶν, ἐστὶ τεθέντων, ὥστε λέγειν ἕτερόν τι ἐξ ἀνάγκης τῶν κειμένων διὰ τῶν κειμένων.—Aristotle.

SYLLOGISM. REASONING.

§ 82. *Syllogism.*

WHEN the state of our knowledge does not warrant us in judging at once whether two conceptions agree or differ, we seek for some other judgment, or judgments, that contains the grounds for our coming to a decision. This is called reasoning, which may be defined "the process of deriving one judgment from another." The technical name for that one single step of the process, of which the longest chains of reasoning are but the repetition, is syllogism, (or computation,) a word which has acquired its present sense from the resemblance between computation proper, *i. e.* gathering the results of a sum, and that gathering of the result of other judgments which we call reasoning. A syllogism has been defined "A sentence or thought in which, from something laid down and admitted, something distinct from what we have laid down follows of necessity." * The form or essence of a syllogism therefore consists, not in the

* *Aristotle,* Pri. An. I. i. I say "a sentence or thought" because λόγος means both *ratio* and *oratio.* The words "laid down and admitted" have no exclusive reference to disputation, for we may lay down judgments for *our own* use alone, when there is no disputant in the case. *Trendelenburg* and *Waitz,* on this passage.

truth of the judgments laid down, or of that which is arrived at, but in the production of a new and distinct judgment, not a mere repetition of the antecedents, the truth of which cannot be denied without impugning those we have already accepted for true.

The new judgment which is to be drawn, and which gives occasion for the reasoning process, is called, *before* proof is found, the question or problem, and *after* proof the conclusion. The judgments used to establish the conclusion are termed the premisses; and the connection between the premisses and conclusion, that entitles us to gather the one from the other, is the consequence; as appears from the phrases "by consequence," "consequently," so often employed in argument. Sometimes the conclusion, as following, "by consequence" has itself the name of consequence, although consequent would be more strictly correct. Latin writers have applied the names *complexio* and *connexio* to the same part of the syllogism.

§ 83. *Immediate and Mediate Inference.*

In some cases we are unable to decide that the terms of the question agree with or differ from one another, without finding a third, called the *middle*, term, with which each of the others may be compared in turn. This is mediate inference. If one suspects that "this liquid is poison," it may be impossible to convert the suspicion into certainty, until one has found that "it contains arsenic;" "containing arsenic" will then be the middle term, which will be compared in a judgment with each of the others in turn; and the whole argument will run, "This liquid contains arsenic; and every thing that contains arsenic is poisonous; consequently this liquid is." We will say nothing at present of the means of finding middle terms, although, as in the given example, long trains of thought or patient observation may be required to secure them.

But sometimes, instead of a third term, differing entirely from the other two, the premiss only need contain the two terms of the conclusion, or some modification of them. Thus from "All good rulers are just" we infer that "No unjust rulers can be good," a judgment introducing indeed no new *matter*, *i. e.* making us acquainted with no new facts; but still distinct from that from which we drew it, as representing the matter under a new form. Here, for purposes of inference, there are not three different terms, because *just* and *unjust*, though they stand for two separate sets of objects, have a particular relation, each implying the existence of the other.* Some Logicians refuse the name of inference to this and similar processes, on the ground that "there is in the conclusion no new truth, nothing but what was already asserted in the premisses, and obvious to whoever apprehends them." † That the conclusion is *virtually* asserted in the premisses, is true not only of these immediate inferences, but of all syllogisms whatever; even in the inductive, the mere consequence—the act of concluding—brings in nothing which is not known potentially as soon as we have the whole grounds before us. So that the objection

* See § 59. † *Mill's* Logic, B. II. ch. 1, 2.

proves too much; as it would disqualify a set of inferences which no one thinks of rejecting. If, however, there is absolutely nothing new—if the concession of the premiss is not only a virtual, but an actual and express declaration of the conclusion, there is no inference, but mere repetition. But who can say that "No unjust rulers are good" is a bare repetition of "All good rulers are just?" In the one we affirm, in the other deny; in the one the subject of thought is "good rulers," in the other "unjust rulers." They are, in these two points at least, distinct judgments, and as the passing of the one makes it possible, without further observation or decision upon facts, to collect the other, there is an inference. In many such cases, it is true, the inference is so obvious, so certain to occur upon the first glance at the premiss, that it seems needless to draw it out; but all the inferences we are about to specify are used from time to time, and this entitles them to our consideration.

The same objection would lie against all attempts to give rules for the immediate inferences, as would be brought against a definition of the colour *blue*, or scientific directions for walking; namely, that the things themselves are so simple that we understand them perfectly without directions. It is easier to discover for ourselves the principle of any case that may arise, than to charge the memory with a list of all the cases and their laws; and therefore few students will go beyond the simple examination of the following sections, which are necessary to the completeness of our analysis of thinking.

§ 84. *Opposition and Inferences depending on it.*

Opposition of judgments is the relation between any two which have the same matter, but a different form, the same subject and predicate, but a different quantity, quality, or relation. Between "No form of government is exempt from change," and "Some forms of government are exempt from change," there is an opposition, called by logicians contradictory, the rule of which is that one or other of the judgments must be true, that no intermediate one is possible, and that both cannot be true together. Hence it results, that if I lay down that "No A is B," I imply the impossibility of laying down "Some A is B," or, in technical phraseology, if I posit the one I remove the other. And again, the refusal to adopt "No A is B," is equivalent to laying down that "Some A is B;" the removal of one implies the position of the other. The doctrine of opposition has to show what may be inferred as to the truth or falsehood of any other kind of judgment, from the truth or falsehood of a given one, the subject and predicate remaining always the same. Arbitrary names, sanctioned by the earliest usage, have been given to the relation between each pair of judgments, to which some addition has been rendered necessary by the new judgments U and Y. But the terms chosen are such as convey their own meaning; and where it was possible, the well-known names have been extended to new relations, instead of introducing new ones.

TABLES OF OPPOSITION OF JUDGMENTS.

I.

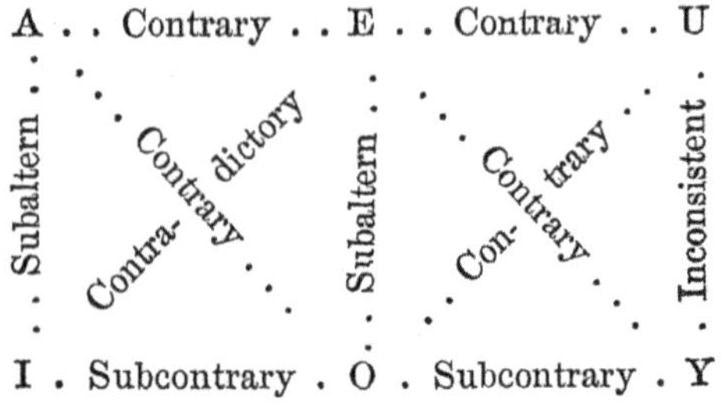

II.

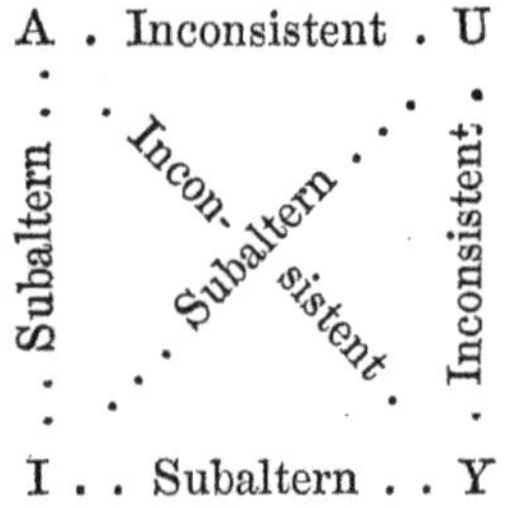

There are five kinds of Opposition; Contradictory, Contrary, Inconsistent, Subaltern, and Subcontrary.

Contradictory opposition * is the most perfect, as we can infer both from the position of a judgment the removal of its contradictory, and from the removal of the judgment the position of its contradictory, as has been shown above. It only exists between the judgments E and I. Other writers describe A and O as contradictories; but the fact is that we cannot tell from the removal of O, whether we ought to replace it by A or U. Let the O "Some men are not rational animals," be re-

* *Aristotle* often called judgments of this kind simply "opposites" (ἀντικείμεναι), as if he considered contradictory opposition the opposition *par excellence*. *Waitz* on Org. xi. b. xvi.

moved, *i. e.* its truth denied, and that removal will not establish the A, " All men are (some) rational animals." A third judgment is possible, namely, that "All men are all rational animals,"—the only rational animals there are, and which of these two is to apply, cannot be inferred from the O, but must be ascertained from the facts of the case.

Contrary opposition exists between affirmative and negative judgments which cannot be true together, but which may be false together; that is, between A and E, E and U, E and Y, U and O, and A and O. From the position of a judgment we are able to infer the removal of its contrary; but the judgment may be removed or denied, without the position of the contrary. If it is laid down that " All men have a right to freedom," it becomes impossible to lay down that " No men have a right to freedom;" but of course it does not follow from the refusal to admit that " All men have the right," that therefore *no* men have.

Inconsistent opposition lies between any two affirmative judgments which cannot be correct together, but may be false together; that is, between A and U, U and Y, and A and Y. Here it becomes necessary to attain a more precise notion of the difference between A and U. Suppose the example of U to be " Animals are things endowed with life and sensation;" which means—that "animals" and "things endowed with life and sensation" are but two modes of representing the same thing, and are therefore interchangeable. Let the example of A be " All men are animals;"—can we say that this judgment has the same properties as the other? can we put " animals" wherever "men" should come into our thoughts? No; "animals" is a very wide class, containing "men" and a vast number of other species. We mean by our judgment, not that men and animals are just the same things, but that men are *contained in* the wider class animals. This relation might be represented to us by making "men" a small circle, within "animals" a large one; whilst the relation between subject and predicate in U would be best conceived as that of two equal circles laid one upon the other. Now every judgment which is really A, and not U, *i. e.* which really has an undistributed predicate, means that the predicate is wider than, and contains, the subject; whereas every U means as certainly that the predicate is no wider than the subject. It is true that we sometimes form an A where we might form a U; as in saying that "All men are (*some*) rational animals," from a belief that in a higher state of being, or in another planet, there may be rational animals to whom it would be improper, from their other characteristics, to apply the name of men; where another, disbelieving the existence of any creatures besides men, to whom the name could apply, may hold that "All men are *all* rational animals." But this does not make the judgment true together. *Which* is true depends upon the facts; and the reason that two persons hold the two judgments together, or one person holds them at different times, is that they know the facts with different degrees of correctness. Where the facts judged upon are fairly and fully known, an A and a U can never represent them with equal correctness, nor can ever be true together. They are inconsistent.

Subaltern opposition is between any pair of affirmative or negative judgments, when the one has fewer terms distributed, that is, taken entire, than the other. That in which there is more distribution is called the subalternant, and that which has less or none, the subalternate; or they may be termed the higher and lower. The inference here is, that when the higher is laid down the lower follows; but nothing follows from denying the higher, or laying down the lower. I is the subalternate to A, O to E, I to U, and I to Y; so that from any A, U or Y, follows an I, and from any E, an O. The name of opposition less properly applies here, as the relation of the judgments is really a partial agreement.

Subcontrary opposition is between particular judgments, of which one is affirmative and the other negative, *viz*: I and O, O and Y. The name subcontrary is altogether arbitrary and without meaning, as the judgments have no real contrariety, but rather a presumption of agreement. They are opposed, according to Aristotle, only in the form of expression.* If "Some men are wise" be *the whole* truth "Some men are not wise," its subcontrary, follows of course; and it has been ingeniously remarked by Toletus, that in this kind of opposition there is not the same subject in the two judgments, for we mean in one "Some men," and in the other "Some *other* men." Each pair of judgments *may* be true together; and I and O cannot be false together. The opposition of Y and O, though we have not given it a separate name, has these pecu-

* An. Pri. II. 15. Ammonius terms them ὑπεναντίας, and Boethius *subcontrarias*.

liar properties, that if Y be true, O must be; and that they may be false together. To distinguish it, we may call it *false*-contrary opposition.

Two judgments * cannot be called opposites, unless the same subject be joined with the same predicate at the same time, and under the same circumstances in both. "The English are very rich," and "The English are not very rich," may be true together, if English *capitalists* are referred to in the former, and *the public revenue* of England in the latter. Moreover, if the judgment imply an act of comparison with some third thing as a standard, the same standard must be preserved in its opposite. It is not uncommon to hear two such judgments as "This house is very large," and "This house is very small," pronounced by two people who are comparing it with two different standards, the one perhaps with his own little cottage, the other with Blenheim or Stowe. But these rules resolve themselves into one —we must be perfectly sure, by distinctly understanding the subject and predicate, that they are in all respects the same in both judgments.

§ 85. *Conversion of Judgments and Inferences from it.*

Conversion is the transposition of the subject and predicate of a judgment, to form a new one. The judgment to be converted is called the convertend, and the new one which results from the transposition,

* *Aristotle* de Interp. ch. vi. § 5. The Latin logicians say that in both judgments we must speak *de eodem secundem idem, ad idem, eodem modo, eodem tempore.*

the converse. By conversion, for example, "Some salts are fusible," would become "Some fusible substances are salts." The converse, as having a different subject of thought (§ 365,) from the convertend, is a new judgment, not merely a different statement of the convertend; for it cannot be the same to think of "salts," and ascertain what can be attributed to them, as it is to think of "fusible substances," and ascertain what is to be predicated of *them*. And as the converse depends entirely for its truth upon the convertend, we must regard it as an inference from it.

In right conversion, the *quality* of the judgment is preserved, and each term that was distributed is distributed in the converse, but no other. Hence we cannot infer from "Some skeptics are vicious" that "*All* vicious persons are skeptics;" we should distribute the term "vicious persons," where the premiss exhibited it undistributed. Remembering this rule, we may dispense with the common division into simple,* and accidental, conversion. The six kinds

* Simple conversion is where the converse is of the same Quantity as the Convertend; conversion *per accidens* where the rule of distribution given above, obliges us to make a particular converse from a universal proposition. Aristotle uses the words *κατὰ συμβεβηκὸς* (*per accidens*) to express "with less propriety—improperly," where a thing *happens* to have a name given to it to which it has no natural (*κὰτα φύσιν*) title. Boethius applied the same Accidental to an irregular conversion, where from our knowledge of the *matter* we bring out a converse not *formally* present, as in converting the conclusion of Bramanity in the common books. Thence later writers apply the name to what Aristotle has called "particular conversion." Simple Conversion is so called properly and naturally, because the proposition suffers no other change than a transposition of terms. But Conversion *per accidens* is called conversion "less properly," because the proposition which was universal before is now particular, so that there is something more than mere conversion. *Berlin Scholia*, 175, a. 27.; *Waitz* on Org. 43, a. 34.; Sir *W. Hamilton*, in Mr. *Baynes's* Analytic, p. 28, *note*.

of judgments give the following converses respectively,—

A is converted to	Y
E	E
I	I
O	η
U	U
Y	A

Upon the conversion of A it may be remarked, that since any judgment and its converse are but two *forms* of the same *matter*, i. e. two modes of thinking upon the same facts, we ought to be able to recover by reconversion the same judgment we at first converted; otherwise, if we are obliged to rest contented with a weaker form, we find that our knowledge of the facts is less now than when we began to convert. By the common rules, A is to be converted to I, and that can only be reconverted to I.

The judgment O is usually considered inconvertible by the ordinary method. But unless we regard the essential difference of subject and predicate, it is hard to see the reason. Unquestionably in such a judgment as "Some substances do not transmit light," there are two terms, the distribution of which we know; why then may we not transpose them into "No things which transmit light are some substances?" Because every judgment should express some new truth concerning its subject, which this converse appears not to do. The former judgment might be the result of experiments, and contains substantial information, namely, that there are substances not permeable by light. But it is useless to know that no things which transmit light are some substances, for after all they may be some *other* substances. We ought to treat O then as inconvertible, because its conversion seems to be fruitless.

§ 86. *Immediate Inference by Means of Privative Conceptions.*

Every conception, we have seen, has a corresponding conception called a privative. The positive conception has marks, but all we know of the privative is that those marks are wanting to it. "Unwise," a privative conception, includes whatever "wise," the positive, does not. Now it is impossible to pass any judgment upon a positive conception, without implying others upon the privative; and hence arise many immediate inferences. They are here submitted in a tabular form,* not of course to be committed to memory, but to be carefully examined, as a preparation for the practice of supplying similar ones to any judgments that occur—an exercise favourable to acuteness, and readiness in interchanging equivalent statements. In the examples, privative words with the prefixed syllable *un* or

* Professor *De Morgan* has furnished the pattern for this Table in his "Formal Logic," p. 61; the additions here made being such as the two additional judgments U and Y made indispensable. No earlier writer has taken the trouble to draw out so carefully and clearly the various judgments in which privatives may be employed. The common books use it in two cases, of which these are examples: "All animals feel," then "Nothing which does not feel can be an animal;" "Some judges are not just," then "Some not-just persons are judges." *Aristotle* omits it. *Leibnitz* (Op. xx. p. 98, *Erdmann* ed.) indicates that there are many forms of privative predication, but does not pursue the subject.

in have been employed, to avoid a multitude of puzzling negative particles. In each group of three judgments, the first is the premiss, and the other two are inferences from it; and in the first division the premiss of each group contains positive conceptions; in the second, privative.

DIVISION I.

A. All the righteous are happy;
Therefore, None of the righteous are unhappy;
And, All who are unhappy are unrighteous.

E. No human virtues are perfect;
Therefore, All human virtues are imperfect;
And, All perfect virtues are not human.

I. Some possible cases are probable;
Therefore, Some possible cases are not improbable
And, Some probable cases are not impossible.

O. Some possible cases are not probable;
Therefore, Some possible cases are improbable;
And, Some improbable cases are not impossible.

U. The just are [all] the holy;
Therefore, All unholy men are unjust;
And, No just men are unholy.

Y. Some happy persons are [all] the righteous;
Therefore, All who are unhappy are unrighteous.
And No righteous persons are unhappy.

DIVISION II.

A. All the insincere are dishonest;
Therefore, No insincere man is honest;
And, All honest men are sincere.

E. No unjust act is unpunished;
Therefore, All unjust acts are punished;
And, All acts not punished are just.

I. Some unfair acts are unknown;
Therefore, Some unfair acts are not known;
And, Some unknown acts are not fair.

O. Some improbable cases are not impossible;
Therefore, Some improbable cases are possible;
And, Some possible cases are not probable.

U. The unlawful is the [only] inexpedient;
Therefore, The lawful is the expedient;
And, The lawful is not the inexpedient.

Y. Some unhappy men are all the unrighteous,
Therefore, No happy men are unrighteous;
And, Some unhappy men are not righteous.

Let it be remarked that the substances we insert into these judgments prove that we do not divide the *whole universe* into happy and unhappy, just and unjust, &c. but some more limited class of existences, such as *cases*, *acts*, *persons* (p. 113). And as to the use of such inferences as these, it may be noticed that men frequently throw a judgment into one of these inferential forms, before they can determine upon its reception or rejection. It would be natural, upon being assured that "All the righteous are happy," to exclaim—"What? Are all the unhappy persons we see then to be thought unrighteous?" Among the above inferences there are no mere conversions, so that from any premiss its converse may be inferred besides.

§ 87. *Immediate Inference by added Determinants.*

Some mark may be added to the subject and predicate, which narrows the extent of both, but renders them more definite—better *determined* (§ 53),

And from the simple judgment, we may infer that which has the additional mark, provided that the distribution of terms remain unchanged. Thus, "A negro is a fellow-creature; Therefore, a negro in suffering is a fellow-creature in suffering." Even two judgments* may be amalgamated upon this principle; thus, "Honesty deserves reward, and a negro is a fellow-creature; Therefore, a negro who shows honesty is a fellow-creature deserving of reward."

§ 88. *Immediate Inference by Complex Conceptions.*

This inference † is parallel to the last; instead of a new conception added as a mark to subject and predicate, the subject and predicate are added as marks to a new conception. For example, "Oxygen is an element, so that the decomposition of oxygen would be the decomposition of an element." Here again, the terms must be distributed in the conclusion or not, according to their distribution in the premiss.

§ 89. *Immediate Inferences of Interpretation.*

It has been shown already (§ 78,) that every judgment may be interpreted in three different ways, ac-

* See *Leibnitz,* Op. xix. Theor. 3. Si coincidentibus addantur coincidentia, fiunt coincidentia. Si A=B et L=M erat A + L=B + M. See also Op. xx. 4.

† See *Leibnitz,* Op. xix. Theor. 3. "Si eidem addantur coincidentia, fiunt coincidentia." This valuable paper would be much clearer, if the great author had distinguished between extension and intension.

cording as we regard it from the side of extension, or of intension, or of denomination. These are not strictly inferences from the judgment, because whenever it is perfectly understood, they are parts of it; but relatively to a mind not fully perceiving all that the judgment really conveys, they are inferential, and we may call them inferences of interpretation.

Lambert* has given one or two other formulæ which may come under the same title. "A is B, therefore B exists," and "A is B, therefore where A is we find B." These may be resolved into one, of which an example may show the use. "Howard exhibited this high philanthropic spirit, therefore such philanthropy really exists," *i. e.* is not merely imaginary. We make a tacit distinction between our notions of real objects and those from imagination or from grounds that are palpably false.† Taking our notions of Socrates, Heracles, and the Chimæra, we see that in the case of Socrates a conviction is implied that he is a *real* person, in that of Heracles that the representation we have of him is at most only partly real, in that of the Chimæra that it is a mere invention of the poets. In all our real notions we imply the mark of existence, and a neglect of it leads invariably to an absurdity. I cannot call it, with M. Duval-Jouve,‡ a judgment, because it is

* Neues Org. I. ch. i. § 259.

† See § 375.

‡ Logique, § 13. Also *Damiron*, Logique, p. 12, who regards judgment as the termination of all the acts of the understanding, whereas in the present work it is treated as preparatory to conception, as undertaken for the sake of more precise and complete notions. But of course an "existential judgment" may be formed, as any other analytic judgment may, with any real conception as the subject; "Man exists, the world exists." Compare *Reid*, Essay vi. ch. I. p. 413, of Sir *W. Hamilton's* Edition.

rather the *result* of a former judgment; when we think of volcanoes, we do not *judge* that they exist, because we have long since done so, and always think of them as existent. Farther, every attribute of a real object is itself real; and therefore when we say that Howard was an exalted philanthropist, we of course imply that the existence of exalted philanthropy is established by the fact of Howard's existence. But where doubts were entertained that our idea of philanthropy had ever been realized, the example before us would have place.

§ 90. *Immediate Inference from a Disjunctive Judgment.*

A disjunctive judgment expresses an act of Division, as "The teeth are either incisors, canine, bicuspid, or molar teeth." According to the rule of mutual exclusion of the dividing members (§ 55) we might infer from the judgment just given, that "The molar teeth are neither incisors, canine, nor bicuspid." According to another rule, that the members must completely exhaust the divisum, we infer that the part of the divisum not contained in one member, must be in some other. "All teeth which are not molar are either canine, incisors, or bicuspid teeth."

FORMULA I.

All A is X Y or Z;
Therefore the X of A is not the Y or Z of A.

FORMULA II.

All A is X Y or Z;
Therefore the not-X of A is the Y or Z of A.

§ 91. *Immediate Inference by the Sum of several Predicates.*

After examination of the properties of any subject, it is necessary to collect the various predicates which have been assigned it, in order to combine them for a definition. The definition of copper, for example, that it is "a metal—of a red colour—and disagreeable smell—and taste—all the preparations of which are poisonous—which is highly malleable—ductile—and tenacious—with a specific gravity of about 8.83," is the result of as many different prior judgments as there are properties assigned. From a sufficient number of judgments in A, having the same subject, a judgment in U may be inferred, whose predicate is the sum of all the other predicates.

§ 92. *Concluding Remark.*

Whilst it is at once admitted that these immediate inferences—syllogisms of the understanding as they are called by Kant, to distinguish them from the mediate syllogism of reason—are obvious enough when they appear singly, the great number and variety of them may be thought a sufficient reason for examining them. Could any person not accustomed to exercises of this kind, draw out fully *all* his own meaning, when he utters the simplest proposition? The judgment "All men are mortal," (a plainer cannot be found,) tells us—that man is one species in the class of mortal beings—that the mark of mortality should always accompany our notion of man—that the word mortal is a name which may rightly be given to man — that, if *all* are mortal, any one man is — that any statement which affirms that no men are mortal must be quite false — that even the statement that *some* men are not mortal is equally false — that since man is contained in the class of mortal things, which is a wider class, it would be wrong to say all mortal things are men — that, however, the assertion " Some mortals are men" would be true enough — even " Some mortals are *all* men" — that no men can be immortal — that any immortal beings must be other than men — that mortality really exists, being found in man, whom we know to exist — that a man with immortal hopes is a mortal with immortal hopes—that (since heaven is immortality) a man expecting heaven is a mortal looking for immortality —that he who honours a man, honours a mortal. Thus from this simple judgment fourteen judgments have unfolded themselves, or, as some would say, the judgment has been put in fifteen different ways, in the last three of which only is any new matter introduced. And yet any man of common sense would say that his proposition really implied them.

§ 93. *General Canon of Mediate Inference.*

The law upon which all mediate inference depends may be thus expressed. *The agreement or disagreement of one conception with another, is ascertained by a third conception, inasmuch as this, wholly or by the same part, agrees with both, or with only one of the conceptions to be compared.* The mediate syllogism, or (as it is usually called) the syllogism, is a comparison of any two notions with a third in order to ascertain whether they agree or not. Suppose the question is whether this disease is mortal; in order to ascertain the agreement of the two notions, so that we may say "This disease is mortal," we find a third notion, that it is a consumption, which we know to be mortal, and then the whole syllogism will be

All consumptions are mortal,
This disease is a consumption;
Therefore it is mortal.

All the properties of a syllogism depend upon the Canon just laid down; as will be seen when they are enumerated.

1. *A syllogism will contain three notions and no more*, namely, the two whose agreement or disagreement we strive to ascertain, and the third which we employ as a means of doing so. They are called *terms;* and the third notion, interposed between the others in order to compare them, is the *middle* term, whilst the other two may be called, from their place in the concluding judgment of the syllogism, the *subject* and *predicate*.

Formerly, the subject of the conclusion was called the *minor* term, and the predicate the *major*, because in one form of inference, supposed to be the most perfect, the major was by its position most extensive, and the minor least; thus, in the syllogism "All men are mortal, Socrates is a man, therefore Socrates is mortal"—mortal, the major term, is more extensive than Socrates, the minor; for, in mortal, we include Socrates and all other men. But in negative inference it is impossible to ascertain the comparative extent of the terms. If the conclusion were "No beasts of prey are ruminant," it would be impossible to ascertain which term were the more extensive,—whether "beasts of prey" applied to more objects than ruminant—inasmuch as the judgment itself declares that they have nothing to do with one another, and one cannot therefore be applied to measure the other. The so-called major term might happen to be a good deal less than the minor. When the concluding judgment is particular, the same absurdity attaches to the names. In "Some brave men are prudent" it is impossible to say whether "brave men" or "prudent men" is the more extensive term. The names of major and minor then are only descriptive, when applied to some particular forms of syllogism. But they are so interwoven with logical phraseology, that it will be better occasionally to annex them in a parenthesis to the less objectionable ones.

2. *A syllogism must contain three judgments and no more.* Since it contains three terms, each of which is to be compared, once only, with every other, there would be three acts of comparison, each expressed by a judgment. Three terms cannot be joined in more than three pairs without repetition.

The two judgments in which the middle term occurs, are called the premisses, and the remaining one the conclusion. That premiss in which the predicate (major term) is compared with the middle, was formerly called the Major premiss, and the other, in which the subject (minor term) occurs, was the Minor premiss. The former was also sometimes called the Proposition, and the latter the Assumption, and sometimes the Subsumption. But all these names are inconsistent with the wider view of inference now taken; and it will be sufficient to call the premisses *first* and *second*, the first being always that in which the predicate of the conclusion occurs, whether it stands first in order or not.

3. *One premiss at least must be affirmative.* The Canon provides that one term at least must agree with the middle, that is, must be united with it in an affirmative judgment; and without this there can be no inference about the two terms which are to be compared. With the premisses "No rash man can be a good general, and Xenophon was not a rash man," we could neither have the conclusion that Xenophon *was* a good general, nor that he was *not*. The premisses afford no data for discovering in what sort of judgment the terms Xenophon and good general may come together.

4. *The* worst *relation of the two terms with a third, that may be established in the premisses, shall be expressed in the conclusion.* Now the best and most intimate relation of two terms is that of absolute identity of matter, as in "An animal is a being with life and sensation;" the next exists where the whole of one term coincides with part only of the other, as in "All organized structures decay;" the lowest relation, where part of one term coincides with part of another, as in "Some flowers are blue." If the two premisses express two different relations, the conclusion must follow the *inferior*. Thus, "All triangles = figures with three sides, A B C is a (some) triangle, Therefore A B C is a (some) figure with three sides;" where the chief predicate though distributed in the premiss is not in the conclusion. The worst

positive relation then which the premisses contain, is all that can be inferred in the conclusion.

5. On a similar principle, *if one of the premisses be negative, the conclusion must also be negative.* The Canon only supposes two conditions, under one of which an inference must be made; that of agreement of two terms with a third, expressed by affirmative premisses, and consequent agreement of the two terms, expressed by an affirmative conclusion; and that of agreement of one term and disagreement of another, with the third term, expressed in an affirmative and a negative premiss, and consequent disagreement of the two terms, expressed in a negative conclusion. The latter condition obtains wherever there is a negative premiss, and therefore the conclusion will also be negative.

6. *The comparison of each of the two terms must be either with the whole, or with the same part, of the third term.* And to secure this (i) either the middle term must be distributed in one premiss at least, or (ii) the two terms must be compared with the same specified part of the middle, or (iii) in the two premisses taken together the middle must be distributed and something more, though not distributed in either singly.

The wise are good,
Some ignorant people are good;
Therefore, Some ignorant people are wise.

This is only a syllogism in appearance, for the two terms have only been compared with part of the third term good; if the wise are *some* good people, and some of the ignorant are *some other* good people, we have compared with two different parts of a term, which is the same as using two different terms —a condition not contemplated by the Canon, and one under which there can be no inference whatever. But in the next example (i) the two terms meet upon common ground in the third term, because the *whole* of it is once introduced.

> All the mineral acids are poison,
> Spirit of salt is a mineral acid;
> Therefore it is a poison.

Here, to whatever portion of the class of "mineral acids" we refer "spirit of salt," it must be a poison, because *the whole class* of mineral acids was brought in as poisonous, so the inference is good. If the first premiss were "*half* the mineral acids are poisons" there would be no inference, because the "spirit of salt" might be in the other half. There would be a comparison with two different parts only of a third term.

The next example (ii) secures a comparison with the same part of a third term, not indeed by bringing in every part of it, but by specifying which part is intended in both premisses alike.

> Certain sciences are classificatory,
> These sciences=Mineralogy, Botany, and Zoology;
> Therefore Mineralogy, Botany, and Zoology are classificatory.

The same part of the term sciences being used, the other two terms must agree. But it is more correct to regard "certain sciences" as the whole of a smaller term (§ 74), than as the part of a larger, sciences in general. The word "certain," marks it off so definitely that we may consider it a distinct conception.

In the next example (iii), that unusual mode of distribution is seen, which is gathered from the two premisses combined, although neither contains it separately.

Three-fourths of the army were Prussians,
Three-fourths of the army were slaughtered;
Therefore some who were slaughtered were Prussians.

For, even supposing that the whole of that fourth that were not Prussians, but (say) Austrians, were slaughtered, there still remain two-fourths, mentioned in the second premiss as slaughtered, who must have been Prussians. And this kind of inference may be drawn wherever the mode of expression satisfies us that something *more than all* the middle term has been mentioned in the premisses; the extent of the agreement between the terms of the conclusion being exactly measured by the excess, over and above the whole of the middle term. Thus, "three-fourths of the army," taken twice, make six-fourths, so that the terms of the conclusion agree to the extent of two-fourths at least of the middle term. Let these three lines represent the terms.

It appears that the middle line, for two-fourths of its length, runs parallel with both the others, and for that distance, therefore, they run along with each other.

7. *Neither term of the conclusion must be distributed, unless it has been so in its premiss.* For, the result of the comparison as stated in the conclusion must not be greater than the comparison itself as made in the

premisses; if therefore *all* of a term appears in the conclusion as agreeing with another, a comparison of all of it with the middle must have been made in the premisses.

Such an inference as

> Pittacus is good,
> Pittacus is wise,
> Therefore *all* wise men are good,

is faulty, because the premisses do not contain "*all* wise men."

These seven general rules of syllogism are not new principles, to be studied as the complement of the Canon. They are directly evolved from it, and are only so many cautions to employ it properly. The Rule of Syllogism is one and one only, but its consequences are various, and they are developed in the general rules.*

§ 94. *Order of the Premisses and Conclusion.*

Although an invariable order for the two premisses and conclusion, namely, that the premiss containing the predicate of the conclusion is first, and the conclusion last, is accepted by logicians, it must be regarded as quite arbitrary. The position of the conclusion may lead to the false notion that it never occurs to us till after the full statement of the premisses; whereas, in the shape of the problem

* They may be remembered by the following hexameters :—

> Distribuas medium, nec quartus terminus adsit,
> Utraque nec præmissa negans [nec particularis]
> Sectetur partem conclusio deteriorem,
> Et non distribuat, nisi cum præmissa, negetve.

or question it generally precedes them, and is the cause of their being drawn up. The premisses themselves would assume a different order according to the occasion. It is as natural to begin with the fact and go on to the law, as it is to lay down the law and then mention the fact. "I have an offer of a commission; now to bear a commission and serve in war is (or is not) against the divine law; therefore I am offered what it would (or would not) be against the divine law to accept." This is an order of reasoning employed every day, although it is the reverse of the technical; and we cannot call it forced or unnatural. The two kinds of sorites, to be described below, are founded upon two different orders of the premisses; the one going from the narrowest and most intensive statement up to the widest, and the other from the widest and most extensive to the narrowest. The technical order cannot even plead the sanction of invariable practice.*

* "In confirmation of the doctrine that the common order of the premisses should be reversed, may be added, what not one of its modern advocates seems to be aware of, that this, instead of being a novel paradox, is an old, and until a comparatively recent period, an all but universal practice. It is not even opposed by *Aristotle*. For to say nothing of certain special recognitions by him of the legitimacy of this order, his usual mode of stating the syllogism in an abstract or scientific form, affords no countenance to the prior position, in vulgar language of what logicians call the major proposition. *Aristotle* is therefore to be placed apart. But in regard to the other ancient logicians, who cast their syllogisms in ordinary language, I am able to state as follows; and this in direct contradiction not only of the implicit assumptions of our later logicians, but of the explicit assertions of some of the most learned scholars of modern times; that the Greeks (Pagan and Christian, Peripatetic, Academic, Stoic, Epicurean, and Skeptic), down to the taking of Constantinople, with very few exceptions, placed first in syllogistic order what is called the minor proposition. The same was done by

Neither the school of logicians who defend it, nor those who assail it, take a comprehensive view of the nature of inference. Both orders are right, because both are required at different times. The one is analytic, the other synthetic; the one most suitable to inquiry, and the other to teaching.

§ 95. *The Three Figures.*

Every syllogism is said to be in one of three *figures*, according to the position of the middle term in the premisses. This may be the subject of the first premiss (major) and the predicate of the second (minor), in which case we say that the syllogism is of the First Figure: or it may be the predicate of both, which constitutes a syllogism of the Second Figure: or the subject of both, which gives the Third Figure. Thus,

I.	II.	III.
M P	P M	M P
S M	S M	M S
∴ S P	∴ S P	∴ S P

It has been usual to call the first figure the most perfect, because it exemplifies most directly a certain law of syllogism called the *dictum de omni et nullo*. The law is to this effect*—" Whatever is affirmed

the Arabian and Hebrew logicians." [I may add the Hindu *Gotama* to these authorities.] "As to the Latins they, previous to the sixth century, were in unison with the Greeks. To the authority and example of *Boethius* I ascribe the change in logical practice. He was followed by the Schoolmen, and from them the custom has descended to us."—*Sir William Hamilton.*

* *Aristotle,* Cat. ch. 5. *Kant* puts it *Nota notæ est nota rei ipsius,* viewing the intention of the judgments. *Leibnitz, Contentum contenti*

or denied of a class, may be affirmed or denied of any part of that class;" so that if one affirms of plants that they require light, one may affirm it also of sunflowers, as a part of the class of plants. This would require three judgments, one to state what we meant to affirm of the class—" All plants need light;" —a second to mention something as part of the class, "Sunflowers are plants;" and a third to affirm the same of the part as had been affirmed in the outset of the whole; "Sunflowers require light." These three judgments, it will be found, have their terms arranged according to the first figure. And on the assumption that the *dictum de omni et nullo* was the paramount law for all perfect inference, and therefore the first figure was alone perfect,* rules have always been given for reducing, as it is termed, every syllogism in the less perfect figures to the first. This can readily be done by changing the order of the terms by conversion (§ 83), or, in the few cases in which conversion will not apply, by substituting a privative for a positive judgment (§ 84), and then converting. But the question was raised—is the *dictum* the sole law of perfect inference? Is it not simply an account of the process of the first figure, and might not each of the other figures have its *dictum* too?

est contentum continentis, viewing (I think) their extension. *Leib.* seems to employ *includere* for the Aristotelian ὑπάρχειν, the word that refers to the intension of terms; but he does not sufficiently distinguish between the two.

* *Aristotle,* Pri. An. I. ch. 5 and 6. *Kant,* in a little Tract, goes over the same ground, contending that all the figures but the first, require the converse of one or other of the judgments to be inserted, to make them pure and natural acts of reasoning. My reason for dissenting will be given in the text.

The discovery of new *dicta** put the process of reduction in a new light. Each of the figures was found to have its own functions, and an attempt to bring the two last to the first figure, only spoilt them as examples of their own rules. Reduction was therefore unnecessary.

We must not suppose that the division of syllogisms according to the figures, is a mere useless subtlety, the result of an arbitrary attempt on the part of logicians to display the middle term in every possible position. For, first, the premisses we choose

* These are not introduced into the text, because they belong to a system of Logic in which no affirmative judgment was held to distribute its predicate, and in which, to comply with the general rules of syllogism, the second figure must always have a negative conclusion, and the third a particular. With our present enlarged list of judgments, they would have a very partial application. However, to illustrate the older treatises they are here given. In the 1st Fig. the dictum given above. The Fig. is useful in arguing from a general to a specific statement. For the 2d Fig. the *dictum de diverso*—"if one term is contained in, and another excluded from, a third term, they are mutually excluded." Useful for showing the differences of things, and preventing confusion of distinct conceptions. For the 3d Fig. the *dictum de exemplo*—"Two terms which contain a common part, partly agree, or if one contains a part which the other does not, they partly differ." Useful for bringing in examples, and for proving an exception to some universal statement. Thus, if it were stated that all intellectual culture improved the heart and conduct, it would be natural to say, in this Figure, "Mr. So and So does not act as he ought, yet Mr. So and So is a person of cultivated mind, therefore one person at least of cultivated mind does not act as he ought." See *Keckermann*, Logic III. ch. 7, 8, and 9. Also *Lambert*, N. Org. I. iv. § 229. But Mr. *Mill* is in an error, shared by *Buhle* (Geschichte, vi. 543,) and *Troxler* (Logik, ii. p. 62,) in thinking that *Lambert* invented these *dicta*. More than a century earlier, *Keckermann* saw that each Figure had its own law and its peculiar use, and stated them as accurately, if less concisely, than *Lambert*. *Keckermann* however ignored the 4th Figure, and *Lambert's* explanation of that may be new.

to establish some conclusion by, may be judgments to which we are so accustomed, that it would be unnatural to take their converse instead, which might be requisite to bring them into the first Figure. It makes some difference whether "Kings can do no wrong" is to be the judgment, or the much more awkward form "Some persons who can do no wrong are kings." But, next, it did not escape Aristotle that the more extensive of two terms ought to be the predicate, that the genus should be predicated of the species. This is the natural, though not invariable, order; and it is worthy of remark that in negative judgments, where from the negation the two terms cannot be set together to determine their respective extension, if, apart from the judgment, we know that the one is a small and the other a large class, the one a clearly determined and the other a vague notion, we naturally take the small and clearly determined conception for our subject. Thus it is more natural to say that "The Apostles are not deceivers," than that "No deceivers are Apostles." So that, if our minds are not influenced by some previous thought to give greater prominence to the wider notion, and so make it the subject, reversing the primary order, the figure of the syllogism will be determined by the extension of the middle term. If this term is obviously wider than the other two, the second will be the natural figure, because there it will be predicated of both. If, again, it is obviously narrower than both, the third, in which it can stand twice as subject, will be the natural figure. Thus, when it was desirable to show by an example that zeal and activity did not always proceed from selfish motives, the natural course would be some such syllogism as the following.

The Apostles sought no earthly reward,
The Apostles were zealous in their work;
∴ Some zealous persons seek not earthly reward.

Admitting that where the extension of the conceptions is not very different, either of them would stand subject as well as the other, we contend that since, in some cases, natural reason prescribes the third figure or the second, and rejects the first, the doctrine of the distinction of three figures is not a mere arbitrary invention, but a true account of what takes place in the mind.

§ 96. *Special Canons of the Figures.*

Although the Canon of Syllogism applies sufficiently to all the figures, it is possible to modify it so as to comprehend the order of the terms in each figure.

Canon of the First Figure.

The agreement or disagreement of a subject and predicate, is ascertained by a third conception, predicate to the former and subject to the latter; inasmuch as this wholly or by the same part agrees with both, or with one only, of the conceptions to be compared.

Canon of the Second Figure.

The agreement of two conceptions is ascertained

by a third conception, which stands as predicate to both; inasmuch as this wholly, or by the same part, agrees with both, or with one only, of the conceptions to be compared.

Canon of the Third Figure.

The agreement of two conceptions is ascertained by a third conception, which stands as subject to both; inasmuch as this wholly, or by the same part, agrees with both, or with one only, of the conceptions to be compared.

§ 97. *The Fourth Figure.*

Besides the three that have been given already, only one other combination of the terms of a syllogism is possible, namely, where the middle is predicate of the first (major) and subject of the second (minor) premiss. The introduction of this combination as a fourth figure, is attributed to Galen on the authority of Averroes.* It would fall into this form—

P M
M S
∴ S P

* The words of *Averroes* are *Et ex hoc planum, quod figura quarta, de quâ meminet Galenus, non est syllogismus super quem cadet naturaliter cogitatio.* (In I Pri. ch. viii. vol. i. p. 63.) I have inspected the Dialectic of *Galen*, published for the first time at Paris in 1844, by Minoides Mynas, a Greek, from a MS. of the eleventh century found in the East; and am of opinion—that *Galen* did not adopt the *fourth* figure, and that an occasional transposition of the premisses in the 1st figure may have led to the erroneous belief that he did. That his modern editor confounds the 1st and 4th figures is beyond dispute.

Many logicians have condemned the use of this figure. It is described as a mere perversion of the first, in which the proper conclusion does not appear, but the converse of it, gained by immediate inference (§ 83). The meaning of this will appear from an example (taken from Abp. Whately's Logic).

What is expedient is conformable to nature,
What is conformable to nature is not hurtful to society,
What is hurtful to society is not expedient.

Here it is contended that the mind naturally expects the converse of the conclusion,—What is expedient is not hurtful to society,—which would bring it at once to a syllogism in the *first* figure, and that we tacitly draw the proper conclusion before passing on to the unnatural one. But whilst it is plain that such a conclusion from such premisses disappoints the expectation, we are unwilling to admit that there is any interpolation of a judgment, without some good reason, especially as Kant supposed the same sort of process to have place in the second and third figures also, where it is certainly not required. The reason now to be given for dismissing the fourth figure as really an indirect way of stating the first, has not, it is believed, been pointed out before. The subject and predicate, we remarked, are different in order of thought, the subject being thought of for itself, and the predicate for the subject. Now in the first figure, the subject of the conclusion was a subject in the premisses, and the predicate was a predicate, so that the order of thought is strictly preserved. So to speak, we do not depose a subject, and set up a predicate in its place. No primary thought becomes secondary, nor any secondary primary

All M is P
All S is M
∴ All S is P

The conclusion no way disturbs the order of terms established in the premisses. But in the second figure, the order is somewhat disturbed; the subject of the conclusion was indeed a subject in the premisses, but the predicate was not a predicate.

No P is M
All S is M
∴ No S is P

This makes the figure one degree less natural than the first; it departs from directness in its use of the predicate (major term). In the third figure the same indirectness occurs; the subject of the conclusion was not a subject in its premiss. But in the fourth figure the order is wholly inverted, the subject of the conclusion had only been a predicate, whilst the predicate had been the leading subject in the premiss. Against this the mind rebels; and we can ascertain that the conclusion is only the converse of the real one, by proposing to ourselves similar sets of premisses, to which we shall always find ourselves supplying a conclusion so arranged that the syllogism is in the first figure, with the second premiss first.

§ 98. *The unfigured Syllogism.*

A syllogism may be stated without making the terms either subjects or predicates; so that it belongs to no figure.* Thus "since copperas and sulphate of iron are identical, and sulphate of iron and sulphate of copper are not identical, it follows that copperas and sulphate of copper are not identical."

§ 99. *Modes of Syllogism.*

The *mode* of a given syllogism is the formal value of its three judgments as to their quantity, quality, and relation. It is expressed by the three letters that denote them (§ 76). These, with the addition of the number of the figure to which it belongs, convey the whole form of the syllogism; thus A I I, Fig. I. is known to mean

All M is P
Some S is M
∴ Some S is P

§ 100. *Table of all the Legitimate Modes in all Figures.*

The following Table is an index of the modes in which a good inference can be drawn.† It is arranged according to the order in which the vowels occur in the alphabet, so that, when any mode has been omitted, as not available for inference, the eye

* Sir *W. Hamilton.*

† It was drawn up by the Author, independently of all assistance from living authorities, in 1841, and published in 1842. Another Table is given below, with such additional modes as contain the doubtful negative judgments η and ω.

can detect and supply it, and the mind examine the reason for its omission.

Fig. I.	Fig. II.	Fig. III.
A A A............	....	A A I
	A E E............	
A I I............	....	A I I
	A O O............	
A U A............	A U Y............	A U A
A Y I............	A Y Y............	A Y A
E A E............	E A E............	E A O
E I O............	E I O............	E I O
E U E............	E U E............	E U E
E Y O............	E Y O............	E Y E
		I A I
I U I............	I U I............	I U I
I Y I............	I Y I............	
		O A O
O U O............	....	O U O
O Y O		
U A A............	U A A............	U A Y
U E E............	U E E............	U E E
U I I............	U I I............	U I I
U O O............	U O O............	
U U U............	U U U............	U U U
U Y Y............	U Y Y............	U Y A
	Y A A............	Y A Y
Y E E............	....	Y E E
	Y I I............	
Y O O............		
Y U Y............	Y U A............	Y U Y
Y Y Y............	Y Y I............	

Some of these modes exemplify different special rules and theorems of logical writers, of which a few are subjoined.

Fig. I. A A A and A A I are the only modes to which the *dictum de omni* directly applies—"Whatever is said of a class may be said of a contained part of the class."

Fig. I. A U A is a formula into which a "perfect induction" might fall, where we affirm something of a whole class, because we have found it true of all the individuals or species which the class contains. Thus

x y and z are P
S = x y and z
Therefore S is P

Leibnitz gives the formula "Cui singula insunt, etiam ex ipsis constitutum inest."

Fig. I. E A E and E I O are the only modes to which the *dictum de nullo* applies. "What is denied of a class must be denied of any part of the class."

E U E and U E E in all figures. "Si duorum quæ sunt eadem inter se unum diversum sit a tertio, etiam alterum ab eo erit diversum." Leibnitz.

Fig. I. and II. U A A. "Quod inest uni coincidentium, etiam alteri inest." Leibnitz.

M = P
All S is M
∴ All S is P

U U U in all figures. "Quæ sunt eadem uni tertio, eadem sunt inter se."

§ 101. *A Mode of Notation.*

To be able to represent to the eye by figures the relation which subsists in thought between conceptions, tends so greatly to facilitate logical analysis, that many attempts have been made to attain it. Of two important schemes, that of Euler and that of Sir W. Hamilton, an account will be given hereafter. The scheme now to be explained is that which Lambert makes use of, in his *Neues Organon.*

A distributed term is marked by a horizontal line, with the letter S, P, or M attached, to denote that it is the subject, predicate, or middle term of the syllogism.

P ————

An undistributed term is marked, not by a definite line, but by a row of dots, to show its indefiniteness, thus

S . . . .

These are the two forms of quantity in which separate conceptions may occur. But when two conceptions are joined in a judgment, another power as to quantity must be represented also. Let the judgment be, " All plants are organized," and let the lower line represent the subject and the upper the predicate; will this representation convey the whole truth?

P . . . .
S ————————

In one point it is inadequate, that the term " organized " is not wholly indefinite. We mean indeed by it, only *some* organized things; but then one part of it is *made* definite by affirming it of plants. We do not know how many, or what, individuals, come into the conception " Some organized things " by itself; but when it occurs in this judgment, we are certain of some individuals in it, *viz:* those which are " all plants." This we are able to express by a line partly definite, partly undetermined, thus

P . . . . . ———————— . . . .
S ————————

Every affirmative judgment may be represented by a line drawn *under* another, the lower being always the subject. Negative judgments, which express that one conception cannot be contained under another, are represented by two lines drawn *apart from* each other, the predicate being a little higher than the subject, thus—

P ————————

S ————————

But in a syllogism there are three terms, so that we require three lines to represent their relations; and the diagram thus drawn will supply some important illustrations of the nature of inference. Suppose the premisses are, "All matter undergoes change, and the diamond is a kind of matter," the relations of the three terms may be thus exhibited.

P . . . ———————— . . . .
M ————————
S ——————

From this notation, besides the two premisses given,

1. All M is P
2. All S is M

we may, by reading downwards, gather that

3. Some P is M, and
4. Some M is S

which are in fact immediate inferences by conversion from each of the premisses respectively. But further, from knowing that M stands under P, and S under M, we have learnt that S stands also under

P, and this we may express, leaving M altogether out of our statement,

5. All S is P
6. Some P is S

the former being the proper conclusion from our premisses, and the latter the converse of the conclusion.

Where one premiss is negative, and by the canon of syllogism one only can be of that quality, the notation will be

```
                         P ________
M . . . ______ . . .
S       ______
```

which would be read thus,

No M is P
All S is M
Therefore, No S is P.

Finally, every universal judgment of substitution, or U, may be expressed by two equal lines

```
P ______________________
S ______________________
```

But when such a judgment expresses a logical division, as "Organized beings are either plants, brutes, or men," the divided character of the predicate may be expressed by breaking up the line which represents it, thus

```
P ______x______y______z
S _____________________
```

which would be read, " All S is either x y or z." The contrary process, of logical composition, which is used to express induction, as " Plants, brutes, and men are the only organized beings " would appear as

P ————————————
S ———x———y———z

and be read "x y z make up the sum of P."—The reader will find great advantage in comprehending the rules of syllogism, from figuring the syllogisms to which they happen to apply, according to these directions.

§ 102. *Equivalent Syllogisms.*

Though the Reduction of Syllogisms, from a so-called imperfect, to the perfect, figure, is no longer requisite now that the power of the *dictum de omni et nullo* is confined to the proper limits, the relations of three conceptions can be expressed, commonly, in more than one syllogism of the same figure, and always in different figures. And the advantage of any adequate system of notation is that it not only represents to us the syllogism itself, which is one way of stating the mutual bearing of three conceptions, but, in making that mutual bearing visible, it furnishes the means of stating it in other syllogisms. An example will illustrate this.

" No agent more effectually imitates the natural action of the nerves, in exciting the contractility of muscles, than Electricity transmitted along their trunks, and it has been hence supposed, by some philosophers, that electricity is the real agent by which the nerves act upon the muscles. But there are many objections to such a view; and this very important one among the rest,—*that electricity may be transmitted along a nervous trunk which has been compressed by a string tied tightly round it, whilst the passage of ordinary nervous power is as completely checked by this process, as if the nerve had been divided.*"* This argument may be thrown into the following syllogism, as the most direct form of statement.

Electricity will travel along a tied nerve,
The nervous fluid will not travel along a tied nerve,
∴ The nervous fluid is not electricity.

This is a syllogism in the second figure, and of the mode A E E, which will be found in the Table in the preceding section, and is therefore a valid mode. The middle term is the conception "able to travel along a tied nerve;" and one of the other terms is under it, and the other not, so that they cannot agree; and this mutual relation may be conceived by the following lines:—

M ————————————
P ——————————   S ———

The question now is—whether having obtained this relation, we cannot find other modes, besides A E E, Fig. II. in which to express it.

As the physiologist is most engaged with the parts and functions of the animal economy, to him "The nervous fluid" would be the most prominent term, the subject of thought, and therefore would very

* *Carpenter*, Animal Physiology, p. 437.

properly be the subject of the whole syllogism. But the *same* three conceptions would be the grounds for arguing—

> The nervous fluid will not travel along a tied nerve,
> Electricity will travel along a tied nerve ;
> ∴ Electricity is not the nervous fluid.

This is E A E, Fig. II. which is also a valid mode ; and it would best suit one who was examining electricity. It is the same as the last statement, except that the present is the converse of the former conclusion. Again, though somewhat less naturally, we may state it,

> Nothing that travels along a tied nerve can be the nervous fluid,
> Electricity travels along a tied nerve ;
> ∴ Electricity cannot be the nervous fluid.

This is E A E, of the first Figure. From what has been said we see that the relations between any three conceptions in our mind are permanent ; that the expression of them is not permanent, but may now assume one mode of syllogism, now another ; that the conditions which determine us to one form as more natural than another are, partly, the difference of extension in the conceptions, where it is ascertainable, partly the greater prominence of one conception in our thoughts at the time, which entitles it to be the subject ; that any one of the syllogisms founded on the conceptions is sufficient to ascertain their relations ; and that by a scheme of notation we may represent not merely *one* of the cognate syllogisms, but the ground of all of them, from which they can afterwards be drawn out separately.

§ 103. *Sir W. Hamilton's Scheme of Modes and Figures of Syllogism.*

A mode of notation proposed by Sir William Hamilton is, beyond doubt, one of the most important contributions to pure Logic which has ever been made since the science was put forth; and I am fortunate in being permitted to annex it.* Its excellencies are—that it is very simple, that it shows the equivalent syllogisms in the different figures at a glance, that it shows as readily the convertible syllogisms in the same figure, that it enables us to read each syllogism with equal facility according to extension and intension, the logical and the metaphysical whole.

In this Table M denotes the middle term; and C and Γ the two terms of the conclusion. A colon (:) annexed to a term denotes that it is distributed, and a comma (,) that it is undistributed. Where the middle term has a : on the right side, and a , on the left, we understand that it is distributed when it is coupled in a judgment with the term on the right, and undistributed when coupled with the other.

The syllogisms actually represented are all affirmatives, being twelve in each figure; and the affirmative copula is the line ——, the thick end denoting the subject, and the thin the predicate, of extension. Thus C : ——, M would signify "All C is (some)

* It is also to be found in Mr. *T. Spencer Baynes's* New Analytic. But the order of the Moods is different, and the present order is that finally fixed on by Sir *W. H.*

SIR WILLIAM HAMILTON'S SCHEME OF NOTATION.

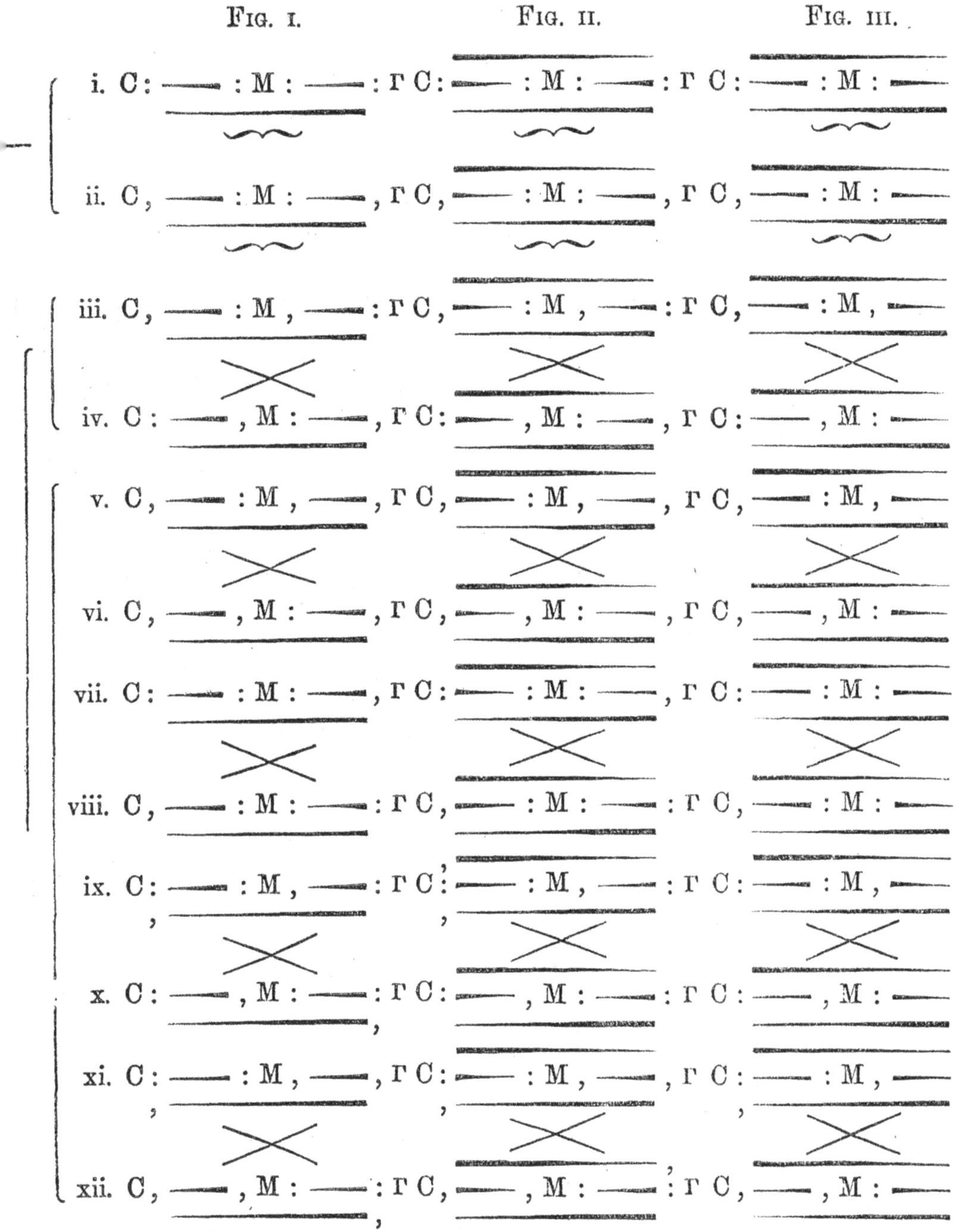

nd ii. are *balanced*. B. The other modes are *unbalanced*. Of these, iii. and iv. are *unbalanced* in terms (not in propositions; the rest in both

M." In reading off the intension, the thin end denotes the subject.

But from each affirmative can be formed two negative syllogisms, by making each of the premisses negative in turn. The negation is expressed by drawing a perpendicular stroke through the affirmative copula; thus —|—. In the negative modes the distribution of terms will remain exactly the same as it was in the affirmatives from which they were respectively formed.

The line beneath the three terms is the copula of the conclusion; and in the second and third figures, as there may be two conclusions indifferently, a line is also inserted above, to express the second of them.

The mark ⏟ under a mode denotes that when the premisses are converted, the syllogism is still in the *same* mode.

But a ✕ between two modes, signifies that when the premisses of either are converted, the syllogism passes into the other.

The middle is said to be *balanced* when it is distributed in both premisses alike. The extremes, or terms of the conclusion are balanced, when both alike are distributed; unbalanced, when one is and the other is not.

According to this scheme there are 12 affirmative Moods in each Figure, and 24 negatives, or 36 altogether. All the *possible* moods of syllogism are here exhibited; but the value of the inference in some of them is so small that they would never actually be employed. For example, by making negative the first premiss of No. v. Fig. II. we have such a syllogism as—

Some stones do not resist the action of acids,
Some metals resist the action of acids;
∴ Some metals are not *some* stones,—

where there is undeniably an inference, but one which can scarcely be said to add to our knowledge of the subject of it. To facilitate a comparison of this Table with the former one (p. 210), its Moods are *translated* into equivalent letters; and an examination will prove that every mood not containing the vowel η or ω,* occurs in both tables, which after deducting the disputed moods so marked, coincide in all respects.

§ 104. *Euler's System of Notation.*

Perhaps the most celebrated plan of notation is that which Euler has described in his *Lettres à une princesse d'Allemagne*.† But, as it only represents the extension of the terms, and not the opposite capacity, of intension, it is inferior to that which has just been described. The sphere of a conception is represented by a circle; an affirmative judgment by one circle wholly or partly contained in another; and a negative by two separate circles. The judg-

* The objections to the employment of the judgments denoted by this will be found in § 77, together with the grounds on which they have been defended. See *Sir W. Hamilton's* Note in Mr. *Baynes's* New Analytic, p. 153, and Discussions in Philosophy, p. 614, by the same author, for further elucidations of this system.

† Made known before *Euler* by *Lange* in his *Nucleus Logicæ Weisianæ*, 1712, and apparently first employed by *Christ. Weise*, who died in 1708. *Ploucquet* employed the square, and *Maass* the triangle instead of the circle. *Drobisch Logik.* § 84.

TABLE OF MODES.

	Fig. I. Aff.	Fig. I. Neg.	Fig. II. Aff.	Fig. II. Neg.	Fig. III. Aff.	Fig. III. Neg.
i.	U U U	E U E U E E	U U U	E U E U E E	U U U	E U E U E E
ii.	A Y I	η Y ω A O ω	Y Y I	O Y ω Y O ω	A A I	η A ω A η ω
iii.	A A A	η A η A η η	Y A A	O A η Y η η	A Y A	η Y η A O η
iv.	Y Y Y	O Y O Y O O	A Y Y	η Y O A O O	Y A Y	O A O Y η O
v.	A I I	η I ω A ω ω	Y I I	O I ω Y ω ω	A I I	η I ω A ω ω
vi.	I Y I	ω Y ω I O ω	I Y I	ω Y ω I O ω	I A I	ω A ω I η ω
vii.	U Y Y	E Y O U O O	U Y Y	E Y O U O O	U A Y	E A O U η O
viii.	A U A	η U η A E η	Y U A	O U η Y E η	A U A	η U η A E η
ix.	U A A	E A E U η η	U A A	E A E U η η	U Y A	E Y E U O η
x.	Y U Y	O U O Y E E	A U Y	η U O A E E	Y U Y	O U O Y E E
xi.	U I I	E I O U ω ω	U I I	E I O U ω ω	U I I	E I O U ω ω
xii.	I U I	ω E ω I U η	I U I	ω U ω I E η	I U I	ω U ω I E η

Sum of all the valid Modes in each Figure.

This Table. Former Table.

I. 36 (= 12 aff. + 24 neg.) — 14 weak neg. = 22
II. 36 (= 12 aff. + 24 neg.) — 16 weak neg. = 20
III. 36 (= 12 aff. + 24 neg.) — 16 weak neg. = 20

ment that "All men are mortal" has the effect of *including* men in the class of mortal beings, which would be represented by a small circle for "men," in a large one for "mortal." The annexed diagram exhibits (I) the Mood A A A, (II) E A E, (III) A I I, and (IV) E I O, all of the first Figure.*

§ 105. *Inference in Intension, Extension, and Denomination.*

That a judgment may be interpreted either in its extension, or intension, or denomination, has been already shown (§ 78). Every syllogism has the same property. Thus,

All metals are lustrous,
Iridium is a metal;
∴ It is lustrous—

may either be read in extension—

The class of metals are some lustrous things,
Iridium is in the class of metals;
∴ Iridium is among lustrous things—

or in intension—

The notion of some lustrous things attaches to the notion of all metals,
The notion of some metal is implied in Iridium;
∴ The notion of some lustrous thing attaches to that of Iridium—

* The system of symbolical notation of *Professor Boole*, of Cork, ought not to be passed over. But it is so intimately connected with his whole work, "*An Investigation of the Laws of Thought*," that an attempt to compress it into a paragraph would only do an injustice to a thoughtful and profound writer.

1

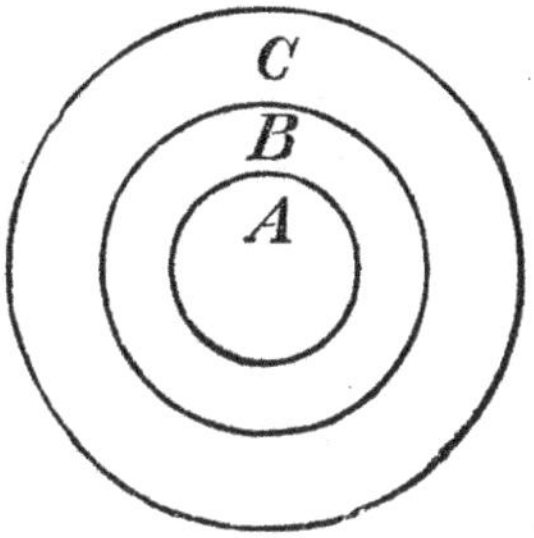

2

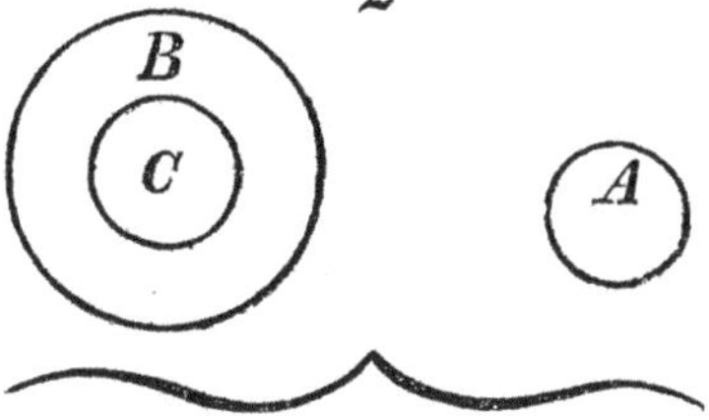

3

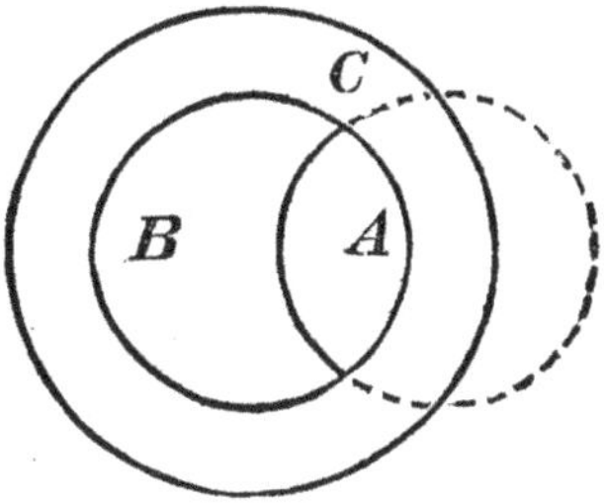

4

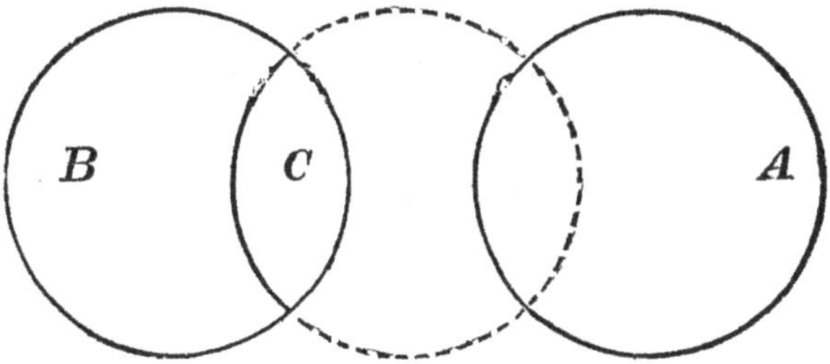

or in less uncouth, but at the same time, less accurate form—

> Lustrousness belongs to our notion of metals,
> Being a metal is part of the notion of Iridium
> ∴ Lustrousness belongs to our notion of Iridium:

or lastly, in denomination

> Metals may be called lustrous,
> Iridium has the name of metal;
> ∴ Iridium may be called lustrous.

Although any argument may be so expressed as to give one or other capacity greater prominence, it is at all times possible to read an argument in any of the three powers, preserving of course the distribution of terms unchanged. The most important term in the extensive point of view is the least in the intensive, because it embraces most objects, but we know least of its nature; in the example, "lustrous" contains the other terms *under* it, and more, but "iridium" implies *in* it the notion of lustrous and much more; "lustrous" therefore has the greatest extension, "iridium" the greatest intension. Where the terms are equal, as in U U U of all Figures, extension and intension are *in æquilibrio.*

§ 106. *Conditional Syllogisms.*

A syllogism in which there is one pure conditional judgment or more (see § 71,) is called a Conditional Syllogism. All arguments of this class come into the scheme of syllogisms already given, when they are properly exhibited. The principal forms are here annexed.

I. In cases where M is N, C is D,
In cases where A is B, M is N;
∴. In cases where A is B, C is D.

II. In cases where C is D, M is N,
In cases where A is B, M is N;
∴. In cases where A is B, C is D.

III. In cases where M is N, C is D,
In cases where M is N, A is B;
∴. In cases where A is B, C is D.

These three forms are composed entirely of conditional propositions. They are in the three different figures; and examples of them will be correct or incorrect according as they do or do not conform to the principles of the syllogism already laid down, as to affirmation and negation, distribution of terms, &c.

IV. In cases where M is N, C is D,
But in the given cases M is N;
Therefore in these cases C is D.

V. In cases where M is N, C is not D,
But in the given cases M is N;
Therefore in the given cases C is not D.

VI. In all cases where M is N, and in no others, C is D,
In the given cases M is not N;
Therefore in the given cases C is not D.

VII. In all cases where M is N, and in no others, C is D,
In the given case C is D;
Therefore M is N.

VIII. In all cases where A is B, M is N,
In the given cases M is not N;
Therefore in the given cases A is not B

IX. In all the cases where A is B, M is not N,
In the given cases M *is* N;
Therefore in the given cases A is not B.

It may facilitate the use of these formulæ if concrete examples of them are added, expressed in the form of ordinary categorical syllogisms.

I. (A A A. Fig. I.)

All cases where law prevails, are cases where the rights of the weaker are secured,
All well-ordered states exhibit such cases;
Therefore in all well-ordered states the rights of the weaker are secured.

II. (A E E. Fig. II.)

All cases where rain falls are cases where clouds obscure the sky,
All cases of heavy dew are cases where there are no clouds;
Therefore cases of heavy dew are not cases of rain.

III. (A A I. Fig. III.)

All cases of ignorance are cases in which a crime is excused,
Such cases are instances of an absence of will or intent;
Therefore some cases of absence of will are cases in which crimes are excused.

IV. (A A A. Fig. I.)

The supposition that matter cannot move of itself implies the existence of a higher moving power,
What we adopt is the supposition, &c.;
Therefore we adopt the view that a higher moving power exists.

V. (E A E. Fig. I.)

The fact that the moon presents always the same face to the earth implies that she has no diurnal revolution on her axis,
But she does present the same face to the earth;
Therefore she cannot go through the diurnal revolution.

VI. (U E E. Fig. I.)

All the times when the moon comes between the earth and the sun, are the sole cases of a solar eclipse,
The 11th of February is not such a time;
Therefore the 11th of February will exhibit no eclipse of the sun.

VII. (U A A. Fig. I.)

All the times when the earth's shadow falls on the moon, are the sole cases of a lunar eclipse,
The 5th of June is such a time;
Therefore the 5th of June will be the occasion of an eclipse.

VIII. (A E E. Fig. II.)

The case of the earth being of equal density throughout would imply its being $2\frac{1}{4}$ times as dense as water,
But in fact, it is not $2\frac{1}{4}$ times as dense as water, but $5\frac{1}{2}$ times;
Therefore it is not of equal density.

IX. (E A E. Fig. II.)

No cases of excessive dew are cases of cloudy night,
But this night is cloudy;
Therefore the dew will not be excessive.

Other modes might be added, but these may suffice to exhibit the nature of the conditional syllogism, together with its affinity to the regular forms. That peculiar connection between two facts which constitutes the one cause and the other effect, offers a problem worthy of the study of the metaphysician,*

* The principal opinions upon the source of our idea of cause and effect may be thus sketched :—

i. *Locke* refers this idea to sensation. We see that one thing has the power to create, or generate, or make, or alter another thing, and such powers we call *causing*, and the things that have them are causes. *Hum. Und.* II. 26, § 2.

ii. *Hume* rejects the notion that the fact which we call a cause

But that the two *are* connected, and that their re-

exercises any power whatever over the effect. But from constantly observing the association or sequence of two facts, we begin to see their invariable connection, and to represent one as the cause of the other (*Essays*, vol. ii. p. 86.) A number of observations is thus a necessary condition of our forming this idea. But why do we give it a name that distinguishes it from sequence, if it is mere sequence? The sunset always follows a flood tide, at a greater or less interval; but no one associates them under the idea of causation.

iii. *Leibnitz* assigns to every thing that exists a certain force or power, and thus constitutes it a cause. Existence, indeed, is measured by power. Whilst *Locke*, as *Hume* remarks, *infers* causation from the fact that things come into being and are changed, *Leibnitz* regards power and causation as primary attributes of all being, not inferred from but implied by it. *Nouveaux Essais*, B. II.

iv. *Kant* considered the notion of cause and effect as one of the forms of the understanding, one of the conditions under which we must think. We are compelled by a law of our mind to arrange the impressions of our experience according to this form, making one thing a cause and another an effect; but whether there exists in the objects themselves that which we mean by a cause and an effect, we cannot determine. (*Critique. Transcendental Analytic.*)

v. The view of *Maine de Biran* is chiefly known through the writings of *Victor Cousin* and others. According to him (and I quote through his critics only), the notion of cause originates with our consciousness of the power of will, which recognizes the will as the cause of our actions; and we transfer this personal power by a kind of analogy to all the operations of nature.

vi. *Sir William Hamilton* traces the idea of causality to that limitation of our faculties which prevents us from realizing an *absolute* commencement or an absolute termination of being. When we think of a thing, we know that it has come into being as a phenomenon, but we are forced to believe that the elements and facts that produced the phenomenon existed already in another form. In the world to which our observations are confined, being does not *begin;* it only changes its manifestations; the stock of forces (so to speak) is not augmented, though their direction and operations alter. By our idea of causation we express this belief; the causes of any thing are the forces and elements of it, before they took shape in it. But see an admirable Conspectus of the theories of Causality with a much fuller account of his own view in *Sir W. H.'s* Discussions, &c. p. 585, *fol.*

lation resembles in many particulars that of subject and predicate in an ordinary proposition, is all that a logician need ascertain. An ordinary proposition asserts that the thought of one thing or attribute draws with it, or implies, the thought of another thing or attribute; the conditional judgment declares that the thought of one fact brings with it the thought of another fact; but whether the connection of the facts is such as to invest them with a particular property, or arises only in the mind, and is one of the forms of thought under which the mind views external impressions, we shall not inquire. If the inferences in the categorical syllogism might be described by the principle *Nota notæ est nota rei ipsius* (see § 93), the corresponding form of conditional syllogism would be explained by *Effectus effectûs est effectus causæ*. And so throughout might the parallel be traced between every categorical mode and a parallel hypothetical.

One distinction of causes must not be forgotten, that which is between the cause of our knowing a fact (*causa cognoscendi*), and the cause of the fact's existence (*causa essendi*). When we say "the ground is wet, because it has rained," we assign to the rain the latter character; it is the cause of the ground actually being in this state. But the cause may change places with the effect; "it has rained because the ground is wet"—where the wetness of the ground is the cause of *our being sure* there has been rain, and this is all that we mean to assert, and not the absurd proposition that the wetness which followed, could bring about the rain which preceded. The inquiry into causes which occupies the inductive philosopher applies to causes of things being, and not properly to causes of our knowing things.

§ 107. *Disjunctive Syllogisms.*

An argument in which there is a disjunctive judgment (§ 71) is called a disjunctive syllogism. A pure disjunctive argument (i. e. one in which no immediate inference has to be supplied) may be at once referred to its proper mode, by ascertaining the quantity and quality of the disjunctive judgment in it. The principal forms of such syllogisms are annexed.

1. (In A U A. Fig. I.)
   C D and E are P,
   All S is either C D or E;
   ∴ All S is P.

2. (In E U E. Fig. I.)
   Neither C nor D nor E is P,
   All S is either C or D or E;
   ∴ S is not P.

3. (In U E E. Fig. II.)
   All P is either C or D or E,
   S is neither C nor D nor E;
   ∴ S is not P.

4. (In E U E. Fig. II.)
   P is neither C nor D nor E,
   S is either C or D or E;
   ∴ S is not P.

5. (In I A I. Fig. III.)
   Either A B or C is P,*
   A B and C are S.
   ∴ Some S is P.

6. (In A U A. Fig. III.)
   C D and E are B,
   C D and E = A;
   ∴ A is B.

Concrete examples of these forms are—

1. Solid, fluid, and aeriform bodies are elastic,
   Every body is solid, fluid, or aeriform;
   Therefore every body is elastic.

2. Neither England, Ireland, Scotland, nor Wales is unhealthy,
   All Great Britain is either England, Ireland, Scotland, or Wales;
   Therefore Great Britain is not unhealthy.

3. A science is either a pure, inductive, or mixed science,
   Astrology is none of these;
   Therefore Astrology is not a science.

4. A question neither affirms nor denies,
   A judgment must affirm or deny;
   Therefore a judgment cannot be a question.

5. Either Christianity or Judaism or Mohammedanism is the true religion,
   Christianity, Judaism, and Mohammedanism are alike monotheistic;
   Therefore a monotheistic religion is the true one.

* This is really a particular affirmative judgment (I); for it means that "Some of A B C are P." It must not be confounded with its apparent converse. "P is either A B or C," which is a universal substitutive judgment (U) and means that P is divisible into A B and C. Thus "a primitive colour must be blue, red, or yellow" is converted into "blue, red, and yellow are the primitive colours," and not into "either blue, red, or yellow is a primitive colour."

6. Oxygen, hydrogen, chlorine, &c. are lighter than water,
Oxygen, hydrogen, chlorine, &c. are the whole of the gases;
Therefore all the gases are lighter than water.*

The complex disjunctives are founded upon the law of distinct division already stated (§ 107). If a genus is divided into so many species, what is in one of the species cannot be in another. In bringing them into the form of common syllogisms, we need only employ a new premiss, gained by an immediate inference under this very principle. Thus—

All A is B or C,
This A is not B;
∴ This A is C—

would become

[All A is B or C, therefore]
All (A that is not B) is C,
This is an (A that is not B);
∴ This is C.

All sciences are either pure, inductive, or mixed sciences,
Astronomy is not a pure or inductive science;
∴ It is a mixed science—

would stand as a syllogism in A A A. Fig. I.

Sciences that are not pure nor inductive are mixed,
Astronomy is a science not pure nor inductive;
Therefore it is a mixed science.

* This is the formula for the Induction by simple Enumeration, where on finding a property to belong to every member of a class singly, we infer that it belongs to the whole class. The worth of such an argument is considered below.

§ 108. *Complex Syllogism. Sorites.*

The simple syllogism is the type of all reasoning, and the test to which all reasoning may be brought. But there are more complex forms of argument, not less natural than the syllogism itself, which do not *require* to be reduced to syllogisms to show their correctness, just as we know ice to be ice without reducing it to the needle-shaped crystals with which freezing commences. Of this kind is the Sorites.

Three or more premisses in which the predicate of each is the subject of the next, with a conclusion formed from the first subject and last predicate of the premisses, have been called a Sorites, or accumulating argument, from the Greek word σωρὸς, a heap. The name is not very appropriate; the German title of chain-argument (*kettenschluss*) expresses better the nature of a process in which the mind goes on from link to link in its reasoning, without thinking it necessary to draw out the conclusions as it passes. Where the premisses are all universal affirmative attributive judgments, not the least confusion can arise from thus postponing till the end the realization of the results. But where the premisses are judgments of different kinds, the reasoning is more difficult to follow, and it may be necessary to draw out each syllogism separately, in order to see whether it is in a valid mood, and, if otherwise, what is the fault in it. This is done as follows :—

All the premisses but the first are leading premisses of so many distinct syllogisms; therefore there are as many syllogisms, minus one, as the Sorites has premisses. For the second premiss of the first syllogism the first judgment of the Sorites must be taken whilst to each succeeding one the conclusion of its predecessor must be the second premiss. A diagram will make this much clearer.

1. A is B,
2. B is C,
3. C is D,
4. D is E,

Therefore A is E.

Reduced to

I.	II.	II.
2. B is C,	3. C is D,	4. D is E.
1. A is B,	[A is C],	[A is D],
[∴ A is C],	[∴ A is D]	[∴ A is E.]

These syllogisms are all in A A A. Fig. I. a valid mode. An invalid mode occurring before the last syllogism would not only be wrong itself, but, as furnishing a premiss to its successors, would vitiate every syllogism that follows.

The number of conclusions which these premisses admit of, is greater than actually appears. We may conclude A C, A D, A E (which appear); and B D B E, C E. Five premisses instead of four would increase the number of conclusions to ten.* There is a form of the Sorites to which the name of Goclenius its inventor has been attached, which is the same as

* Com. *Arist.* Pri. An. I. 25. The formula for ascertaining the number of conclusions is this :—

Let the number of premisses = n, the number of terms = n + 1; then the number of conclusions $= \frac{n\,(n-1)}{1.2}$

the common form, except that the premisses are reversed. It would run

D is E,
C is D,
B is C,
A is B,
∴ A is E.

In the Goclenian Sorites extension is made more prominent, by starting with the premiss which has the two widest terms; in the common form intension predominates, as the narrower terms precede. The former descends in extension from the predicate of the conclusion; the latter ascends in intension, from the subject. The Goclenian form suits deduction best; the common or Aristotelian form, induction. The Goclenian descends from law to fact; the common ascends from fact to law.*

This will be clearer from a pair of examples.

* A "pretty quarrel" long existed amongst logicians, which of the two was to be called *progressive* and which *regressive*. Till *Kant's* time, the Goclenian was called progressive, the common regressive. *Kant* reversed it, followed by *Kiesewetter* and others. *Jacob* reversed it again, followed by *Krug* and others. *Troxler* ii. 100. It was a mere strife about words. If we are discovering truth by the inductive method, the Aristotelian form is progressive; if we are teaching truth, or trying our laws upon new facts, we use deduction, and the Goclenian form is progressive. In an apt but familiar figure—if I am on the ground floor, and wish to fetch something that is above, my going up stairs is my progress towards my object, and my coming down is a regression; if the positions of myself and the thing are reversed, going down would be progress, and returning up, regress. The inductive truth-seeker is on the ground-floor of facts, and goes up to seek a law; the deductive teacher is on a higher story, and carries his law down with him to the facts.

GOCLENIAN OR DESCENDING SORITES.	ARISTOTELIAN OR ASCENDING SORITES.
Sentient beings seek happiness, All finite beings are sentient, All men are finite beings, Caius is a man; Therefore he seeks happiness.	Caius is a man, All men are finite beings, All finite beings are sentient, All sentient beings seek happiness; Therefore Caius seeks happiness.

In the following example a mixed order prevails:—

That which thinks is active,
That which is active has strength,
That which has strength is substance,
The soul thinks;
Therefore it is substance.

The premisses of the Sorites may be, all or some of them, hypothetical; indeed as this argument is but an aggregation of simple syllogisms, the rules for the construction of simple syllogisms apply to its several parts; with this one caution, that in the Sorites each foregoing syllogism furnishes a premiss, not expressed, to the next succeeding one, and therefore we must see not only that each is good in itself, but that it will furnish an available premiss to its successor. This may be tried by altering one of the higher premisses in any of the examples into a negative; at the next step, an error will be apparent.

§ 109. *The Dilemma.*

The Dilemma is a complex argument, partaking both of the conditional and disjunctive. It is *a syllogism with a conditional premiss, in which either the antecedent or consequent is disjunctive.* It may prove a negative or an affirmative conclusion; in the former case it is said to be in the mode of removal (*modus tollens*), because it removes or refutes some conclusion that has been proposed for proof: in the latter it is in the mode of position (*modus ponens*), because the proposed question is *laid down* as proved. The following forms of it, with the manner in which they are presented as syllogisms, may be sufficient.

I.

If A is B or E is F, then C is D,
But either A is B or E is F;
∴ C is D.

II.

If A is B, then C is D or E is F,
But neither C is D nor E is F;
∴ A is not B.

III.

If some A is B, either the m that are A or the n that are A, are B,
But neither the m that are A nor the n that are A are B;
∴ A is not B.

The same regarded as simple syllogisms.

I.

[The cases of A being B and E being F] are [cases of C being D],
This is [a case of A being B or E being F].
∴ This is [a case of C being D].

II.

[The case of A being B] is [a case of C being D or E being F].
This is not [a case of C being D or E being F];
∴ This is not [a case of A being B].

III.

Neither m of A nor n of A are B,
All A is either m or n;
∴ No A is B.

The word Dilemma means "double proposition," so that the whole argument takes its name from the one mixed judgment in it. When this is *more* than double, as in "If a prisoner is legally discharged, either the magistrate must refuse to commit, or the grand jury ignore the bill, or the common jury acquit, or the crown exercise the prerogative of pardon," the argument has been called a Trilemma, Tetralemma, or Polylemma, according to the number of members the judgment may have.

The following are concrete examples of the formulæ.

I. If the king is moved or if he is covered, I am checkmated the next move; One or the other must be; Therefore I shall be checkmated.

II. If a man cannot make progress towards perfection, he must either be a brute or a divinity; But no man is either; Therefore every man is capable of such progress.

III. If some science can furnish a criterion of truth, either a formal or a real science must do so; But (for different reasons) neither the formal sciences nor the real do so; Therefore science affords no criterion of truth.

TRILEMMA. If the system of the universe is not the best possible, we must suppose either that the Creator willed not a better one, or that he knew no better one, or that he could not create a better. The first cannot be true (it is against His goodness). The second cannot be true (it assails His wisdom). The third cannot be true (it limits His power). Therefore the system of the universe is the best.

The popular notion of a Dilemma, that it is a choice of alternatives, each of them fatal to the cause or the character of an adversary, is countenanced by many logicians, but can have no place in pure Logic, into which the object to be gained by arguments, or the personal consequences which follow from admitting them, ought not to enter, and the properties of the arguments themselves are the sole object of consideration.

If the criminal knew the consequences of his act, he was wicked; if he did not know the consequences, he was insane.

This is really two distinct hypothetical judgments, associated because they happen to have a common term—"the criminal;" and because one or other of them must be true; and two distinct syllogisms would be founded upon them, as the counsel for the defence would probably take for his second premiss —"He did not know the consequences of his act, therefore he is insane," while the counsel for the prosecution would maintain that "He did know the consequences, and therefore was guilty." No doubt it is a great detriment to a prisoner to be found either guilty or insane, but this does not appear upon the face of the argument, and therefore pure Logic does not take it into account. A new judgment would be required to show the connection of the two notions; so that besides the two conditional syllogisms, contained in the argument itself, a third is tacitly admitted, that shows the connection of the other two. This sort of argument, a great favourite with the Sophists and old logicians, is called also *Syllogismus Crocodilinus*, and *Syllogismus Cornutus;* and "the *horns* of a dilemma" are known even to common language.

§ 110. *Incomplete Syllogisms.*

The arguments used in thinking, speaking, or writing, are never drawn out in strict technical form, except by practised logicians, desirous of exhibiting their art to those who, like themselves, are conversant with it. A sentence which contains the materials of a syllogism, not technically expressed, has been called an enthymeme, or an enthymematic sentence. Aristotle understands by enthymeme a syllogism such as would be used in rhetoric where the full and orderly expression of premisses and conclusion would seem laboured and artificial. And as the omission of one of the premisses is a common, perhaps the commonest, feature of enthymemes, logicians have defined them as syllogisms with one premiss suppressed. But we may also omit the conclusion, or invert the order of premisses and conclusion; and unless we extend the name enthymeme to these cases we put a considerable restriction upon its original meaning. Let the enthymeme then be defined—*an argument in the form in which it would naturally occur in thought or speech.*

§ 111. *Prosyllogism and Episyllogism.*

In a chain of reasoning, one of the premisses of the main argument may be the conclusion of another argument, in that case called a prosyllogism; or the conclusion of the main argument may be a premiss to a supplementary one, which is called an episyllogism. Let us take the syllogism which a coroner's jury might have to go through. The *question* is, "Has A. B. been poisoned?" and the syllogism is, "A man who has taken a large quantity of arsenic has been poisoned, and A. B. is found to have done so, therefore he has been poisoned;" with the addition of a prosyllogism and episyllogism the reasoning would run—"A man who has taken arsenic has been poisoned; and A. B. has taken arsenic, for the application of Marsh's and Reinsch's tests discover it (Prosyl.); therefore A. B. has been poisoned and therefore we cannot return a verdict of death from natural causes." (Episyl.) A prosyllogism then is *a syllogism whose conclusion is a premiss in a given syllogism;* an Episyllogism is *one, whose premiss is a conclusion in a given syllogism.* The Sorites, Prosyllogism and Episyllogism, deserve our attention as the joints of thinking by which the various members, the acts of immediate and mediate inference, are knit together in an organic connection. Of them, however, the first can rarely be employed; the two last meet us continually.

OUTLINE

OF THE

LAWS OF THOUGHT.

PART IV.

APPLIED LOGIC.

"Mais, parce que l'esprit se laisse qulequefois abuser par de fausses lueurs, lorsqu'il n'y apporte pas l'attention nécessaire, et qu'il y a bien des choses que l'on ne connâit que par un long et difficile examen, il est certain qu'il serait utile d'avoir des règles pour s'y conduire de telle sorte, que la recherche de la vérité en fût et plus facile et plus sûre; et ces règles, sans doute, ne sont pas impossibles."—ARNAULD.

APPLIED LOGIC.

§ 112. *Province of Applied Logic.*

IN the foregoing pages the Laws of Thought have been considered solely in themselves; and their connection with the objects they belong to has been studiously kept out of view. It has been shown that every conception consists of marks, without any attempt to explain how the marks are to be obtained; that a judgment of a given quantity, quality, and relation, can be converted or opposed, no matter whether it is a true judgment with reference to the matter it sets forth; that a given form of syllogism is correct and its proof cogent, whether or no the premisses it draws from are frivolous, or even incorrect. In order to understand aright the laws of thinking in themselves, this procedure was necessary; for we must distinguish between faults in the forms themselves, which we have the means of correcting without travelling beyond them, and faults in the materials of thinking, that cannot be corrected without a reference to the objects that supplied them. For example, "some men are infallible," is a judgment correct in form, but false in matter, as our knowledge of humanity teaches us; again, to convert "some men are philosophers," into "all philosophers are men," is wrong in form, although it happens that the latter judgment, erroneously produced, is materially correct.

Applied Logic teaches the application of the forms of thinking to those objects about which men do think These objects arrange themselves under three great divisions, Man, the Universe, and Absolute Being. When the views we take of objects are substantially correct, when our thoughts correspond with facts, we are said to be in possession of the truth; and thus we return to a definition of Applied Logic already proposed. It is the science of the necessary laws of thought as employed in attaining truth.

§ 113. *Science.*

These laws may be applied to the fragmentary knowledge and scattered information gathered by every one in his passage through the world; they are unconsciously applied in this way every instant. But it would be a higher application of them to erect by their means a complete structure of the truth that related to one object or set of objects, as Zoology contains all that relates to animals, Geology all we know of the earth's structure, and Psychology all that pertains to the human mind and soul. Such a system of the truths that relate to one set of objects is called a science, which has been defined (p. 26), a system of principles and deductions, to explain some object-matter. To fulfil its intention every science must have attained to true statements concerning its object-matter, so far as the nature of the case and the present means of examination allow; it must be able to define the object-matter, and its several subordinate parts, with clearness and precision; and it must be able to indicate the extent of the domain the object-matter covers; and lastly it must exhibit these results in a systematic and harmonious shape. For the first it must employ Induction and Deduction; the second is the province of Definition; the third is provided for by Division; and the fourth may be referred to Method.

§ 114. *Is a Philosophic Criterion of Truth possible.*

The search after truth cannot long dispense with any one of these instruments; and even with the free use of them, the history of science shows how slow has been the advance, how largely (to use Leibnitz's image) the sand and mud of error have been mixed with the gold grains of truth. All of them in their degree have to do with evidence, with the proof of propositions; Induction and Deduction chiefly with the discovery and appreciation of evidence, and Definition and Division chiefly with the statement and arrangement of its results. Hence, if we have to answer the question whether a Criterion of Truth, *i. e.* a standard for judging of the truth of propositions, is possible,* we answer that evidence

* *Plato* speaks of "Experience, prudence, and reason," as affording conjointly a κριτήριον of truth (Pol. 582 A.). This for the sense of the word. For other proposed criteria, not mentioned in the text, we have that of *Wolff*, *determinabilitas prædicati per notionem subjecti* (but it applies only to explicative judgments—see p. 175); that of *Descartes*, "that is true which is clearly known and perceived," but he admits that the test is somewhat vague; and lastly that of *Plato*, "truth is conformity with the ideas." *Evidence* is used by the Cartesians, sometimes in the sense of evidentness; but we employ it to mean "the grounds which make evident."

is the sole means of establishing, and therefore the sole standard for testing, the truth of any proposition, and that all the operations connected with evidence contribute their share to the criterion. But such a maxim as that "a judgment must rest upon sufficient evidence" is too abstract to be of use by itself as a test of truth. In fact no shorter rule, no more portable touchstone can be indicated, for the examination of objective truth, than the whole science and rules of evidence. And in the special cases where other criteria appear to be applied, as in the discussion whether religious truth is to be tried by external testimony or internal conviction, whether historical evidence or the religious sentiment is the best criterion, the dispute is only as to the kind of evidence that shall take precedence.

Four principal criteria of truth have been in different forms advocated by logicians; the reader is now in a position to estimate their value.

1st CRITERION. *The principle of Contradiction.* "The same attribute cannot be at the same time affirmed and denied of the same subject." Or "the same subject cannot have two contradictory attributes." Or "the attribute cannot be contradictory of the subject."* To illustrate this—at a particular time facts were observed as to the motions of the planets, which were inconsistent with the received theory that these motions were circular. The theory was consequently modified, first by the introduction of epicycles, and finally by the substitution of the

* The first mode of statement is *Aristotle's*, *τὸ γὰρ αὐτὸ ἅμα ὑπάρχειν τε καὶ μὴ ὑπάρχειν ἀδύνατον τῷ αὐτῷ καὶ κατὰ τὸ αὐτό.* Metaph. IV (Γ) iii. The second is Aristotelian; the third is *Kant's*.

theory of elliptic revolution; because otherwise the astronomer must have affirmed of the planets a circular and a non-circular motion, or in other words must have assigned to a subject, to which he had already given "circular motion," a predicate contradictory of this.

2d Criterion. *The principle of Identity.* "Conceptions which agree can be united in thought, or affirmed of the same subject at the same time." This principle is the complement of the former.

3d Criterion. *The principle of the Middle being excluded* (lex exclusi medii). "Either a given judgment must be true, or its contradictory; there is no middle course."* So that the proof of a judgment forces us to abandon its contradictory entirely, as would the disproof of it force us upon a full acceptance of the contradictory. This law, among other uses, applies to the dialectical contrivance known to logicians as *reductio per impossibile.*

4th Criterion. *The principle of sufficient* (or *determinant*†) *reason.* "Whatever exists, or is true, must have a sufficient reason why the thing or proposition should be as it is and not otherwise." ‡ From this law are educed such applications as

* This is the *ἀντίθεσις ἧς οὐκ ἔστι μεταξὺ καθ' αὑτήν*, of *Aristotle*, (An. Post, I. i. *καθ' αὑτὴν*, "as appears *per se* from the nature of the assertion." *Trend.*) Compare Metaph. IV. (Γ.) 7, and *Alexander's* comment.

† *C. A. Crusius*, in a tract on this subject, finds fault with the ambiguity of "sufficient," which might seem "sufficient for this effect" without excluding it from the possibility of producing some other. According to him, this principle involves absolute necessity, and destroys morality.

‡ *Leibnitz*, Theod. I. § 44. Upon this principle, and those of Contradiction and Identity, *Leibnitz* has based his Logic.

these :—1. Granting the reason, we must grant what follows from it. On this depends syllogistic inference. 2. If we reject the consequent, we must reject the reason. If we admit the consequent, we do not of necessity admit the reason.

Now the distinction between formal and material truth, or in other words between self-consistency in thinking, and conformity with facts, assists materially in forming an estimate of the worth of these principles. A judgment may be formally true, and materially false; as in the inference "No men err, Socrates is a man, therefore he cannot err," which is correctly drawn, yet proves a falsehood from a falsehood: or it may be materially true, yet formally false, as, "Socrates is a man, Socrates erred, therefore all men err;" where a true judgment has been drawn from two true judgments, yet not correctly. The four criteria in question are useful in securing formal truth, that is, in keeping our thoughts in harmony with each other; but for the discovery of material truth, for giving us thoughts that are true representations of facts, they are either useless, or only useful as principles subordinate to the higher criterion of which all applied Logic is but the expansion, that every proposition must rest upon sufficient evidence. The principle of contradiction has been already implied in the doctrine of privative conceptions in the theory of disjunctive judgments and inferences and in other places. The principle of the excluded middle is the canon of the inference from contradictory opposition upon which the refutation of a false conclusion must rest. The principle of the sufficient reason is implied in the syllogistic canon that every conclusion must follow from and depend on sufficient premisses; it is employed in other forms, in hypothetical reasonings in particular. And in these purely formal applications the criteria have their importance, but that not the highest.

Viewed as instruments for judging of material truth, they sink into mere rules for the reception of evidence. The first is a caution against receiving into our notion of a subject any attribute that is irreconcilable with some other, already proved upon evidence we cannot doubt. The second is a permission to receive attributes that are not thus mutually opposed, or a hint to seek for such only. The third would compel us to reconsider the evidence of any proposition, when other evidence threatened to compel us to accept its contradictory. The fourth commands that we seek the causes and laws that have determined the existence of our subject, for the subject cannot be adequately known except in these. So that the vaunted criteria of truth are rules of evidence; and there is no one means of judging of truth, except what the whole science of Evidence affords.

A. Construction of Science.

§ 113. *Induction and Deduction.*

Induction* is usually defined to be the process of

* Opinions are somewhat divided both as to the meaning of ἐπαγωγή, the word of which Induction is the English equivalent, and the nature of the argument that bears the name. 1. It is supposed to be a *persuasive* argument to which a person is *induced*

drawing a general law from a sufficient number of particular cases; Deduction is the converse process, of proving that some property belongs to a particular case, from the consideration that it comes under a general law. More concisely, Induction is the process of discovering laws from facts, and causes from effects; and Deduction that of deriving facts from laws, and effects from their causes. *E. g.*, that all bodies tend to fall towards the earth is a truth which has been obtained by considering a number of bodies where that tendency has been displayed, by induction; if from this general principle we argue that the stone we throw from our hands will show the same tendency, we deduce. If it were always possible duly to examine the whole of the cases to

(*ἐπάγεται*) to assent. Comp. Πρόσεχε *μή σε ἡττήσῃ τὸ προσηνὲς αὐτοῦ καὶ ἡδὺ καὶ ἐπαγωγόν* (*Epictetus*, Ench. 34), where the last word means *persuasive, alluring*. Compare *Cicero* (de Inv. I. 31.). "Inductio est oratio, quæ rebus non dubiis *captat assensiones ejus* quicum instituta est; quibus assensionibus facit, ut illi dubia quædam res, propter similitudinem earum rerum, quibus assentit, probetur." 2. It is the *bringing in* (*τὸ ἐπάγειν*) examples or comparisons, Τὸ *εὖ τὰς εἰκόνας ἐπάνεσθαι*—(*Xenophon*, Œcon. 17, § 15.) This latter derivation finds most favour. Then the process itself is sometimes described as if it were a way of proving particular unknown facts from particular known facts. "Cum plura interrogasset [Socrates], quæ fateri adversario necesse esset, novissime id de quo quærebatur, inferebat, cui simile concessisset." (*Quinctilian*, V. 11.) The logician will see that this comes close to the logical Argument from Example. Both in Induction and Example, however, there is an appeal to a general law, expressed or implied. Our definition is that of *Aristotle* (Top. I. 12.), "Induction is the process from particulars to universals." In using the phrase "the syllogism from induction," A. hints at that wider view of syllogism, as the simple element of *all* reasoning whatever, which it is one main object of this book to develop. See *Heyder*, Darstellung, pp. 60, 219; *Ernesti*, Lex. Techn.; *Trendelenburg*, Excerpta, § 20; but chiefly *Reinhardi* Opuscula, I. 212.

which a law applies, and to see by intuition the significant and important parts of each, the process of Induction would be simple enough. But a complete inspection of all the cases is very seldom possible; even the laws on whose invariable operation the strongest reliance is placed, must have been laid down upon the evidence of a number of cases very limited when compared with the whole; that men must all die, and that heavy bodies tend to fall towards the earth, are statements which no one can boast of having verified by enumeration. The perfect certainty with which they are believed, rests upon far less than the millionth part of the cases that might be brought to bear witness about them. Nor again are the significant and essential circumstances easy to observe, in the few cases that lie within the reach. Either they escape notice altogether, as did the fact of the earth's revolution in the early days of Astronomy; or they are so entangled or overlaid with a mass of other facts that their importance does not at first appear, like the action of cold in the production of dew, before Dr. Wells's observations, or the influence of an open drain in producing and sustaining fever, till within the last few years. It appears then that the pure inductive syllogism, that argument by which a law is laid down as the exact sum of all the single cases, will not suffice for scientific research. To take an example—

Gold, silver, copper and the rest will combine with oxygen,
Gold, silver, copper and the rest are the only metals;
Therefore all metals combine with oxygen.
(A syllogism in A U A, Fig. III. p. 227.)

This argument could not be formed until people discovered what at first no one suspected, that oxygen was the cause of the rusting and tarnishing of metals; and it still stands open to dispute if a metal should be hereafter discovered that refuses to combine with oxygen. Yet it might be selected as one of the inductions that approach most near to perfect enumeration. The logic of science then must employ other instruments than this syllogism, so very limited in its application, so very liable to question. Four principal questions require to be answered by Applied Logic.

1. How are the causes of facts to be distinguished, amidst a multitude of other facts, all open to observation?

2. How are causes discovered which are less open to observation than the effects?

3. When should an incomplete enumeration (or induction) of facts be deemed sufficient, and on what principle?

4. How should new laws be expressed and recorded?

The following sections contain an indication of the answers to these four inquiries, but by no means a full exposition of them.

§ 114. *Search for Causes. Inductive Methods.*

All men are apt to notice likenesses in the facts that come before them, and to group similar facts together. The similarities are sometimes so obvious that the most careless observer is arrested by them; the rise of the tide to-day and yesterday, the tendency to fall which a stone from the hand, an acorn from an oak, and a hailstone from a cloud exhibit alike, and the power of growth exhibited by a grain of corn and a tulip root, afford groups of cases which seem so to classify themselves as to leave the mind little room for inquiry. The faculty by which such similarities are apprehended is called observation; the act of grouping them together under a general statement, as when we say "All seeds grow—all bodies fall," has been already described as generalization.

Now if any obvious generalization be examined, as for example "bodies tend to fall," we see that this only furnishes us with the sum of several distinct facts; that "bodies fall" is only a shorter form of stating that this body falls, and that body, and that other, and so on till every single body has been mentioned. *Why* all bodies tend to fall has not been stated. In other words a law has been laid down; but the cause of its operation remains to be ascertained. A law or rule is a general principle embodying a class of facts; when it is regarded in its connection with theory it usually has the former name, and when it is concerned with practice, the latter. The formation of such general propositions is the first procedure in the formation of science; at the same time they are of little service unless accompanied by the ascertainment of causes.

What then do we understand by the cause of any given fact or thing? We mean the sum of the facts or things to which it owes its being. We know that the various phenomena that engage us are not so many beginnings or new creations, but are parts of a long sequence of events, brought about by many facts that have passed already, and destined in their turn to bring about other phenomena. In this sequence, no new force is gained or lost; there is commutation of forces, but, so far at least as we can see, neither increase nor diminution. When we inquire into causes, we are only seeking one step higher up in the sequence for the forces now combined in the new phenomenon under examination; we wish to know what concurring agencies they were, which brought this fact about. Now the older writers attempted not merely to find out these antecedent phenomena, but to assign the kind of share which each took in producing the result, by dividing causes into efficient, formal, material, concomitant, and the like. This is partly founded on a wrong view of causation, and it is partly beyond our reach. If we attempt with them to pronounce that the producing or efficient cause of any thing (*causa principalis*, κύριον αἴτιον) is to be sought in one particular antecedent fact, whilst the other facts whose concurrence was no less required for the result, must take subordinate places as instrumental or impelling causes, we are in danger of the double mistake of elevating almost into a personal agent one of our phenomena, and of slighting others which have equally conduced to the end. All we know for certain is, that there are certain antecedents, the want of any one of which would have made the phenomenon wholly, or in its present shape, impossible. We must therefore apply universally, what the scholastic writers admitted in some cases, the principle that all the facts or elements from which a new fact or thing draws its existence, *i. e.* all the associate causes (*causæ essentialiter sociatæ*) of it, make up what we term its cause, on the scholastic maxim that "several partial causes concurring for one effect, must be regarded as one" (*causæ partiales in toto concursu stant pro una*). The cause of an explosion of coal-gas is not the lighted candle alone, nor the gas which it kindles, nor the admixture of common air which makes the gas explosive, but it is the concurrence of all three.

The cause of any phenomenon is only then truly assigned when account has been taken of all the precedent phenomena. It remains to observe that common language is not always framed upon this complete view. If I shake an apple-tree and an apple fall, I am spoken of as the *cause* of the fall; yet all that I did was to give an opportunity for the law of gravitation to act. In fact my action is selected as the cause, where a little thought would have shown that several causes concurred. This arises partly from the obvious sequence, in point of time, of the fall to my action. But although we say that the cause is antecedent to its effect, we must not understand this as implying invariable antecedence in point of time. The vices of the court and government concurred to cause the French Revolution, and were antecedent to it in time; the law of gravitation causes the fall of the apple, and the oscillations of a pendulum, but it is not antecedent to these in point of time, but actually present in them. The antecedence of the cause is one of relation, rather than of time; if it were otherwise, that act alone which preceded in time a given phenomenon must be reckoned as its cause, where perhaps it only gave the occasion for the chief and constant cause to operate. He who applied the match to the powder would be the one cause of all the destruction that followed the explosion of the mine.

Where it is proposed to inquire for the cause of a phenomenon, it is not implied that one cause can have determined it alone; but that, most of the conditions being known, one unknown fact has had a great influence upon the result, and that our search is therefore confined to this.

The principal rules which regulate, consciously or not, the search after the cause, are as follows:—

1. The cause (or causes) must be sought among the invariable concomitants of the effect.

But it must not be forgotten that the same effect may follow from causes entirely different; as ebullition from the escape of steam and the disengagement of carbonic acid. In order to reduce our search to a single cause, we must narrow down our description of the effect, so as to exclude similar, but not identical phenomena.

2. The cause cannot be any thing which is present in other cases where the given effect is not produced, unless the presence of some counteracting cause shall appear, to account for its non-production.

3. The cause is generally suggested by analogy or resemblance, from cases in which the connection of a cause and an effect is better known.

4. The cause is frequently indicated by a variation of degree corresponding to a variation of the degree of effect.

5. The cause will be more likely to appear from considering as many forms of the effect as possible.

6. A suspected cause may be tested by allowing it to operate in circumstances of less complication, to see whether the effect is produced.

7. Where complications exist, the effects must be

narrowly estimated, to determine whether the causes discovered or suspected account for the whole of them; if there is any residual effect, even in the form of a modification of the effects of the known causes, we must seek for its cause also.*

A few examples may be given in illustration. The Danish astronomer Römer was engaged in a course of observations on the revolution of one of the moons of Jupiter, in order to determine its precise time by observing the intervals between its eclipses. He assumed that the interval between any two disappearances of the satellite in the shadow of its planet, would give the precise time of its revolution. But in order to secure the greatest accuracy he continued the observations through several months. Had there been nothing to qualify the assumption, one observation, free from error, would have enabled the astronomer to predict the times of all the future eclipses of the satellite. But Römer found that his predictions were invariably wrong; the observed time was later than the predicted time, and it was not long before he perceived that the error in this direction gradually and regularly increased. By and by he found a decrease in the amount of difference between fact and calculation set in, as gradual and regular as the increase had been; until at length the two became coincident. Now, here was a phenomenon of which the cause was to be discovered. There was one fact which, Römer well knew, accompanied the phenomenon, and varied with it in degree; and that was the

* In drawing up these rules I have derived much aid from *Sir J. Herschel's* Preliminary Discourse on Natural Philosophy, a work which every student would do well to read carefully.

change of the position of the earth in her orbit, and consequently a change in the distance of the earth from Jupiter. It was difficult not to associate these phenomena together, even before the causal connection of one with the other was perceived. But Römer was able to suggest the mode of their correction. The apparent retardation of the eclipse was not a retardation of the satellite itself, but of his perception of it. The light took time to travel; and the difference of the time of the eclipse, when seen from one part of the earth's orbit, nearest to Jupiter, and its time when seen from another part, most distant, would be exactly the time which light took to travel across a distance equal to the diameter of the earth's orbit. But this distance being known, Römer was able to determine the velocity of light; although it formed no part of his purpose in commencing the observations.

It might be difficult to find a better example of the search after causes. Here the corresponding variations of degree of two phenomena distinctly indicated their connection; this variation was a residual phenomenon, not at all expected in the outset, and one which a perfunctory observer might have passed over as insignificant, or set down as the result of some error of his own. The need of embracing as many forms of a phenomenon as possible in our observations also becomes indirectly apparent. It would be most difficult to measure the velocity of light upon the surface of our own planet, because that velocity is so great, not less than 192,000 miles in a single second. But by including a set of observations where the distances are vast, the calculation becomes comparatively easy; for even at this almost incredible speed, the last beam of the satellite as it became extinguished in the shadow, took 16 minutes and 26 seconds to traverse the interval of space which came into the observations.

The third rule, obvious as it is, has much influence on the progress of philosophy, according as it is well or ill observed. That the laws of nature are throughout uniform and harmonious, will be insisted on below; and science sees, as yet at least, no limits to the application of this maxim, for the relations between forces, which were hitherto considered quite distinct, if not opposed, are daily becoming more evident to observant eyes.* Hence there is no more abundant source of scientific improvement than the process of extending the causes of known phenomena to explain the unknown. "Galileo opened the path of all true astronomy, by the simple maxim that the same laws of motion which hold good on the surface of the earth, apply also throughout the celestial spaces; and Lyell did the same thing for geology, by maintaining that the analogy of real and existing ought to be extended through all the immeasurable periods of past time."† The extension of the theory of types, already accepted in physiology, to chemistry also, is probably opening out great results for that science.

Under the sixth rule are included all the varieties of experiments, and of simplified observations. We are sure that the pitch of different musical tones depends on the number of vibrations of the air in

* See *Grove's* Correlation of Physical Forces.

† *Professor Powell's* Unity of Worlds

each, when in the instrument called the Sirene, we cause the vibrations and find that the proper musical note results. We know that the theory of double vision is correct, when in Wheatstone's stereoscope the eyes do actually receive the impression, even exaggerated, of a solid body, from two plain pictures taken from different points, as the two eyes would see them. That the column of mercury in the Torricellian tube was counterpoised by a column of air, was proved by Pascal when he caused the instrument to be carried up the mountain, and found that as the ascent gradually diminished the height of the column of air above it, so was the column of mercury it was able to sustain, diminished in proportion. Dr. Buckland was confirmed in his surmise that certain bones, bruised and mangled, were the relics of the prey of hyenas, when a living beast of the same species reduced before his eyes the bones of an ox to a condition precisely similar.

In Sir Humphry Davy's experiments upon the decomposition of water by galvanism, it was found that besides the two components of water, oxygen and hydrogen, an acid and an alkali were developed at the two opposite poles of the machine. As the theory of the analysis of water did not give reason to expect these products, they were a *residual phenomenon*, the cause of which was still to be found. Some chemists thought that electricity had the power of *producing* these substances of itself; and if their erroneous conjecture had been adopted, succeeding researches would have gone upon a false scent, considering galvanic electricity as a *producing* rather than a *decomposing* force. The happier insight of Davy conjectured that there might be some hidden cause of this portion of the effect; the glass vessel containing the water might suffer partial decomposition, or some foreign matter might be mingled with the water, and the acid and alkali be disengaged from it, so that the water would have no share in their production. Assuming this he proceeded to try whether the total removal of the cause would destroy the effect, or at least the diminution of it cause a corresponding change in the amount of effect produced. By the substitution of gold vessels for the glass without any change in the effect, he at once determined that the glass was not the cause. Employing distilled water he found a marked diminution of the quantity of acid and alkali evolved; still there was enough to show that the cause, whatever it was, was still in operation. Impurity of the water then was not the sole, but a concurrent cause. He now conceived that the perspiration from the hands touching the instruments might affect the case, as it would contain common salt, and an acid and an alkali would result from its decomposition under the agency of electricity. By carefully avoiding such contact, he reduced the quantity of the products still further, until no more than slight traces of them were perceptible. What remained of the effect might be traceable to impurities of the atmosphere, decomposed by contact with the electrical apparatus. An experiment determined this; the machine was placed under an exhausted receiver, and when thus secured from atmospheric influence, it no longer evolved the acid and the alkali.

A formal analysis of these beautiful experiments will illustrate the method of applying the rules of pure Logic in other cases.

I. Statement of the case, the *residual* cause being still undiscovered.

"The decomposition of water by electricity produces oxygen and hydrogen, with an acid and an alkali."

II. Separation of the *residual* from the principal cause.

a. "The decomposition of water produces oxygen and hydrogen.

b. "The production of an acid and an alkali in the decomposition of water *may be caused* by action on the glass vessel containing the water." (Problematical Judgment—A.)

III. The latter Judgment—b—disproved by a syllogism in Mood E A O, Fig. III. with a conclusion that *contradicts* it.

"A case in which I employ a vessel of gold cannot involve any decomposing action on a glass vessel,

"A case in which I employ a gold vessel still gives the acid and the alkali;

"Therefore cases of the production of the acid and alkali are not always cases in which glass is decomposed."

IV. Another attempt to suggest the residual cause.

"The acid and alkali are produced by the decomposition of impurities in the water employed."

Syllogism in A A I, Fig. III. *tending to* prove this.

"An experiment with *distilled* water must admit *less* impurity,

"An experiment with distilled water gives *less* acid and alkali;

"Therefore sometimes with less impurity we have less acid and alkali."

V. "The contact of moist hands" may be an additional cause of the residual phenomenon.

Improved syllogism in A A I, Fig. III. to include this concurrent cause.

"An experiment with distilled water, and apparatus kept from contact of hands will admit *still less* impurity,

"An experiment, &c. results in the production of still less acid and alkali;

"Therefore sometimes with still less impurity we have still less acid and alkali."

VI. Amended syllogism. A A A, Fig. III.

"A case where we use these precautions *in vacuo* is a case of *no* impurity,

"A case where we use, &c. *in vacuo* is a case of *no* acid and alkali;

"Therefore a case of no impurity is a case of no acid and alkali."

VII. Immediate inference from last conclusion.

"Cases of no-impurity are cases of non-production of acid and alkali,

"Therefore" (according to the example in p. 186, Division II. of inference from A)

"All cases of production of acid and alkali are cases of some impurity;"

which was to be proved.

An example like this brings into a strong light many of the characteristics of inductive reasoning Forms usually considered to be deductive are here freely employed. The later steps tend to confirm the earlier, on which, however, they themselves depend; so that a mutual confirmation is obtained from setting them together. When the chemist substituted gold vessels for the glass, and inferred from the continuance of the effect under this change that the glass could have nothing to do with its production, it was formally possible in the then state of knowledge that the glass might be the cause in the one experiment, and the decomposition of the gold in the other. But the later steps, which showed that the effect varied with the variations in a circumstance wholly distinct from the decomposition of glass or gold reduced the possibility of maintaining such a view to the very lowest amount. Even the premisses of particular syllogisms in the chain are sometimes tested and corrected by the conclusion, although formally the conclusion should entirely depend upon the premisses. The experimenter expected to find that the use of distilled water would exclude *all* impurity; and he intended that his premiss (See No. IV.) should assert as much; but when it turned out in the conclusion that the supposed products of the impurity were still present, he was reduced to the choice between abandoning that cause and recasting his premiss so as to admit that the cause was still present—" the use of distilled water gives *less* impurity."

§ 115. *Anticipation.*

The next question to be answered is—how are causes discovered which are not obvious, even after repeated inspections of the facts in which they lie hid? By a power or combination of powers granted only to a few, which has been called Anticipation. It is the power of penetrating into the secrets of nature, before the evidence is unfolded; it is enjoyed, as one might expect, by those only who have long and deeply studied the laws of nature already laid open, but not by all of these. It is no mere power of guessing, but an active imagination, supplied with materials by a clear understanding carefully disciplined. The system of anatomy which has immortalized the name of Oken, is the consequence of a flash of anticipation which glanced through his mind when he picked up, in a chance walk, the skull of a deer, bleached and disintegrated by the weather, and exclaimed after a glance, "It is part of a vertebral column!" When Newton saw the apple fall, the anticipatory question flashed into his mind, "Why do not the heavenly bodies fall like this apple?" In neither case had accident any important share ; Newton and Oken were both prepared by the deepest previous study to seize upon the unimportant fact offered to them, and show how important it might become; and if the apple and the deer's skull had been wanting, some other falling body, or some other skull, would have touched the string so ready to vibrate. But in each case there was a great step of anticipation; Oken thought he saw the type of the whole skeleton in the single vertebra and its modifications, whilst Newton conceived at once that the whole universe was full of bodies tending to fall; two truths that can scarcely be said to be contained in the little occurrences in connection with which they were first suggested.

The discovery of Goethe, which did for the vegetable kingdom what Oken's did for the animal, that the parts of a plant are to be regarded as metamorphosed leaves, is an apparent exception to the necessity of discipline for invention, since it was the discovery of a poet in a region to which he seemed to have paid no especial or laborious attention. But Goethe was himself most anxious to rest the basis of this discovery upon his observation rather than his imagination, and doubtless with good reason.*

A mistaken notion prevails that this rapid antici-

* *Whewell's* Hist. Sci. Ind. III. 477. As with other great discoveries, hints had been given already, though not pursued, both of Goethe's and Oken's principles. Goethe left his to be followed up by others, and but for his great fame, perhaps his name would never have been connected with it. Oken had amassed all the materials necessary for the establishment of his theory ; he was able at once to discover and conquer the new country.

pation does not belong to the philosophic cast of mind—that it is precisely what Bacon condemns as the method which "hurries on rapidly from the particulars supplied by the senses to the most general axioms, and from them as principles, and their supposed indisputable truth, derives and discovers the intermediate axioms." It is thought that caution, and deliberate examination of every particular we can find, before we allow ourselves to form any conclusion whatever, are the conditions of all sound physical inquiry. There is here a confusion of two distinct things. Scrupulous caution should be exercised before an hypothesis is considered to be *proved;* and the law that we believe to be true should be applied to every fact where it can be supposed to operate, and to every other law with which it might interfere, in order to verify exactly what was at first only a happy conjecture. Bacon meant to complain that this sober process did not always follow the bright thought and brilliant suggestion; and perhaps that the bright thought itself was not suggested in the region of facts but in that of words. When the ancient Astronomy, rushing to the general axiom that "the circular motion is the most perfect," deduced from it the intermediate axiom that the motion of the heavenly bodies must be the circular, it might be reasonably charged with undue use of anticipation; because the highest axiom, having no precise and definable meaning, cannot have really sprung from the contemplation of any facts, nor do it and the axiom drawn from it square with the facts they pretend to embrace. Where these conditions are obeyed, Anticipation is, as it has been called, the mother of science. "To try wrong guesses," says Dr. Whewell, "is, with most persons, the only way to hit upon right ones. The character of the true philosopher is, not that he never conjectures hazardously, but that his conjectures are clearly conceived, and brought into rigid contact with facts. He sees and compares distinctly the ideas and the things;—the relation of his notions to each other and to phenomena. Under these conditions, it is not only excusable, but necessary for him, to snatch at every semblance of general rule,—to try all promising forms of simplicity and symmetry." Anticipation then is the power whereby the mind presages a truth before it is fairly proved, before she makes the attempt to establish it by exact and cautious methods. Philosophy proceeds upon a system of credit; if she never advanced beyond her tangible capital, her wealth would not be so enormous as it is. She works with a principle as true before she knows it to be so, because in watching how it operates upon facts consists the best means of establishing its truth; but she must be prepared at the same time to abandon and dismiss it whenever it is found to be in direct and irreconcilable conflict with established facts.

§ 116. *Inductive Conception, Colligation, Definition.*

Upon the nature of the Conception which Anticipation furnishes, and its share in the formation of science, much controversy has been raised, one party maintaining that the mind must be content with recording the facts, and another, that a Conception must anticipate the facts, and furnish us with a key to their language. Granting on the one hand that a theory or conception to explain facts will be worthless, unless it shall prove to be itself a fact, we must admit on the other that great steps of inductive discovery are made with the help of a preconception, and not by merely throwing observations together. "That the fact of the elliptical motion of the planet Mars," says Dr. Whewell, "was not merely the *sum* of the different observations, is plain from this, that other persons, and Kepler himself before his discovery, did not find it by adding together the observations. The fact of the elliptical orbit was not the sum of the observations merely; it was the sum of the observations, *seen under a new point of view*, which point of view Kepler's mind supplied."

Such a conception, of which several instances have now been given, effects the *Colligation* (to borrow Dr. Whewell's name) of the facts to be explained. But in order to connect itself with the facts, the conception itself must be capable of Explication or Definition, not indeed of *adequate* definition, since we shall have to alter our description of it from time to time with the advance of knowledge, but still capable of a precise and clear explanation. For example, a large class of facts is bound together by the notion of "chemical affinity," and could not be understood and arranged without the thread of this Conception to run through them. To refer them to this, their proper Conception, is one operation; to give a proper Explanation of chemical affinity another.

DEFINITION.—Chemical affinity is the power by which the particles of one elementary body are made to cohere with those of another, so as to produce a new substance, with characters either distinct from or opposed to those of the constituents separately.

PROPOSITION.—The tarnishing of metals, the neutral salts, &c. &c. are instances of the action of chemical affinity.

Therefore we expect to find in them the characters mentioned in the definition.

This is a syllogism in U A A, Fig. I.; and whilst our reasoning faculty can draw it out and appreciate its truth and applicability, reason alone could not have suggested the premisses. No rules can be given for the discovery of the appropriate conception that explains our facts; "such events," says Dr. Whewell, "appear to result from a peculiar sagacity and felicity of mind—never without labour—never without preparation; yet with no constant dependence upon preparation, upon labour, or even entirely upon personal endowments." The suggestion of the conception may be due almost entirely to accident; the explication of it, often by far the more difficult step, cannot be accidental, but will proceed from a natural sagacity highly disciplined by scientific pursuits.

Conceptions not wholly correct may serve for a time for the Colligation of Facts, and may guide us in researches which shall end in a more exact Colligation. The theory of *circular* motions of the heavenly bodies was of this kind; and in its turn the conception of epicycles. The theory of Phlogiston in chemistry made many facts intelligible, before the correcter one of Oxidation superseded it. So with the theory of "Nature abhors a vacuum," which served to bring together many cognate facts, not previously considered as related. Any incorrect conception of this kind has a place in science, whilst and in so far as it is applicable to facts and renders them intelligible. As soon as facts occur which it is inadequate to explain, we either correct, or replace it by a new one.

§ 117. *Complete and Incomplete Induction.*

The third question that demanded an answer was —on what principle are incomplete inductions, *i. e.* examinations of facts that stop short of complete enumeration, sufficient to establish general laws? The answer will contain the most interesting and important of the principles of Logic. All our experience teaches us that in the universe, the "Cosmos," whose very name means order, regularity and uniformity prevail, and caprice and uncertainty are excluded. Whilst it is conceivable that any one of the natural laws in which we place most confidence might be reversed, while it is certain that many of them have been miraculously suspended for purposes proportionably great and important, our present belief in their permanence is almost unlimited. The thought that there might be no more daylight, if our planet ceased to revolve whilst one side of it was averted from the sun—that a draught from the spring would to-day destroy the life which it recruited yesterday—that a stone thrown from the hand would remain suspended in mid-air instead of falling—never enters our minds, except perhaps as an amusing fancy; yet each of these things is formally possible. Our confidence in the uniformity of natural laws is embodied in the Canon, that *under the same circumstances and with the same substances the same effects always result from the same causes.* This great inductive principle is itself proved by induction, and partakes of the same formal defect that may be charged against other inductive results, viz: that its terms are wider than our experience can warrant. Many groups of facts, connected as causes and effects, have not been examined; and in them it is conceivable at least that there may be capricious causes producing opposite effects at different times. If this were otherwise—if the canon were the result of a simple enumeration of all possible cases, its present value as a rule would disappear; since it is to unknown and unexamined cases that we chiefly wish to apply it. We draw a universal canon from an experience less than universal, and then employ it to justify us in drawing other universal truths from other particular experiences.

The difficulty, however, in applying this Canon is to discover the existence of a law of nature in any set of facts, and how far the interference of other laws permits it to operate. And here the relation between Deduction and Induction, between Synthesis and Analysis, is of great service. These pairs of terms correspond exactly, as names for the same two processes; but Induction and Deduction give prominence to the law, Analysis and Synthesis to the fact. Thus we call the law of gravitation an inductive law, and speak of deductions from it, thinking more in both cases of the universal than of the particular cases it referred to. But we ana lyze a fact or a substance, and make a synthesis (or *placing together* of elements) to reproduce the fact or substance. Using the two former names, the universal, the law, the world of conception, the abstract is made prominent; using the two latter, we give prominence to the single case, the phenomenon, the world of the senses, the concrete. The supposed general principle may be tried by applying it to a new particular case; the analysis of a fact into its elements may be tested by putting the elements together anew, and seeing if the fact is reproduced; the correctness of the observations may be confirmed by careful experiment. And such attempts offer a twofold advantage. If, on applying some general principle of which we are still uncertain, to a new particular case, we find that it helps to explain the particular, this is one fruit of the process; and another is that our confidence in the general principle is materially strengthened. Law explains fact; fact confirms law. And after this alternate ascent and descent has been a few times performed, our belief in the correctness of its results is quite complete.

This process can be understood most readily from examples. The metal called Potassium was discovered in acting on potash by the voltaic battery; and thus far the two judgments—

Potash is an alkali,
Potash yields Potassium—

would seem sufficient to describe the result. But not so; a mind disciplined to scientific inquiry saw at once that this single fact was an indication of a law. In the system of nature is no caprice; if the power of yielding a metal belonged to this alkali *as such*, beyond doubt other alkalies would participate in it. These two judgments therefore become premisses to an act of inductive reasoning.

(A A A, Fig. III.)

Potash yields a metal,
Potash is an alkali;
Therefore *all* alkalies contain a metal.

Now this syllogism is formally incorrect; for we cannot argue from a single alkali to the whole, and the property we have discovered may belong to this alone in connection with some undiscovered peculiarity. How shall this be ascertained? By trying how the conclusion, upon which suspicion rests, will apply to new cases; by experimenting on another alkali, as if the universal law were already established, by deducing from it, as we have induced to it.

(A A A, Fig. I.)

All alkalies contain a metal,
Soda is an alkali;
Therefore it must contain a metal.

The experiment is tried, and answers perfectly And the success of the prediction operates strongly to raise our belief in the conclusion on which it proceeded. That alkalies in general have a metallic base was indicated at first by one case alone, that of potash; but the chemist was guided by that case to a second attempt, and now a second one strengthens his belief that a law exists. To extend the trials to the alkaline earths, is suggested by their similarity to alkalies; with them too the experiments are successful, and the law is considered to be established. And though ammonia furnishes an apparent exception, as it has been found impossible from the volatile nature of that substance to procure ammonium from it, I suppose that no skilful chemist doubts that ammonium exists, so strong is the general conviction that nature's laws are uniform, and that where most substances alike in their general character, exhibit some striking property, it has been granted to them all without exception.

Two principles then are established, that the correctness of synthesis is proportionate to that of the preceding analysis; and that a doubtful analysis may be confirmed by a synthesis. In other words, a correct induction furnishes the premiss for a sound deduction, and a doubtful induction must be verified by deductions from it. Examples of these may be found on every side. The artilleryman, when he points a gun according to known rules, executes a synthesis of several principles, the law of gravitation, that of momentum, that of atmospheric resistance; if his shot misses, it will be either because some element has been left out of the analysis, the comparative force perhaps of different sorts of powder, and the windage of a loose ball in the barrel of the piece; or because the influence of each of the known laws has not been duly apportioned. The theory that marble is carbonate of lime fused under pressure has been made highly probable by the (synthetic) experiments of Sir James Hall, who made a substance closely resembling marble by those means. A correct analysis of *lapis lazuli* was suspected to be erroneous, because there seemed to be nothing in the elements assigned it, which were silica, alumina, soda, sulphur, and a trace of iron, to account for the brilliant blue colour of the stone; accidental synthesis, which was followed up by intentional, reproduced it, and thus the analysis was found to be correct, whilst the synthesis is now daily performed for commercial purposes. The law that the planets are retained in their orbits by an attractive force that varies inversely as the square of their distance from the sun has been worked out to its theoretical results, and these have been compared, synthetically, with the known facts. Theory was found not to correspond with fact in all respects, and thus it became necessary to revise the analysis, and discover the residual causes that produced the variation; which astronomers have succeeded in doing.

By the mutual coöperation then of these two processes, the physical sciences are advanced.* If no attempts were made to draw a conclusion and see what use could be made of it, till grounds formally complete were before us, conclusions would never be drawn. The certainties by which the chemist, th

* *Table of the relation of these processes.*

	By Deduction	By Induction
	or Synthesis	or Analysis
	in Teaching	in Learning
	or Verification	or Invention
	or γένεσις (*Ar.*)	or εὕρεσις (*Ar.*)
	we proceed	
From	Law	To Fact
	Rule	Example
	Cause	Effect
	διότι (*Ar.*)	ὅτι (*Ar.*)
	ἀπὸ τῶν ἀρχῶν (*Ar.*)	ἐπὶ τὰς ἀρχάς. (*Ar.*)

astronomer, the geologist conducts his operations with composure and success, were once bare possibilities, which after being handed back and forward between Induction and Deduction, turned out to be truths. This leads on to other considerations, first as to the Modality of Judgments, that is, the degree of our belief in them, and next as to the use of the Syllogism in the procedure just described.

§ 118. *Belief, and Degrees of Belief.*

In forming any judgment we cannot avoid attaching to it a particular degree of credence, which might be, and often is, expressed by the insertion of some adverb to qualify the copula; thus "To-morrow will (possibly) be fine," and "Two straight lines (indisputably) cannot enclose a space." Although one of these judgments admits a degree of doubt, which the other excludes, the difference lies in our knowledge of the things spoken of, rather than in the things themselves. To-morrow will be fine or will be stormy, and it is fixed by the laws of nature which shall happen; but *to us* the matter is purely doubtful, because we cannot see into the order of nature as to this particular. Doubtful statements may become certain, without any alteration in the facts to which they relate, by changes in our knowledge. A child sees with wonder a lunar eclipse, and thinks that *possibly* another may happen to-morrow; when he has learnt Astronomy he may be able to say from exact calculations upon what day one may positively be expected. Yet here the order of things remains the same. The amount of belief which we have in our judgment has been called its Modality, as being the *mode* in which we hold it for truth. Arranging the degrees of Modality in an ascending scale, we find that a judgment may be

1. Possible, where upon the first view we have no cause to think that the predicate may not be truly said of the subject, but have not examined. Does this amount to a judgment or is it the step which must precede the formation of the weakest kind of judgment?

2. Doubtful, where we have tested it in some cases, and found that some seem to confirm it, whilst some are doubtful.

3. Probable, where all the trials we have made are favourable, but the number of them is not sufficient to warrant certainty.

4. Morally certain for the thinker himself; where from examination of the matter, or prejudice, or interest, he has formed his own belief, but cannot put forward sufficient grounds for it, so as to control that of others.

5. Morally certain for a class or school; where the judgment rests upon grounds which are sufficient for all men of the same habits of thought, or the same education, as the thinker.

6. Morally certain for all; as for example the belief that there is a future state, which though not absolutely demonstrable, rests upon such grounds that it ought to influence the conduct (*mores*) of every man.

7. Physically certain, with a limit; where the judgment is grounded on an induction supposed to be complete, but with the possibility that future induction may supersede it.

8. Physically certain without limitation; as our belief in the law of gravitation, the law of chemical affinity, &c.

9. Mathematically certain; where doubt cannot be admitted. *Ex. gr.* the axiom—Two straight lines cannot enclose a space; or the theorem—The angles at the base of an isosceles triangle are equal.

All these degrees of belief may, upon a broader principle of division, be resolved into three.

Our judgments, according to Aristotle, are either problematical, assertive, or demonstrable; or in other words, the results of Opinion, of Belief, or of Science.

The problematical judgment is neither subjectively nor objectively true, that is, it is neither held with entire certainty by the thinking subject, nor can we show that it truly represents the object about which we judge. It is a mere opinion. It may however be the expression of our presentiment of certainty; and what was held as mere opinion before proof, may afterwards be proved to demonstration. Great discoveries are problems at first, and the examination of them leads to a conviction of their truth, as it has done to the abandonment of many false opinions. In other subjects we cannot from the nature of the case advance beyond mere opinion. Whenever we judge about variable things, as the future actions of men, the best course of conduct for ourselves under doubtful circumstances, historical facts about which there is conflicting testimony, we can but form a problematical judgment, and must admit the possibility of error at the moment of making our decision.

The assertive judgment is one of which we are

fully persuaded ourselves, but cannot give grounds for our belief, that shall compel men in general to coincide with us. It is therefore subjectively, but not objectively certain. It commends itself to our moral nature, and in so far as other men are of the same disposition, they will accept it likewise.

The demonstrative judgment is both subjectively and objectively true. It may either be certain in itself, as a mathematical axiom is, or capable of proof by means of other judgments, as the theorems of mathematics and the laws of physical science.

§ 119. *The Syllogism both deductive and inductive.*

It is a great misfortune for Logic that the Syllogism has been regarded as an instrument for deduction only. An error of Aristotle's, for the correction of which his many-sided mind has itself supplied hints, has been tenaciously preserved; and according to it, four modes of syllogism, in which we start from a general law as our main premiss, have been regarded as the only perfect forms, and opinions have been pronounced upon the whole syllogistic system from these four specimens. We need not wonder then that modes only adapted for teaching truth, have been pronounced useless for discovering it; that when deductive arguments are selected, it should be easy to prove that they will not do the work of inductive. But it is wonderful that so few should have perceived how absurd were the attempts to turn the so-called imperfect modes into perfect ones. It has been shown already (p. 210), that the modes of each figure in the old arrangement had their proper use, that the first served for deducing facts from laws, the second for establishing differences, and the third for bringing in examples and exceptions. Yet logicians have persisted in torturing syllogisms of the second and third figures into the first, by the help of Conversion, without perceiving that they turned a natural argument into a distorted monster. To say—

(A A I, Fig. III.)

Lead is fusible,
Lead is a metal;
Therefore some metal is fusible—

is natural enough; but it partakes far more of the nature of induction than deduction, because it is advancing from a single observation towards a more general statement, which may end probably in a universal. Now to establish the erroneous assertion that all syllogisms are deductions, logicians are bound either to deny that such an argument is a syllogism, or to attempt to reduce it to one of the deductive modes. They adopt the latter alternative, thus—

(A I I, Fig. I.)

Lead is fusible,
Some metal is lead;
Therefore some metal is fusible.

But this unnatural form is no more like deduction than before; there is no reasoning from a law to facts, from a general to a particular statement, and all that has been done is to give us for a second premiss an unnatural judgment such as logicians have taught us already to avoid as much as possible.

The syllogism is not confined to deductive arguments. Every one of the inductive methods already described, falls easily into an appropriate syllogistic form; and we can no more reason without making syllogisms than we can speak and argue without forming sentences. What Grammar does for speech Logic does for thought; it ascertains its simple elements and exhibits them, and if it be found that the inductive processes do not fall readily under the old forms, it would be right to consider first whether the forms could be amended or enlarged, rather than to abandon at once one half the territory of thought, the whole of which Logic has always by its names and definitions seemed to claim.

To assign one half the domain of Logic to Induction is not strictly correct. There is in truth a third process, of some subordinate advantage in investigation, whereby no advance is made towards general laws, as in Induction, nor towards the application of laws to facts, as in Deduction, but the matter of knowledge is exhibited under a new and more convenient form. It has been appropriately named Traduction.* The modes U U U in all the figures are those which exemplify it most perfectly.

§ 120. *Employment of defective Syllogisms.*

The difficulty in answering the question—how does Logic aid by the syllogism in adding to our stock of knowledge? has been caused principally by studying only the complete forms of syllogism,

* By Mr. *James Broun,* in an able letter in Prof. *De Morgan's* Formal Logic, p. 332.

whereas in discovery it is necessary to accept defective forms, only suspending our adoption of them until they are fortified by other evidence. The fact that such suspense is necessary proves that the forms are imperfect; the fact that we have attained new truths from evidence formally insufficient to establish them by itself, proves their usefulness. This will appear from a description of some of the best known forms of defective syllogism.

The RHETORICAL ENTHYMEME as described by Aristotle, is "a syllogism from probable propositions or from signs." The probable proposition (εἰκὸς) is that sort of statement which must satisfy us in matters where universal assertions are impossible; as in human affairs, that "injured men will seek revenge —men are active where their interest is concerned," and the like. Any syllogism into which a proposition of this sort, general but by no means universal, enters, can only supply a general and therefore uncertain conclusion. The sign (σημεῖον) according to Aristotle, is a proposition in which some one fact or mark that accompanies, precedes, or follows, another fact or conception, is adduced as a necessary or probable indication that the other is present. (Pri. An. ii. 27.) In describing a sign as "a proposition," some violence is done to language, since it can always be expressed as a single term. As no account is taken of negative signs, indications, that is, that a given thing does *not* exist, all the Enthymemes based on signs will be positive or affirmative; and as they are to prove the existence of a given fact without limitation, their conclusions will also be universal. Now some of them are found to furnish demonstrative proof of the point they would establish; and these are called Proofs. Others only afford a presumption more or less valid that the conclusion is true. This difference becomes manifest from the use of the three Figures; the Proofs will only be found, where the mode and figure of the syllogism, made out of the terms of the question with the sign for a middle term, are logically valid. Where they are invalid, the sign will fall short of a Proof to the extent of that invalidity. Thus, of three Enthymemes; (I.) Dionysius must fear because he is a tyrant; (II.) This man is the murderer, because he was near the murdered man; (III.) As we see from the case of Lord Bacon, contemplative men are competent to the affairs of life;—each falls into a different figure.

(I. A A A.)

All tyrants fear,
Dionysius is a tyrant;
∴ He must fear.

(II. A A A.)

The murderer would be near,
This man is near;
∴ He is the murderer.

(III. A A A.)

Lord Bacon was a practical man,
Lord Bacon was contemplative;
∴ All contemplative men are fit for practical life.

Of these the first alone is formally conclusive, because it violates no syllogistic rule; it amounts therefore to a scientific proof. Not so the second; it has not distributed the middle term; it should have shown not only that the murderer must be near, but that he *alone* could be so. The third again draws a conclusion far too wide for its premisses; what is true of Lord Bacon need not be so of the whole class from which he has been selected. On reference to the table (p. 210) it will be found that A A A is omitted both from the second and third Figures, in consequence of these defects. But are these imperfect modes quite useless? Far from it. A single argument of this kind establishes a presumption of agreement between the terms of the conclusion, and instigates to the search for other confirmatory signs. But several concurrent Enthymemes are often as cogent as a demonstrative syllogism. In the investigation of the authorship of the letters of Junius, Mr. Taylor employs of necessity a string of enthymemes in the second Figure, each in itself defective, but altogether forming a very strong case. Thus,

The author of "Junius" wrote a particular hand,
Sir Philip Francis wrote the same kind of hand;
Therefore Sir Philip Francis is the author of "Junius."

The author of "Junius" made certain mistakes in correcting proof-sheets,
Sir Philip Francis made the same mistakes;
Therefore Sir Philip Francis is the author of "Junius."

The author of "Junius" had a particular style,
Sir Philip Francis wrote the same style;
Therefore Sir Philip Francis is the author of "Junius."

The author of "Junius" is guilty of an anomalous use of certain words,
Sir Philip Francis is guilty of the same;
Therefore Sir Philip Francis is the author of "Junius."

The author of "Junius" employs certain images,
Sir Philip Francis employs the same;
Therefore Sir Philip Francis is the author of "Junius."

The author of "Junius" ceased to write at a particular time,
Sir Philip Francis must have ceased to write at the same time;
Therefore Sir Philip Francis is the author of "Junius."

The results of these and several similar arguments are summed up in a syllogism which most people, unless they could assail the truth of some of the statements, would think conclusive, to the effect that two persons who in so many points are not found to differ must be one and the same. Circumstantial evidence falls naturally into a series of Enthymemes of the second figure. Those of the third figure are employed in inductive reasoning; and a series of them might afford a very high degree of probability that the conclusion common to all was true. Aristotle's doctrine of Enthymemes differs from the ordinary view of syllogism, only as to the order of statement of these as distinguished from common syllogisms, and the license allowed to employ provisionally, defective arguments, where better cannot be found. In any syllogism whatever, if we regard the question or conclusion first, as Aristotle does in this case, we may call the middle term a sign of its truth: but it is an important admission that signs may be used which do not prove the question, and only establish a presumption stronger or weaker in its favour.

The Example is an argument which proves something to be true in a particular case from another particular case. Thus "Harvey might expect to be persecuted for his discovery of the circulation of the blood, because Galileo was for *his* discovery." But the connection between two distinct facts can only depend upon their coming under some common law and therefore in the Example the proof is not of one particular judgment by another, but of a particular by means of a universal, for which another particular is the sign. Thus

(Enthymeme in A A A, Fig. III. with Episyllogism in A A A, Fig. I.)

Galileo was persecuted,
Galileo was a discoverer in science;
Therefore *all* discoverers are likely to be persecuted.
Harvey is a discoverer,
Therefore he too will be persecuted.

This argument is called "rhetorical induction;" it differs from induction* proper in bringing in only one example instead of many, and in going on to prove another particular case, instead of stopping at the general law. The flaw in it is obvious; but the nearer the predicate of the second premiss approaches to distribution, the less probable is an error. If it could be shown that "Galileo was a fair sample of *all* discoverers," the mode would become A U A, Fig. III. which is formally correct. But in its weaker form it is perpetually employed.

THE INDUCTION BY IMPERFECT ENUMERATION is an argument which establishes a general law or rule from a number of examples of it less than the whole. Thus

(In A A A, Fig. III.)

Gold, silver, and copper melt,
They are metals;
Therefore *all* metals will melt.

* This difference disappears if with Diogenes Laertius, and Cicero, we describe Induction as an argument from particulars to like particulars. *Heyder*, Dartstellung, p. 60.

Its formal fault is the same as that of the Enthymeme of the 3d Figure (p. 285), with which it is almost identical; the conditions on which it may be employed have been explained above.

§ 121. *Syllogism of Analogy.*

Analogy has been defined "The similarity of ratios or relations;" and as each relation supposes two cognate things, a comparison of relations would imply four things and four terms to express them. Thus (to employ one of Archbishop Whateley's examples) when Mandeville uses as an argument against popular education, that, "If the horse knew enough he would soon throw his rider," he intends to imply two pairs of related terms—

As the horse is to its rider, so is the people to its rulers—

and to assert further that since the one relation depends upon the continuance of ignorance on the part of the horse, the other depends upon ignorance also. Common sense suggests the refutation of such an argument; we deny that the relations *are* similar, or at least that the similarity reaches so far as to warrant such an assertion as is founded upon it. Similarity of relations may exist, however, where there is no resemblance between the related *things.*

But in popular language we extend the word analogy to include resemblances of things, as well as of relations. Analogy in this sense has exercised an immense influence on the formation of language. In innumerable cases visible or tangible things lend their names to invisible and spiritual, from a resemblance more or less striking between them. *Transgression* in its primary sense means the crossing over a visible boundary; *right* means straight, and *wrong* means twisted. We speak of a *clear* statement, a *lofty* mind, and a *deep* thought, all these adjectives being drawn from the analogies of the material world. Whilst we can exhibit them in the form of a statement of proportions, so as to vindicate the original sense of analogy, it is not necessary, nor in all cases natural, to do so. We may consider therefore that similarity of attributes, as well as of relations, may have the name of analogy.

Employed as an argument, analogy depends upon the canon—*The same attributes may be assigned to distinct but similar things, provided they can be shown to accompany the points of resemblance in the things, and not the points of difference.* But since the presupposition of a power of discerning to what part of the things the attributes belong, is indispensable, the argument itself depends for its weight upon something external to itself, and sinks into a mere exposition. In a syllogism proving that the metropolis, as the heart of a state, should not be suffered to become too large, because a large heart is diseased, the real dispute would not be about the syllogism itself—

The heart in relation to the body should not be too large,
The heart in relation to the body = (partly) the metropolis in relation to the state;
Therefore the metropolis to the state should not be too large.

This inference (in E U E, Fig. III.) is faultless, provided we admit that the partial identity established between the heart and the metropolis includes the point of size; and to decide this, other arguments will be requisite, which, if unsuccessful, will render the present one false; if successful, needless. And therefore arguments of this kind, founded on a questionable resemblance, are used rather to suggest comparisons, and so persuade, than to compel conviction; and philosophers have had great cause to complain of the many fallacies which become current through false "metaphorical analogies."

But where the resemblance between two things is undoubted, and does not depend on one or two external features, analogy tends much more strongly to persuasion at least, though it cannot amount to demonstration. Its principle would be—*When one thing resembles another in known particulars, it will resemble it also in the unknown.* The expression of their agreement must be a *qualified* judgment of identity—a U. They must not be of the same kind, but only of a similar one, otherwise the argument is a mere case of Example. Neither must the usual tests have been applied (see p. 258,) to prove that the known particulars invariably accompany the unknown, otherwise, as Mr. Mill observes, we trench upon the ground of Induction. In venturing thus to assign attributes to a thing, because other things of a different class have them, we show our dependence on the regularity and consistency of creation. When the geologist discovers a fossil animal with large strong blunt claws, he infers that it procured its food by scratching or burrowing in the earth, trusting that a conformation which in other kinds of animals accompanies this particular mode of life, would not be arbitrarily and exceptionally assigned in this case to an animal of different pursuits. The following example, from Bishop Butler, of a false analogy, and its refutation, will show the syllogistic treatment of analogies :—

"There is little presumption that death is the destruction of human creatures. However, there is the shadow of an analogy, which may lead us to imagine it is—the supposed likeness which is observed between the decay of vegetables and of living creatures. And this likeness is indeed sufficient to afford the poets very apt allusions to the flowers of the field, in their pictures of the frailty of our present life. But, in reason, the analogy is so far from holding, that there appears no ground even for the comparison, as to the present question; because one of the two subjects compared is wholly void of that which is the principal and chief thing in the other, the power of perception and of action; and which is the only tning we are inquiring about the continuance of. So that the destruction of a vegetable is an event not similar, or analogous, to the destruction of a living agent."

This may be resolved into two syllogisms.

I. Analogy—in A U A, Fig. III.

The decay of vegetables is total destruction,
The decay of vegetables=(for present purposes) the decay of living creatures;
Therefore the decay of living creatures is total destruction.

II. Refutation—in A E E, Fig. II.

The decay of animals is that of living, acting creatures,
The decay of vegetables is not that of living, acting creatures;
Therefore the decay of vegetables is not the same as that of animals.

The conclusion E of the latter syllogism is opposed as a contrary to the premiss U of the former.

§ 122. *Syllogisms of Chance.*

Chance* may be described as the amount of belief with which we expect one or other, out of two or more uncertain events. Uncertain events are those wherein no cause or law appears, to determine the occurrence of one rather than of another. As all questions into which this notion enters demand a numerical statement, the doctrine of Chances is usually regarded as a branch of mathematics; and its intricacies can only be explained by persons deeply conversant with that science, who have turned their attention to this special branch of inquiry. Only the bare elements of it can be given here, with a few of the simplest examples.

1. The first principle is that *the probability of an uncertain event is represented by the number of chances favourable to an event divided by the total number of chances.* Thus the chances that a pictured card will be drawn out of a pack at random, the first attempt, are $\frac{12}{52}$, because there are fifty-two cards that may be drawn, and only twelve pictured

* The materials of this section are taken entirely from *Quetelet* on Probabilities (of which most interesting work there is a readable and spirited translation by Mr. *G. O. Downes*), and from the Formal Logic of Professor *De Morgan*, whose researches, there, in the Cambridge Philos. Trans., and in the Encyclopædia Metrop., are spoken of by those better able to follow them than myself, as very acute and profound. Professor *Donkin* (Philos. Mag. May, 1851) has developed with great clearness the view, common to him and to the writers I have named, that "the subject-matter of calculations in the theory of probabilities is *quantity of belief.* In every problem a certain number of hypotheses are presented to the mind, along with a certain quantity of information relating to them: the question is—in what way ought belief to be distributed among them?" His researches did not come under my notice till the text was written.

cards to furnish the desired result. If it is wished to balance the chances on each side, the twelve favourable must be subtracted from the whole fifty-two, and forty unfavourable are found to remain. Applying this principle, we should see without much consideration that a proposition absolutely certain must be represented by a unit, because there is no difference between the number of favourable events and the whole events. That the card drawn will be of some suit or other is certain; then its chance is $\frac{52}{52}=1$. It is equally clear that the symbol of a wholly uncertain judgment is $\frac{1}{2}$, for the two chances are that it may come to pass or not, and the former of them is the one favourable chance. Thus that a red card will be drawn, and not a black, will be $\frac{26}{52}=\frac{1}{2}$.

To take a familiar, yet somewhat more difficult problem—what are the chances, in tossing up a halfpenny, that it will give a head at or before the third throw? We assume that the sides of the coin evenly balance each other, which by the way is not the case. Now here are eight events, any one of which may occur in three throws—

1. No head may be thrown.
2. The 1st throw only may be a head.
3. The 2d ———————
4. The 3d ———————
5. The 1st and 2d ———————
6. The 1st and 3d ———————
7. The 2d and 3d ———————
8. All three may be heads.

Out of the eight, the first alone is adverse; in all

the rest a head *is* thrown at or before the third trial; and according to the axiom, the favourable chances are seven (events) to one (event); or $\frac{7}{8}$ of the cases make for us.

That this result is fairly calculated may be gath ered from another mode of proof. Suppose that eight distinct trials are made, to see at what throw the first head comes; we may calculate that in seven out of the eight trials it is likely to occur at or before the third. As heads are as likely to be thrown as tails, we expect that in half, that is, four cases, heads will make their appearance the first time. The same principle applies to the other four cases, in which we must go on to a second throw; in half of the second throws, that is, two, we expect heads. There remain only two cases in which it will be necessary to proceed to a third trial, to get the head; and half of them, or one, will be heads. Thus—

In 4 cases, a head first throw.
In 2 ——, —— second ——.
In 1 ——, —— third ——.
—
7

leaving only one of the eight trials in which it will be necessary to go further. Here again we have seven favourable events to one unfavourable; in common language the odds are seven to one.

There is no difficulty in stating the result thus attained, in a syllogism.

$\frac{7}{8}$ of the groups of three throws give a head,
This trial is to be a group of three throws;
Therefore this trial ($\frac{7}{8}$) will give a head.

The fraction written after the subject of the conclusion is to be read "It is 7 chances out of 8;" or, taking the numerator for the chances on the one side, and the difference between it and the denominator for those on the other, "The chances are 7 to 1."

The origin of the axiom is involved in the same difficulty as attends the axioms of geometry. How do we come to expect that in the long run head and tail will nearly divide the throws between them? Why do we not look for a long unbroken series of one or the other? Experience, no doubt, first suggested this absolute indifference of nature to two events, neither of them having any known cause that should give it a preponderance. But it may still be questioned whether the intricate calculations founded on this axiom are mere generalizations of experience, and whether our faith in the necessary truth of the axiom be not more than the sum of our experiments. Certain it is that experience confirms it. In experiments made by Buffon, by Professor de Morgan, and M. Quetelet, the results coincided very closely with the *à priori* calculation. But to verify the doctrine of chances by experiment, a wide range of facts is required, because a series of a few cases often exhibits great aberrations from a rule that never fails to vindicate itself in a longer course on trials. An Insurance Office, with five or ten clients only, might be ruined in a year by two deaths. In some of the experiments alluded to above, a head was not thrown till the 10th, the 14th, and the 16th throws. It is not unusual to find a family with six or eight sons and no daughters; and yet the whole number of male is very nearly equal to that of female births throughout the world.

2. Where the probability is a compound one, that is, where one uncertain event depends upon another, the rule is that *the whole probability is ascertained by multiplying the chances of the separate events together.* Imagine a gold, a silver, and a leaden urn, the first containing four white and two black balls, the second and third six white balls each; and suppose that a man is to draw one ball blindfold from one of the three urns, he knows not which,—what are the chances of his fixing on a black ball? The black ball can only be drawn from the golden urn; and the chance that he goes there at all is $\frac{1}{3}$: if he finds that urn, the black balls in it are $\frac{2}{6}$ of the whole; then the chances of his drawing a black ball are $\frac{1}{3} \times \frac{2}{6} = \frac{2}{18} = \frac{1}{9}$. By way of proof that the sum total of the chances is not altered by their having been distributed over two events, it is to be noticed that if all the 18 balls were in one urn, the chances would be exactly the same. The syllogism would be—

My drawing from the golden urn is $\frac{1}{3}$ of the possible cases,

My drawing a black ball is $\frac{2}{6}$ of the possible drawings from that urn;

Therefore my drawing a black ball is $\frac{1}{9}$ of the possible cases. Or—

B is $\frac{1}{3}$ A,
C is $\frac{2}{6}$ B;
$\therefore$ C is $\frac{1}{9}$ A.

In other words, there are 16 to 2, or 8 to 1, against my drawing a black ball.

3. To find the chance of the recurrence of an event already observed, *divide the number of times the event has been observed, increased by one, by the same number increased by two.* If an inlander coming to the sea, observed the phenomenon of the tide ten times in succession, the chance to him that at the next period the tide would again rise would be $\frac{10+1}{10+2}=\frac{11}{12}$; or 11 to 1. Every certainty is represented by a unit, as has been shown; and so many units are added to the possible cases (denominator of the fraction) as there have been events, and so many to the favourable cases (numerator) as there have been favourable events. "Or, if we represent," says M. Quetelet, "the number of times that the event has occurred by a similar number of white balls that we throw into an urn, adding also one other white ball and one black ball, the probability of the reproduction will be equal to that of drawing a white ball."

4. In order to calculate the probability that an event already observed will be repeated any given number of times, the rule is, to *divide the number of times the event has been observed, increased by one, by the same number increased by one and the number of times the event is to recur.* Thus, if the tide had been observed 9 times, the chance that it would recur ten times more would be $\frac{9+1}{9+10+1}=\left(\frac{10}{20}\right)=\frac{1}{2}$. "This is the same thing as if each reproduction of the observed event corresponded to putting a white ball in an urn where there were already, before commencing the trials, a white ball and as many black balls as it is supposed that the event observed should re-occur times."

5. The probability that there exists a cause of the reproduction of any event observed several times in succession is expressed by *a fraction which has for its denominator the number 2 multiplied by itself as many times as the event has been observed, and for its numerator the same product minus one.* This has been called Bayes's rule, and its validity is not so generally admitted as that of the preceding ones. Thus, supposing the two tides only had been observed, the chance of a cause would be

$$\frac{2\times2\times2-1}{2\times2\times2}=\frac{7}{8}.$$

Where the observations have not all been favourable, in order to estimate whether the event will occur once more, the rule is to divide the number of times the event has been *observed to happen increased by one, by the total number of observations increased by two.* Thus, if out of 26 metals known to the chemist, 24 are heavier than water and 2 lighter, the chance that the next discovered, assuming as certain the fact of discovery, will be lighter than water will be $\frac{2+1}{26+2}=\frac{3}{28}$; or 25 to 3.

Other examples of these formulæ may readily be found, to make the use of them easy, and to verify their truth. In applying the doctrine of chances to that subject in connection with which it was invented, —games of chance—the principles of what has been happily termed "moral arithmetic" must not be forgotten. Not only would it be difficult for a gamester to find an antagonist on terms, as to fortune and needs, precisely equal, but also it is impossible that with such an equality the advantage of a considerable gain should balance the harm of a serious loss. "If two men," says Buffon, "were to determine to play for their whole property, what would be the effect of this agreement? The one would only double his fortune, and the other reduce his to naught. What proportion is there between the loss and the gain? The same that there is between all and nothing. The gain of the one is but a moderate sum,—the loss of the other is numerically infinite, and morally so great that the labour of his whole life may not perhaps suffice to restore his property."

The theory of chances assists materially in giving a clear conception of modality (p. 278). A proposition may pass from absolute uncertainty where there is as much against as for its truth ($= \frac{1}{2}$) up to absolute certainty ($= 1$) through an infinite number of deepening shades of probability ($\frac{3}{5}$, $\frac{4}{5}$, $\frac{99}{100}$, and so on). These refinements in estimating evidence are little used in ordinary thinking, it is true; and broader lines of distinction suffice. But they seem to justify those who exclude modality from the *form* of judgments, since otherwise one judgment would seem to be capable of being modified into a hundred, the expression remaining the same, and the evidence only varying.

Hume in his "Essay of Miracles" has overlooked one property of highly probable judgments—that the favourable evidence for them not only preponderates over, but utterly expels, the unfavourable, and especially in matters where the moral nature is concerned. The probable evidence that the sun will rise daily for the next ten years is exceedingly strong: and consequently, from "the days of Noah" to the present, people have acted as if the weaker probability had no existence. If a jury find a man guilty, because ten credible witnesses have sworn against him, and one or two for him, they consider that the testimony of the ten annihilates that of the two; were it otherwise, they must give the prisoner the benefit of their doubt. A son does not estimate the balance in favour of the truth of a father's statement, nor a friend of a friend's: because to doubt at all is not to believe. When he asserts that in the case of miracles, "there is a mutual destruction of arguments [for and against them], and the superior only gives us an assurance suitable to that degree of force which remains after deducting the inferior," he neglects the distinction between mathematical and moral subjects; in the one, both favourable and adverse chances must be preserved; in the other, that is, where we have to *act* on probabilities, adverse arguments must, when once we have made up our minds, be ignored entirely, because to permit them the smallest influence would weaken and fetter our actions. The rest of his argument has been fully refuted. Writers on probabilities have shown how rapidly the scale of belief ascends with the addition of each new independent witness; and Paley has exposed the fallacy of reasoning from what is contrary to one's own experience to what contradicts the universal experience of men.

The numerical mode of statement illustrates the operation of the will in moral actions. The action entirely indeterminate, in which there is an exact equilibrium between the motives for and those against a particular course, is represented by (say) $\frac{50}{100} = \frac{1}{2}$; though some maintain that except in the case of the ass of Buridanus, whose "two bundles of hay" are no longer worthy of the dignity of philosophy, so nice a balance cannot occur. The necessary action, where all the motives are on one side, is represented by $\frac{100}{100} = 1$. Between these extremes a vast number of degrees must exist; and though human justice draws a broad line where criminal responsibility begins, its decisions must needs be rough and inaccurate.

The application of the doctrine of chances to real cases must be made with great caution. Our illustrations have been drawn for the most part from artificial cases, where causes have been studiously excluded that might have disturbed and complicated the results: in nature these are hard to find.

§ 123. *Syllogisms of Classification.*

Classification, which enters into all sciences, is the basis of some of them, as Botany, Mineralogy, and Zoology. In every act of classification two steps must be taken; certain marks are to be selected, the possession of which is to be the title to admission into the class, and then all the objects that possess them are to be ascertained. Where the marks selected are really important, and connected closely with the nature and functions of the thing, the classification is said to be natural; where they are such as do not affect the nature of the objects materially, and belong in common to things the most different in their main properties, it is artificial.

A class cannot always be defined in words, so as to describe *every* species in it. From the lowest of ts subdivisions to the highest, we pass through so many shades of difference, that we had a difficulty in perceiving and expressing the likeness between the extremes; and properties which were prominent at the bottom of the scale, are in the higher steps forgotten, as nobler ones come into view. To distinguish the polyp, the lowest species in the animal series, from a plant, it must be defined as "having a digestive cavity;" whereas the definition usually given for higher animals, and for the conception animal in general, conveys that they are "beings endowed with life and sensation." Still we group them together by our perception of likeness; which though not so obviously applicable to the ends of the series viewed together, and apart from the intermediate links, become so when we pass regularly along the chain. We might not be able to prove that the polyp had sensation at all, if there were not creatures a little higher in the scale of being, resembling the polyp in other particulars, and exhibiting more plainly the sense of feeling. We presume that it exists in the lower, because we see it in the higher, and though it decreases as we descend, we cannot show that it has ceased. The definition of a genus is the adequate definition of its lowest species only, since one which included any higher properties than the lowest exhibits, would of course exclude it. But in classification, the definition is not so much used as the *type*, by likeness or unlikeness to which we arrange the others, and assign them a higher or lower degree.

Though the species in any great class rise by the steps of a regular arrangement, the same series must not be continued from the highest of one kingdom to the lowest of the next above it. The highest plant is often considered next below the lowest animal, whereas it is much more like, though infinitely inferior to, the highest animal. The animal, vegetable, and mineral kingdoms rather resemble ladders of equal height resting upon three different steps of a house, than ladders raised one upon the other. The lowest animal, the lowest plant, and the lowest mineral answer to each other; and the complex animal organism, the tall and beautiful tree, and the regular group of crystals correspond in some measure at the top of the respective scales.

A syllogism like the following is adapted to express classification.

(U A A. Fig. i.)

All beings endowed with life and sensation = animals,
The polyp . . . . the man have life and sensation;
Therefore they are animals.

§ 124. *Nomenclature.*

The fourth question to be answered was—How shall new laws be expressed and recorded? It has been shown already (p. 44) that names are useful in preserving the results of new discoveries and reasonings, and that without such means science could never secure its gains, nor reproduce them with the necessary celerity. Let any one consider how much is meant by *chemical affinity*, *atomic weight*, *capital*, *inverse proportion*, *polarity*, *means*, *and limits*; how theories are here gathered up into a single word, and passed readily from mind to mind; and he will admit the parallel between words and that paper money by which the ponderous wealth of the world may be enclosed in envelops, and passed swiftly from hence to the antipodes. Hence every progressive science must constantly enlarge its store of names and words. Four ways are open to it of doing so.*

1. Names already in use may be adapted to new meanings, by fresh definitions. Thus *salt* has been extended, from the condiment still known by that name, to a great class of compound bodies known to the chemist. *Force*, *attraction*, *affinity* afford other examples.

2. Names that contain their own explanation may be formed, to represent new ideas; as *isomorphism* for the identity of the crystalline forms of some chemical bodies; προαίρεσις, to express the *previous choice* or purpose which makes our actions morally imputable to us; *homœopathy* for the system of medicine that professes to cure by medicines that produce *effects like* the disease. Names so constructed will often embody a theory, and should be discarded if it turns out to be untrue.

3. The invention of a wholly new name, unmeaning in itself, but accompanied by a precise definition, is free from some of the dangers that beset the other modes; for old words are often used vaguely, because they have obtained a footing before their scientific meaning has been given them, and new names that convey their own explanation are often cumbrous,

* For fuller illustrations, see *Whewell's* Philosophy of the Inductive Sciences.

and in some cases do not permit the erroneous theory they carry on their face, to be amended. An attempt of this kind has been made by Von Reichenbach, in designating a new force he believes that he has discovered by the name *Od*-force. Such a name, whatever be thought of the theory it belongs to, seems well devised; it is short and easy of use, and it enters readily into compounds, as Odyle, Thermodyle, and so on.

4. Chemistry affords good examples of the mode of forming new names by systematic alterations of old well known ones. Thus from *sulphur* we have *sulphide*, *sulphite*, *sulphate*, *bisulphate*, &c. and each of these is appropriated to a particular chemical constitution. Such a plan seems to obviate the objections on the score of novelty, vagueness, and transitoriness, to which other methods are open.

§ 125. *Sources of Principles.*

The inductive and deductive processes presuppose some principles from which they may commence. A principle might be defined as that from which reasoning begins.

Observation, either by means of the senses unaided, or by the assistance of instruments, furnishes the principles of inductive reasoning. Where isolated observations are of less value, from their fluctuations, as in estimating the temperature of the country, the weight of the atmosphere, and the like, *the doctrine of means* is applied to an extended series of observations. By it, the sum of the results of the observations is divided by the numbers of observations taken, and the quotient is *the mean.* Although this may happen not to correspond exactly with a single observation, yet in a large number of them it is found that the majority range themselves closely round the mean, and that the number diminishes with surprising regularity as we approach either extreme. Thus, if the mean temperature on a given day in the year be 60° Fahrenheit, as ascertained from the observation of a hundred years, and 50° and 70° be the extremes on either side, we shall find on arranging the single observations that most of them cluster as it were around 60°, whilst one or two only coincide with each extreme; and that as the mean is approached, say by intervals of two degrees, the number of coincident observations grows greater at each step till the mean is reached. A full explanation, intelligible to all, of this most interesting subject, is given in Quetelet's work "On Probabilities." Where a mean is taken, without any need for arranging the several observations according to their approach to it, it has been called *an average;* the results of the harvest, and the prices of corn, are estimated in this way every year, the former roughly, the latter with arithmetical accuracy.

Historical records are observations which rest upon the testimony of others; of these the most important are the records of religious history, which rest upon outward testimony accepted and confirmed by the inward religious consciousness.

Deductive principles are certain universal propositions gained in various ways. *Theological principles* are the truths of the divine law, made known to man by inspiration; universal, but not generalized from experience by observation. *Natural principles* are propositions in morals, government, and the like, upon which there is a general agreement founded upon a natural instinct. *Mathematical principles* are propositions about space and number, to which the reason cannot but assent, without requiring to verify them by new trials; such are the *definitions* and *axioms* of geometry. *Positive principles* have been gained by reasoning upon former experience; they are either *the definitions* of the mixed sciences, or *divisions* of their subject matter, or *hypotheses* laid down to be verified by future comparison with facts.

TABLE OF PRINCIPLES.

N.B. This is not a perfect logical division; *ex. gr.* "Observations" may depend on testimony and so be "historical."

- Principles
  - Inductive
    - Simple Observations
      - Without instruments
      - With instruments.
    - Aggregate Observations
      - Scale of means and limits.
      - Simple averages.
    - Historical Records.
  - Deductive
    - Theological
    - Mathematical
    - Natural
    - Positive
      - Definitions
      - Divisions
      - Hypotheses.

§ 126. *Errors and Fallacies.*

Not one logical principle can be put in practice without the possibility of error. Where an error is latent, and tends to deceive either the thinker or those to whom he offers it, the name of *fallacy* is given to it. A complete list of fallacies would include one or more for every one of the processes of thinking; and, after all, the exposure of material errors can only be effected with advantage by each separate science for its own department, as has been done for Political Economy in the "*Sophismes Economiques*" of M. Bastiat. Formal errors are only deviations from the laws of thought already laid down, as, for example, by making an incomplete division, or by holding contradictory judgments together, or by drawing a conclusion too broad for the premisses.

§ 127. *Dealing with Errors.*

When opposing arguments are to be dealt with, we may either assail one of the premisses by an *Instance* (ἔνστασις) to the contrary of what it asserts; or we may *dissolve* (λύειν) the argument by showing its unfitness for proof because of some formal defect, as where a universal is proved from a few particulars. Or, admitting the apparent correctness of the opposing argument, we may prove the contradictory of its conclusion by an unassailable argument of our own, which is then called an *Elenchus* (ἔλεγχος). Or lastly, we may fortify our own argument by "a reduction to impossibility," that is, by showing that something impossible or absurd follows from contradicting our conclusion; this is called *indirect* demonstration, as it goes round to prove that a thing is by showing what absurdity would follow if it was not, and thus differs from the direct mode, which proves directly from premisses that the thing is.*

B. Arrangement of a Science.

§ 128. *Method. Definition and Division.*

As method in the highest sense is a natural gift rather than a technical system, it can be best understood by studying a few examples, which have proceeded from minds of the highest order. It will be found that whilst the deductive and the inductive orders have been followed, with the aid of definition and division, none of these means has been exclusively employed; and the due admixture of them, and the degree of preponderance to be assigned to any one, have been regulated by the imagination and taste of the constructor. In "Euclid's Elements," the nature of the subject, which is independent of verification from facts, permits an almost exclusively deductive order to prevail, which proceeds from definitions and axioms, and dispenses with division. In "Plato's Republic," one of the noblest examples of method, successive definitions of justice are brought to the test and rejected; and then division preponderates, in the enumeration of the powers of the human soul, and of the classes in a state that answers to them; as well as of the declina-

* Instance, Pri. An. II. 26; Solution of an Argument, Rhet. I. 2, Pri. An. II. 27; Elenchus, Pri. An. II. 20; Reduction to Impossibility, Pri. An. I. 23, Post. An. I 26.

tions through which the perfect polity, if it could be constructed, would have to pass. The whole is fused together and adorned by a dramatic element, in such a manner as to render this dialogue the finest work of pagan philosophy. In the "Nicomachean Ethics" of Aristotle, definition predominates but with considerable aid from division. Thus he enumerates the opinions of men about "the good," and rejects all but the right one; defining that, under the name of "happiness," he is led on to define the parts of his first definition; and in the case of the moral and intellectual virtues he does not consider his explanation complete without an enumeration (or division) of both classes. In subordinate portions, good examples of division are also found; and in the concluding chapters of Book VI., and in other places, discussions upon nominal definitions, or the senses which various Greek nouns bear, are also introduced. The text-books of chemistry, mineralogy, botany, and zoology, will afford good examples of division, based upon definition; a class or type is defined, and the species enumerated and examined.

The close relationship between definition and division will be evident to the student who examines such examples carefully. In truth, wherever a division is made upon some natural, and not merely accidental ground, every step of it furnishes some distinctive mark, which will naturally make its appearance in a definition afterwards. Again, as every definition properly so called, sets forth distinctive marks of the conception defined, it gives at the same time the means of dividing or separating it from other classes. In order to secure this mutual coöperation, Aristotle lays down, that in dividing in order to define, a real genus should be taken, to which the differences should be added in regular order; that every dividing species should be enumerated; and that each new difference should be founded upon, and divide, the foregoing one (διαφοραὶ διαφορῶν)—thus, it would be better, after dividing bodies into living and not living (p. 105), to subdivide living bodies into those which have sentient life, and those without it, rather than into terrestrial and aquatic, which would have nothing to do with the former difference.*

§ 129. *Subordinate Parts of a Science.*

Judgments that relate to speculation only, are called theoretical; those which refer to practice are practical. Judgments that require or admit of proof, are called demonstrable; those which are manifest from the very terms, are indemonstrable. Thus much being premised we can define certain subordinate parts of a science.

An Axiom is an indemonstrable theoretical judgment. A Postulate is an indemonstrable practical judgment. A Theorem is a demonstrable theoretical judgment. A Problem is a demonstrable practical judgment. A Thesis is a judgment proposed for discussion and proof (but with Aristotle it sometimes means an axiom of some special science or disputation). An Hypothesis is a judgment provisionally accepted as an explanation of some group of facts, and is liable to be discarded if it is found

* See An. Post. II. xiii. 7 (97, a.); Met. VII. 12, (1038. a)

inconsistent with them. A judgment which follows immediately from another, is sometimes called a Corollary or Consectary. One which does not properly belong to the science in which it appears, but is taken from another, is called a Lemma. One which illustrates the science where it appears, but is not an integral part of it, is a Scholion.

§ 130. *Categories.*

Whilst pure Logic neglects the *real* nature of the things it deals with, and attaches to them only a *formal* value, logicians in almost every age have endeavoured to form schemes of classification in which things should be arranged according to their real nature. Logic deals, as we have seen, with second intentions, but it has been found desirable to make classes for first intentions also. To these classes the name of Categories, or as we might render it Attributions, has been given; for whilst they are classes of things and not of propositions, so that they do not properly attribute any quality to a subject, they are constructed with a view to the more ready discovery of attributes when required. They are intended, like the labelled drawers in a cabinet, to be a well-arranged repository of the treasures of thought and knowledge, in which they may be kept secure and ready for use. Such a system of arrangement for things and the attributes of things is essentially metaphysical, and if admitted into Logic at all, must belong to the application of it, wherein we employ the pure forms of thought to discover the nature of things.

We require of a good system of Categories that it provide a place for every simple notion, and that its heads or divisions be specific enough to furnish real help in finding the attributes of any subject; in two words, that it be exhaustive and suggestive. Tried by this test, such divisions as that into Substance, Mode, and Relation, will be rejected as comparatively useless; if complete and exhaustive, they are too vague to offer any tangible suggestions. Even the more elaborate division of Aristotle is open to this charge; not to dwell upon the accusations sometimes made, that it is confused and incomplete. He divides words and notions into ten classes, viz: Substance, Quantity, Quality, Relation, Place, Time, Position, Mode of Being, Doing, and Suffering. Trendelenburg finds an exact correspondence between these and the grammatical division of the parts of speech, the first four corresponding to Substantives and Adjectives, the next two to Adverbs, and the last four to the active, passive, and neuter Verbs; but perhaps he pushes a good suggestion, that Aristotle sought in language the groundwork of his arrangement, somewhat too far. Another important suggestion would reduce the number of the principal Categories to four, Substance, Quantity, Quality, and Relation; of the last of which the remaining six are only subdivisions, for Place and Time are the relation of things to each other in space and time, and the remaining four imply connection with other things.*

* See *Stallbaum, Parmenides,* Prol. p. 170. For the history of Categories see Professor *Trendelenburg's* Geschichte der Kategorien.

Another division of Categories may be just attempted.

TABLE OF THE CATEGORIES.

- Conceivable Things are
  - SUBSTANCE
  - Attribute
    - QUANTITY
    - QUALITY
    - Relation
      - of TIME
      - of SPACE
      - of CAUSATION
      - of COMPOSITION
      - of AGREEMENT and REPUGNANCE
      - of POLAR OPPOSITION
      - of FINITE TO INFINITE.

§ 131. *Division of the Sciences.*

No subject has attracted more discussion, than that of the right classification of the Sciences; on no subject has discussion produced less agreement. Some have proposed to classify according to the purpose to which sciences are to be applied; others according to the faculties through which the knowledge is derived to us. The former would divide sciences into theoretical and practical, according as speculation or useful application is to be the result

lehre, and for the Hindu System of Kanâda, see the Appendix to the present work.

of each ; but this barren division ends here, as it can only be carried further by importing some new principle to assist. The latter would be grounded on such distinctions as whether a science were rational or experimental, and the like. But it is not true that each science has a separate set of faculties set apart to its use; and in the more complicated sciences, the whole mind, with all its powers, finds a sufficient employment.

The most natural ground of classification is that according to the subject-matter of the sciences. Every science is separated from the rest, in virtue of its having for its subject some one set of facts and laws, bound together by one conception of which it can give an account. Astronomy is the science which takes account of the heavenly bodies. Physiology, that which has for its study the phenomena of life. Descartes was probably the first who insisted that sound knowledge should advance from the simpler to the more complex phenomena; and in this remark lay the germ of a sound arrangement of the sciences, which scarcely however seems to have begun to bear fruit before the time of Ampère and Comte. The writer last named, whatever may be thought of the general tenor of his principal work, or of his later aberrations, has thrown much light upon the present subject.

On the principle which Descartes laid down, the following would be the order of the principal sciences; and it is accepted substantially by the principal writers who have attended to this mode of arrangement, such as Comte, Isidore Saint-Hilaire, and Cournot. Mathematics, or the science of quantities, is at once the most simple in its elements and the most general in its application, entering more or less into all the sciences of nature, and constituting almost the whole of that which comes next it in the order of dependence. Astronomy, or the science of the heavenly bodies, is the application of mathematical truths to the laws of matter and motion; matter and the motions of material bodies being the new conception which belong to this science. Physics, being the science, or rather group of sciences, which is conversant with the general laws of the world, so far as they relate to beings without life or organization, would come next; and it imports, in addition to the conceptions of Astronomy, those of light, of heat, of sound, of electricity, of magnetism, and many others. Chemistry would rank next, which is the science of the decomposition and combinations of the various substances that compose and surround the earth. Next in order of complexity would rank Physiology, founded on the additional conception of vegetable and animal life. To this would succeed Anthropology, or the science of man's nature; and to this Social Science, which ascertains the laws that govern men when combined in cities and nations. Each of these departments may be divided into many branches; as Physics into Acoustics, Optics, Electricity, and the like; or Social Science into Morals, Politics, Political Economy, Law, and the like.

On comparing scientific works, differences in the mode of teaching the same subject become apparent. In one the pure theory of Astronomy is presented; in another the striking features of its historical progress as a science, with speculations on the historical sequence of the phenomena themselves; in a third the practical applications of which the science admits in respect to the comfort and progress of mankind. This threefold mode of treatment runs through all the sciences; and in a table of them might well be expressed. The classification would thus embody all that is valuable of another system of classes, that according to the purpose towards which the science was directed.

A classification which advances on Descartes' principle, from the more simple to the more complex subjects, which commences from the notions of extension and quantity, and proceeds through material things, up to living, intelligent, and moral agents, ought to coincide with the order in which the sciences themselves have reached maturity. And this it certainly does. Mathematics had made good its ground when aetronomy was yet in its infancy; physics began to obtain a sure footing later than either; whilst the sciences which relate to life are still very immature; and some of the main problems of social science are yet matter of controversy even in our own days.

There is besides a general correspondence between this classification and the order in which the various objects of science came into being. The heavenly bodies were first appointed their paths in the celestial spaces; then the surface of our earth was prepared for living creatures; then they were created after their kind, and man the last. The social life of man grew up last of all, when his race was multiplied on the globe; and ever as new elements appear, the conditions of society are being modified even to the present time.

So far, all the sciences enumerated have been such as have the visible universe for their subject. But the thought of man is not circumscribed by the limits even of the universe; nay, according to the celebrated argument of Descartes, it cannot help advancing from the futile and imperfect to the idea of the infinite and complete Being. The relations of the world and of man to this Being is the subject of another science, which we may call Religious Philosophy. That our knowledge of this is less precise, and more open to dispute on the part of others, arises from the nature of the object and the kind of evidence we have of it. The knowledge of God begins in an inward need of his aid, and according as that is stronger or weaker, will be the disposition to discern Him as the Author of the universe, and to consider the facts of nature as so many manifestations of Him. The evidence we have in the other sciences is direct and primary; for it is derived from the direct contemplation by the senses of facts offered to them. But the evidence on which religious philosophy must proceed is indirect and secondary: for it turns on the conviction which arises in us from the contemplation of our own mind and the universe around us, that there must exist something which is neither our mind nor the universe, but the external ground and source of both. For this reason Religious Philosophy must take its place, not as one step in the series of the sciences, but rather as something parallel to, yet distinct from, the whole of them.

We are now in a position to sketch the table of the Sciences.*

CLASSIFICATION OF THE SCIENCES.

Group.	*Mode of Treatment.*		
I. MATHEMATICS	Theoretical.	Historical.	Applied
II. ASTRONOMY	Theoretical.	Historical.	Applied
III. PHYSICS	Theoretical.	Historical.	Applied.
IV. CHEMISTRY	Theoretical.	Historical.	Applied.
V. PHYSIOLOGY	Theoretical.	Historical.	Applied.
VI. ANTHROPOLOGY	Theoretical.	Historical.	Applied.
VII. SOCIAL SCIENCE	Theoretical.	Historical.	Applied.

RELIGIOUS PHILOSOPHY.

§ 132. *Conclusion.*

These hints may be sufficient to guide a student in applying the principles of Pure Logic to the practice of analysis.†

If this little work is hastily examined and cast aside, of course the reader will not have become a logician; he will have learnt the unimportant fact

* The number of writers on the Classification of the Sciences is very great. In drawing up the present section, I have derived assistance from the works of *Comte, Ampère,* and *Isidore Saint-Hilaire.* The plan of *M. Cournot* I only know through the last-named writer; the threefold mode of treatment belongs to his arrangement. Besides these have been consulted Dr. *Whewell's* works, *Weise's Architectonick,* and a Tract on the subject by Mr. *George Ramsay.*

† They are not intended to supersede a reference to such works as Whewell's Inductive Sciences, Herschel's Preliminary Discourse, and Mill's Logic; to induce the reader to carry his researches on to these and similar productions is their chief object. These writers have allotted a larger space for the most part to the special sciences and their history than was compatible with the present attempt, even if sufficient learning and ability had been at command.

that upon this or that disputed doctrine the author held this or that opinion, and his knowledge will go no further. Instead of learning Logic, he will know an insignificant fact in logical history. The mistake is not uncommon;—we inquire what Aristotle and Bishop Butler said on morality, and think that we have studied Moral Philosophy; we read the Organon, and call ourselves logicians. History presides over these and other facts; we are in *her* domain when we use our books in this narrow spirit. Philosophy does not exist until the mind of the student begins to work for itself with the principles it receives historically; to decompose and to compose anew, to criticize the arguments employed, to essay at least to push the confines of truth farther into the wilds and error of ignorance, and to leave her a wider territory.

If Grammar is learnt by speaking and writing, if a man cannot become an orator without repeated efforts to speak in public, nor a poet without practising the mechanism of verse till he can use it with ease, it seems absurd to expect that a course of lectures heard, with a string of definitions learnt, will make a logician.

Let those who wish to possess the intellect they have received from above, in the depth and clear ness, the sober composure, the calm activity which a high degree of culture can alone bestow, venture to study Logic in a larger spirit than the merely historical. Let them become dialecticians; not in the sense which the sophist attached to that name, but rather in that which the scourge of sophists gave it. Let them not use so excellent a weapon as the reason in mere play, with a guarded point and bated edge, but let them keep it sheathed, sharpened, and shining, till a battle has to be fought against an error. Let them watch for themselves the processes gone through in completing any science. If the rules given in books are erroneous, let them try to correct; if imperfect, to complete them: or if experience verifies their truth and utility, let them be regarded with a degree of trust greater than could have been awarded to them before, when they stood in books, the mere historical record of other men's philosophy. No one who has studied Logic in this conscientious spirit has ever found it trifling or useless.

APPENDIX.

ON INDIAN LOGIC.

ON INDIAN LOGIC.*

THE sciences of Logic and of Grammar were, as far as history allows us to judge, invented or originally conceived by two nations only, by Hindús and Greeks. All other nations, if they ever cultivated these sciences, received the first impulse from without. The Romans from the Greeks, the Germans from the Romans, the Arabs from the Greeks, the Jews from the Arabs.

That the two most highly gifted nations of the world, the Hindús and the Greeks, should both have been led, each in its own way, to a study of the laws of thought and the laws of language, seems in itself perfectly natural.

At the time, however, when the different systems of Hindú philosophy became first known to the scholars of Europe, at the beginning of this century, every thing that came from the East was looked upon as of extreme antiquity. There had been vague traditions of Indian philosophy long before the time of Aristotle. There were reports of early Greek sages travelling to India as the fountain-head of ancient wisdom. Alexander himself had found himself in India face to face with a whole nation of philosophers. It was readily admitted, therefore, that the Hindú system of Logic was more ancient than that of Aristotle, and that the Greeks borrowed the first elements of their philosophy from the Hindús. Alexander, who had been himself in conversation with the Logicians of India, might have sent some of their treatises to his tutor at home, and Aristotle would have worked them up into a system of his own. This view was actually taken and defended by men like Görres.† They were struck

* Communicated by Professor Max Müller.

† Görres undertook to prove that the Greeks had borrowed some technical terms from the Sanskrit. Indian philosophers admit five elements, and the fifth is called *akâs*, ether. This ether has quite a different meaning from the *αἰθήρ* which some Greek philosophers considered as the fifth or highest element. Görres, however, quotes (without giving a reference) a

by many points of coincidence in both systems of Logic. In each there were Categories, Genus, and Species, and even Syllogisms! It could not be otherwise—the Greeks must have borrowed it from the Hindús. That two nations, if they once conceived the idea of analyzing the laws of thought, could possibly arrive at similar results even on the most general points, and that it would require coincidences in many minute details or in palpable errors, to prove beyond doubt that the two systems had a common origin, seems never to have occurred to these enthusiastic Orientalists.

But on the other hand, does it show a higher power of logical reasoning or historical criticism, if we find men like Niebuhr taking the opposite view of the matter, and deriving Indian philosophy from Greece? Niebuhr is reported to have said in his Lectures on Ancient History, "If we look at Indian Philosophy, we discern traces of a great similarity with that of the Greeks. Now as people have given up the hypothesis, that Greek philosophy formed itself after Indian philosophy, we cannot explain this similarity except by the intercourse which the Indians had with the Græco-macedonic kings of Bactra."

To Niebuhr and to most Greek scholars it would naturally be next to impossible to believe that Greek Logic and Greek philosophy in general were of foreign origin and a mere importation from India. They know how Greek philosophy grew up gradually, how its course runs parallel with the progress of Grecian poetry, art, and civilization. They know that it is a home-grown production as certainly as that Plato and Aristotle were Greeks and not Brahmans.

But, then, a Sanskrit scholar has just the same conviction with regard to Indian philosophy. He can show how the first philosophical ideas, though under a vague form, existed already in the mind of the early poets of the Veda. He can trace their gradual development in the Brâhma*n*as and Upanishads. He can show how they gave rise to discussions, how they took a more distinct form, and were at last fixed and determined in the most scientific manner. He too is as certain that Indian philosophy was a native production of India, as that Gotama and Ka*n*âda were Hindús and not Greeks.

Until, therefore, it can be proved *historically* that Greeks received their philosophy from India or Indians from Greece—or until coincidences can be pointed out which it is impossible to explain otherwise, it will be best to consider both Greek and Indian philosophy as au-

passage from Aristotle, where this fifth element is mentioned under the name of *ἀκοτ-ονοματον*, and this he translates by "akâs-nominatum,"—*ἀκοτ-ονοματον* being evidently an ingenious conjecture for *ἀκατονόμαστον*.

tochthonic, and to derive from their mutual similarities only this consolatory conviction that in philosophy also there is a certain amount of truth which forms the common heirloom of all mankind, and may be discovered by all nations if they search for it with honesty and perseverance.

According to the accounts which the Brahmans themselves give of the history of Indian philosophy, there have been, and there still exist, six systems of philosophy. They are called the Sânkhya, Mîmânsâ, Nyâya, Yoga, Vaiseshika, and Vedânta. These systems are not represented to us in a successive order, they do not apparently arise one upon the ruins of the other, like the schools in the history of Greek and German philosophy. They always seem to run parallel, each maintaining its place side by side with the others, and each representing a distinct view of the Universe, and of the relation of the seeming to the real world. Even at the present day the Brahman unites three or more of them in his course of study.

Each of these systems is complete in itself. Each contains something of what we should call Physics, Metaphysics, Logic, and even Ethics. In one system, however, certain topics occupy a more prominent place and are discussed at greater length. Thus, while the Mîmânsâ is more theological, and the Sânkhya more metaphysical, the Nyâya system, in which the reasoning faculties of man are more closely examined, has become known to us by the name of "Indian Logic." In India also, a Naiyâyika, or follower of the Nyâya, means as much as a Logician, or a man who understands the laws of reasoning, and still more the art of logical wrangling. The other systems refer to the Nyâya, whenever logical questions have to be settled.

Nevertheless, it would be wrong to call the Nyâya, Logic, in our sense of the word. The Nyâya, as well as the other systems, has for its highest object the solution of the problem of existence, and only as a means towards accomplishing this object, does it devote particular attention to the instruments of knowledge—and, as one of them, to syllogistic reasoning.

In order to explain what in the mind of a Hindú philosopher would correspond to our Logic, it will be necessary to give a short sketch of the Nyâya. We shall there see the exact place which Logic occupies in the system of Hindú philosophy, and be able to judge how far it corresponds to that which Aristotle and other philosophers after him have assigned to this philosophical discipline. The reason why the Nyâya is chosen in preference to other systems, is not because it alone contains an account of the syllogism. The syllogism finds its place in the Vedânta and Sânkhya as well; but it is more fully treated by the Naiyâyikas. Again, Kanâda's work, called the Vaiseshika philosophy, is chosen in preference to the Nyâya-sûtras of Gotama, because there is so much of minute technicality in the latter, that it would be very difficult to give a complete account of it in a short compass.

Kanâda starts boldly by declaring that he is going to explain how a man can obtain the most exalted and exalting knowledge of reality, and by means thereof arrive at a state of complete blessedness, the Summum Bonum. The way to blessedness, according to him, is knowledge, but knowledge of a particular kind, that is to say, a discriminating knowledge of the seven * Categories.

These Categories are, Substance, Quality, Action, Genus, Individuality, Concretion, and Non-existence.

The Sanskrit word which has been translated by category is "padârtha," which in common usage means a thing. The etymological signification, however, is "meaning of word," which, if interpreted philosophically, comes to express "the most general meaning of words," "what is common to all words," what is predicated by words without any regard to their special meaning, as given in the Dictionary. Like the Categories of the Greek system, the Padârthas are wide classes of "first intentions." They are the last and highest predicates, and the only thing that can be predicated of them according to Visvanâtha, is their "perceptibility."

But does this perceptibility involve their reality? We must hear the objections which the Hindú-Materialist raises against this supposition. Taking the first category, that of substance, he says, "All we really perceive, if we speak for instance of water, is water. We do not perceive any thing of water being a substance. Therefore you have no right to speak of substance as a category." But, answers the Vaiseshika, though we do not perceive substance with our eyes, yet we perceive that there must be something in which qualities can reside; something which remains unchanged though the qualities change;—which rests the same whether it becomes a cause or an effect. This then we call substance.

* Originally there were but six, Non-existence being omitted in Kanâda's Sutras. The statements given here are taken from Annambhatta's Tarkasangraha, published at Benares without the name of the editor. This publication, and many most valuable works lately issued from the Sanskrit College of Benares, are due to Dr. Ballantyne, the Principal of this College. A Hindostani translation, together with an English translation, was also published at Benares, from the hand of Mr. F. Edward Hall, though without his name

Quality, again, is what resides in a substance. Quality itself has no qualities, but substance has.

Quality produces by itself no change. What produces change, or combination and separation of qualities, is what we comprehend under the third Category, or Action, and this also resides in substance only.

These are the three principal categories, and they seem to correspond very nearly with Aristotle's *οὐσία*, *ποιόν* and *ποσόν*, and *ποιεῖν*. After these three, follow the two categories of Genus and Individuality.

Genus resides in Substance, Quality, and Action, and it is twofold, higher or lower. The *highest* genus, which is shared by every thing, is "being," the summum genus. Next to it we get as *lower* genus that of being a category, of being substance, earth, a clod, &c.

Individuality is endless. It resides in substance only, and as we shall see, in substance before it becomes material and perceptible by the senses, that is to say, in atomic substances. Individualities mutually exclude each other.

The next category stands as it were by itself, and forms the top of the pyramidal arrangement of the categories, which tapers from the fundamental three, to the qualifying two, and ends in that which we translate by "Concretion." It is peculiar to Indian philosophy and difficult to be rendered into the philosophical language of Europe. It expresses the intimate relation of things which cannot exist separately. A quality, for instance, cannot exist by itself, but only as the quality of a substance, nor can substance exist except with reference to qualities. Now, substance and quality are not considered as merely together, but as interwoven, as inseparable, and mutually dependent; and this relation is expressed by the category of Concretion. The same relation exists between the whole and its parts, between Genus and Species, between cause and effect.

The last category, which, as we saw, is omitted by some of the Vaiseshikas, is that of Non-existence. It is of four kinds, according as it applies to things: 1. Which are not yet, but may be afterwards; 2. Which are no more, but have been; 3. Which are not, and never will be; 4. Which are not what something else is, *i. e.* which differ.

Of these seven categories, which exhaust the universe of knowledge (omne scibile), Substance comprehends the five elements, earth, water, light, air, and ether; it comprehends time and space; soul and self.

The five elements may be either eternal, uncreated not percep tible by the senses, but established by inference; or created, perceptible and destructible. In the former state they exist as infinitely small, in the latter they are products. Considered as products again, the elementary substances are threefold: organic, organ, or inorganic. Earth, which is determined as that which has the quality of Odour, exists, as organic, in animal bodies. As organ it is the apprehender of odour. As inorganic it consists in stones. In this manner we get five organs: the organ of hearing corresponding to the substance of ether; that of feeling to the substance of air; that of seeing to light; that of tasting to water; that of smelling to earth. Ether has one quality, and the organ of hearing apprehends one quality, that of sound. Air has two qualities, and the organ of feeling apprehends two, those of sound and tangibility. Light has three qualities, and the organ of sight apprehends three, those of sound, tangibility, and colour. Water has four qualities, and the organ of taste apprehends four, those of sound, tangibility, colour and savour. Earth has five qualities, and the organ of smell apprehends five, those of sound, tangibility, colour, savour, and odour.

Here then we have something very like the doctrine of Empedocles,

Γαίῃ μὲν γὰρ γαῖαν ὀπώπαμεν, ὕδατι δ' ὕδωρ,
Αἰθέρι δ' αἰθέρα δῖον, ἀτὰρ πυρὶ πῦρ ἀΐδηλον,
Στοργὴν δὲ στοργῇ, νεῖκος δέ τε νείκεϊ λυγρῷ,

only carried out to too great an extent, and thereby caricatured. The only remark which it is necessary to make, is that "ether" is treated differently from the other elements. While the other four elements exist both in an atomic and in a terrestrial state, ether never leaves its transcendental reality, but is eternal, one, and infinitely great (all-pervading).

The next two substances, which, like ether, exist as eternal only, as one and all-pervading, are Time and Space. Time is the cause of what we call Past, Present, and Future. Space is the cause of what we call East, West, North, South, &c. Both time and space being eternal substances, and eternal only, it follows that they are never perceptible by the organs of the senses.

The eighth substance is Self. It is the substratum of the qualities of knowledge, wish and will. It is twofold, the living Self and the Supreme Self. The Supreme Self is the Lord, the Omniscient; He is One only, free from joy and sorrow. The living Self is attached to different bodies, but it is still eternal and all-pervading. Wherever the body is, there is the living Self; but the living Self itself remains uncreated and eternal. Its existence can be proved, but it cannot fall under the cognition of the senses.

The last substance is Soul, the cause of perception, of pleasure and pain, and the passions. As Self, though attached to bodies, is all-pervading and infinite, we should not be able to account for the fact of our successive or discursive knowledge. Self, like the Omniscient, would know every thing at once, unless there was the soul, through which all impressions must pass in succession and become individualized. Soul, too, is eternal only, but it is endless;—not infinitely great, but infinitely small, and attached, not to the Supreme, but to living Selves only.

It is not necessary to enter into a more detailed account of the substances, for it is clear that there is only one Substance which will fall under our more immediate consideration, the Substance of Self, and this only as the substratum of the quality of knowledge. It is where the quality of knowledge is examined, that we shall recognize what by European philosophers is treated as Logic.

Before we proceed, however, to that Chapter, we must at least cast a glance at the different headings of the two categories of quality and action.

Qualities are, 1. Colour; 2. Savour; 3. Odour; 4. Tangibility; 5. Number; 6. Dimension; 7. Distinction; 8. Conjunction; 9. Disjunction; 10. Priority; 11. Posteriority; 12. Weight; 13. Fluidity; 14. Viscidity; 15. Sound; 16. Perception; 17. Pleasure; 18. Pain; 19. Desire; 20. Aversion; 21. Effort; 22. Merit; 23. Demerit; 24. Faculty. They are eternal if residing in eternal substances, and non-eternal if residing in material bodies. Knowledge, Pleasure and Pain, Desire and Aversion, Effort, Merit and Demerit, are qualities of the Self only. Perception, Desire, and Effort are eternal as qualities of the Supreme Self, but non-eternal as qualities of living Selves.

Actions are, Lifting up, Throwing down, Contraction, Expansion, and Procession. They exist only in the four elements and in Soul.

The fourth Category, or Genus, is something which resides in substance, qualities, and actions, but is eternal, and as such not sensuously perceptible. It is one, but it always resides in many. It is that by which it becomes possible to comprehend several things into one class, and to predicate something of them, which they have in common. We call this an abstraction; but to the Hindú the Genus of things, or the General, is something real, inherent in substance, or quality, or action, though of course not material or perceptible by the senses. The Genus, therefore, or the cause of what we call general, is conceived as something independent of single objects, though it is known to us only as inherent in the objects of intuition. It is inherent in substances, qualities, and actions, and is perceived by us as we perceive either substances, actions, or qualities. What Ka*n*âda means by calling Genus inherent, is that substances, qualities, and actions cannot exist, not even in their eternal state, without the Genus. The same applies to Individualities, only that they do not inhere in qualities and actions, but in substances only. Individuality is what makes a thing to be itself, and not any thing else. And if we hear Ka*n*âda expressing his opinion, that "individualities which mutually exclude one another, exist in substances only," we almost seem to read the words of Aristotle, *τὸ τί ἐστιν ἁπλῶς τῇ οὐσίᾳ ὑπάρχει.*

These five categories would apparently exhaust the meaning of every word (padârtha). If we take, for instance, the word lightning, and ask Ka*n*âda what is expressed by it, he would say, first, a substance, and more particularly, an elementary substance. Secondly, a number of qualities, like colour, distance, or dimension. Thirdly, action, and here the action of throwing down, which cannot be a quality, because qualities are always conceived as at rest. Fourthly, a genus; because when we speak of lightning, we imply that it exists not once only, but as a class, which class is a lower genus if compared with light. Fifthly, an individuality; because we mean this particular lightning, which never existed before and never will exist again. Nevertheless, says Ka*n*âda, these five categories do not yet contain all that we mean by the word lightning. It is not the mere agglomerate of substance, quality, &c. that constitutes a real conception—but these categories must again be intimately connected or interwoven, before they represent or constitute a reality. The juxtaposition of categories would be a mere abstraction, and it requires the category of concretion to make all the other categories concrete and real. With it, we predicate, not, first substance, then quality, and so on, but we predicate substance as necessitating quality, quality as inseparable from substance, genus inherent in both, and individuality supported by genus. Thus only does a real conception become fully exhausted by categorical analysis.

We now return to a consideration of the qualities, and more especially of that which is called "Knowledge." Knowledge is a quality of the Self in the same manner as colour is of light. It is inseparably connected with it, and is explained as the cause of every conception that is expressed in language. Knowledge is either remembrance or perception. Perception is twofold, right or wrong. Right perception represents the thing such as it is, silver as silver. This is called truth (pramâ). Wrong perception represents the thing as the thing is not, mother-o'-pearl as silver.

Right perception is fourfold, sensuous, conclusive, comparative, and authoritative. It is produced by the senses, by inferring, by comparing, and by revealed authority. This fourfold division of knowledge is taken from Gotama and not from Ka*n*âda. Ka*n*âda admits but two sources of knowledge, perception (pratyaksha) and inference (laingika); that is to say, he comprehends all knowledge which does not arise from the senses, under the general title of inference. The different systems of Hindú philosophy have been arranged by Colebrooke, according to what each considers to be the only trustworthy means of knowledge. The *K*arvâka or Materialist admits but one source of knowledge, sensuous perception. The Buddhist and the Vai*s*eshika admit two, perception and inference. Manu (xii. 105) and Sânkhya philosophers admit three, for they acknowledge, besides perception and inference, the authority of revelation. The followers of Gotama add comparison as a fourth instrument of knowledge; the Prabhâkaras presumption as a fifth, and the Mîmânsakas privation or negation as a sixth. To the Self it is indifferent whether its knowledge is produced by any one of these instruments, as long as each represents the thing such as it is.

We pass over the chapter on causation, which serves as an introduction to the chapter on sensuous perception. Nor do we enter into the intricacies of sensuous perception, of which six different kinds are enumerated and explained. They arise from the different ways in which the organs of sense are brought into contact with their objects, which objects may be either substantial matter, or qualities and actions, as inherent in substance, or the Genus, as inherent in substances, qualities, and actions.

After sensuous knowledge comes conclusive knowledge, which is gained by means of inferring. Conclusive knowledge is, for instance, "This mountain is a volcano," whereas our sensuous perception is only that the mountain smokes. In order to arrive from this at the conclusion that it is a volcano, we must be in possession of what is called a pervading rule, or a Vyâpti. This pervading rule, which sometimes might be called a law, is, that smoke is inseparably connected with fire, or, as the Hindú calls it, that smokiness is pervaded by fieriness, that wherever there is smoke there is fire. If we possess this Vyâpti, which we may remember by such instances as a culinary hearth, &c. then, in order to arrive at conclusive knowledge, we only require consideration (parâmarsa) in order to find out in any sensuous impression something which can be pervaded, something which can make the mountain the member (paksha) of a Vyâpti, this something being, in our case, the smoke. If we know that the smoke which we perceive, is qualified to become part of a Vyâpti (this Vyâpti being, "wherever there is smoke there is fire"), then we know conclusively that this mountain is fiery, because it smokes.

It would have been easy to translate these definitions into more technical language. We might have clothed Ka*n*âda in a Grecian garb, and made him look almost like Aristotle. Instead of saying, that conclusive knowledge arises from a consideration that there is something in an object which is pervaded by something else, and that the pervading predicate is predicable of all things of which the pervaded predicate is, we might have said, the conclusive knowledge that S is P, arises from the consideration that S is M, and M is P, or with Aristotle, *ὁ συλλογισμὸς διὰ τοῦ μέσου τὸ ἄκρον τῷ τρίτῳδείκνυσιν*. What Ka*n*âda calls member of a pervasion (paksha, e. g. mountain), we might have translated by subject or terminus minor; what pervades (vyâpaka or sâdhya, e. g. fieriness), the predicate or terminus major; and what is to be pervaded (vyâpya, e. g. smokiness), the terminus medius. But what should we have gained by this? All that is peculiar to Indian philosophy would have been eliminated, and what remains would have looked like a clumsy imitation of Aristotle. *Multa fiunt eadem sed aliter*, and it is this "aliter" which constitutes the principal interest in a comparative study of philosophy. Even such terms as conclusion or syllogism are inconvenient here, because they have with us an historical colouring, and throw a false light on the subject. The Sanskrit Anumâna is not *συμπέρασμα*, but it means "measuring something according to something else." This is done by means of "parâmarsa," which means "groping," or trying to find in an object something which can be measured by something else, or which can become the member of a pervasion. This corresponds to the discovery of a terminus medius. In Kapila's system (I. 61), the principal object of inference is said to be transcendental truth. Things which cannot be seen with our eyes, are perceived by inference, as fire is from smoke, and he defines inference (I. 101) by "knowledge of the connected, arising from perception of a connection or a law." But, again, the relation of what pervades and what is pervaded is very different from what we should call the relative extension of two conceptions. This will become more evident by what follows. For the present we have learnt, that the act of proving (anumâna) consists in our knowing that there is on the mountain fire-pervaded smoke. Through this we arrive at *anumiti* or conclusive knowledge, that the mountain is a volcano.

What follows is translated from Annambha*tt*a's Compendium

"The act of concluding is twofold, it being intended either for one's own benefit or for others. The former is the means of arriving for ones's self at conclusive knowledge, and the process is this. By repeated observation, as in the case of culinary hearths and the like, we have obtained the general rule (vyâpti), that wherever there is smoke there is fire. We now approach a mountain, and wonder whether there might not be fire in it. We see the smoke, remember the general rule, and immediately perceive that the mountain possesses fire-pervaded smoke. This is, as yet, called only groping after signs (linga-parâmarsa). But from it arises the conclusive knowledge, that the mountain itself is fiery. This is the actual process when we reason with ourselves."

"If we try, however, to convince somebody else of what we know to be conclusively true, then we start with the assertion, The mountain is fiery. Why? Because it smokes; and all that smokes, as you may see in a culinary hearth and the like, is fiery. Now you perceive that the mountain does smoke, and hence you will admit that I was right in saying, that the mountain is fiery. This is called the five-membered form of exposition, and the five members are severally called, 1. Assertion, the mountain has fire; 2. Reason, because it has smoke; 3. Proposition, all that has smoke has fire; 4. Assumption, and the mountain has smoke; 5. Deduction, therefore it has fire. The means of inference in both cases is the same. It is what was called the groping after signs, or the handling of the demonstrative tokens, in which the essential process of inferring consists."

What is called by Annambha*tt*a the conclusion for one's self corresponds *totidem verbis* with the first form of Aristotle's syllogism:

All that smokes is fiery,
The mountain smokes;
Therefore the mountain is fiery:

What is called the conclusion for others seems more irregular, on account of its five members, and of the additional instances, which seem to vitiate the syllogism.

We must not forget, however, that whatever there is of Logic in these short extracts, has but one object, that of describing knowledge as one of the qualities of the Self. Knowledge, as Ka*n*âda has shown, is not confined to sensuous perceptions, and therefore knowledge gained by inference is examined next. The question is, how is it that we know any thing beyond what we perceive with our senses? The answer is, by inferring. If we place ourselves on this point of view, which Ka*n*âda has taken, it becomes clear, first, that we cannot expect from Ka*n*âda a treatise on formal Logic. The formal Logician takes a purely scientific interest in the machinery of the human mind. He collects, arranges, and analyzes the functions of our reasoning faculties, as they fall under his observation. But the question which occupies Ka*n*âda is, how is it that we know things which we do not see, and how can we prove that we do know them? Now the instrument by which we know things which we do not perceive with our senses, is inference. Hence, Ka*n*âda has to explain first, what inference is, and how we do infer; secondly, how far inference can be made to yield the same certainty as our sensuous impressions. For this purpose, it seems that neither the deductive nor the inductive syllogism, if taken by itself, would have been sufficient. Deductive reasoning may in itself be most valuable for formalizing facts, it may give a variety of different aspects to our knowledge, but our knowledge will never be substantially increased, no new fact will ever be discovered by it. And if on one side Ka*n*âda cannot use deduction because it teaches nothing new, he cannot use induction either, at least not in its general acceptation, because it teaches nothing certain.

The only object of all knowledge with Ka*n*âda, as we saw before, was absolute truth, or pramâ. Now Aristotle does not make a secret of it, that the *ἐπαγωγή*, in order to prove the *ὅλως*, must be *διά πάντων*, and that this is impossible. Knowledge gained by epagogic reasoning is, strictly speaking, always *ἐπί τὸ πολύ*, not what Ka*n*âda would call pramâ. The conclusion which Aristotle gains by way of induction, "Animals which have little bile are long-lived," might be called a Vyâpti. Aristotle arrives at this, by saying, man, horse, and mule (C) are long-lived (A); man, horse, and mule (C) have little bile (B); therefore all animals with little bile are long-lived. But Ka*n*âda would express himself in a different way. He would say, wherever we perceive the attribute of little bile, we also perceive the attribute of long life, as, for instance, in men, horses, mules, &c. But here he would not stop, but he would value this vyâpti merely as a means for establishing a new fact; he would at once use it as a means of deduction, and say, "now the elephant has little bile, therefore is he long-lived."

One thing can be said in favour of the Indian method. If we go on accumulating instances, as in the case before mentioned, if we add horses, mules, men and the like, we approximate more and more towards a general rule, but we never eliminate real exceptions, not to speak of possible exceptions. The Hindú, on the contrary, by saying, "Wherever we see the attribute of little bile, we observe long life," and then giving a number of instances by way of illustration, excludes the reality, though he does not exclude the possibility, of exceptions. He states it as a fact, that wherever the one has been, there has been the other, which throws the *onus probandi* as to a case to the contrary, upon the other side. In our system, there is nothing to force an opponent to admit a hundredth case, because in ninety-nine cases the rule happened to be true—while, if it is impossible to attack the "Wherever" of the Hindú, there is in this Wherever a real power that brings conviction for every case that comes under it. If it can be proved that there never was an instance where smoke was seen without fire, the mutual inherence and inseparable connection of smoke and fire is established more stringently than by any number of accumulated instances where the two have been seen together. The conditions under which it is allowed to form a Vyâpti, that is to say, to form Universals, have occupied the attention of Hindú philosophers more than any other point in Logic. They distinctly exclude the mere accumulation of observations. For things, they say, may be together a hundred times, and may still not be mutually inherent. They make exceptions for practical purposes. There repeated observations may be turned into a general rule, but not in philosophical discussions. Volumes after volumes have been written on this subject, and though I do not believe they will throw new light on the question of the origin of Universals, yet they would furnish a curious parallel to the history of the European Intellect.

It will be necessary, before closing these remarks, to say a few words in answer to the attacks which have been made on Indian Logic.

It has been said that the instances which occur in the third member of the five-membered argument, vitiate the conclusion. The proposition that wherever there is smoke there is fire, was supposed to lose its universal character if it was followed by an instance, "as in the culinary hearth." Against this we have to remark, first, that, according to Hindú logicians, this instance is not essential, and is therefore occasionally left out altogether. Next, the instance is never used to confirm the universal proposition, but to illustrate it, and for this very reason it is chiefly used in rhetorical inductions. From the Sûtras of Gotama (I. 35), it might certainly appear, as if the object of the third member was to give an instance. He says, "the proposition, or the third member, is an instance which, from the fact that smoke accompanies fire, shows that fire must be there." However, the Commentator explains that this is not strictly a definition of the third member, but merely an explanation. What the third member supplies is a statement that fieriness pervades smokiness, together with an example to make the connection between them more apparent.

In the original work of Ka*n*âda, of which the Library of the East India House possesses a MS., containing text and commentary, we see still more clearly that the third member is simply an universal proposition. We read there (p. 76, a.) : " Inference is twofold, either for one's self or for others. That for others consists of five sentences, which are called Assertion, Reason, Proposition, Assumption, and Deduction. Assertion does not mean more or less than the wording of the conclusive knowledge which is to be established. Reason is that member which expresses in the ablative the means of proof. Proposition is the third member, which shows that the means of proof and what has to be proved by it, are *never* one without the other. The Assumption shows that the means of proof (heretofore determined as inseparable from what is to be proved) belongs to the subject of our assertion. And the Deduction shows that therefore what is to be proved belongs to the subject. The argument therefore proceeds in the following way, A word is non-eternal, because it is composed ; whatever is composed is non-eternal ; a word possesses the quality of being composed, such quality being pervaded by non-eternity ; therefore a word is non-eternal." He further states that the names of the five members mean with the Vaiseshikas, Promise, Pretext, Authority, Scrutiny, and Repetition.

In Ka*n*âda's system, therefore, it would seem as if the instance, belonging to the proposition, was altogether ignored, and we might feel inclined to admit that it occurs only incidentally in Gotama's philosophy. But if we inquire more carefully, we find that the instance in Gotama's syllogism has its own distinct office, not to strengthen or to limit the universal proposition, but to indicate, if I may say so, its modality. Every Vyâpti must, of course, admit at least one instance. These instances may be either positive only, or negative only, or both positive and negative. If it is said, " The jar is nameable, because it is knowable ; every thing that is knowable is nameable ;" we can only have positive instances, as tree, table, and the like. It is impossible to bring a negative instance of something which is not provable, because every thing is provable. On the contrary, if we have a case, like " the earth is different from all the other four elements, because it has odour," it is impossible to go on—" All that is different from the other elements has odour,"—because the only case in point would again be " earth." Therefore we must here employ the negative Vyâpti, and say, Whatever is not different from the other elements, has no odour, and then it is possible to add an instance, namely, water, light, &c. After this the Hindú proceeds, Now earth is not so (not inodorous) ; Therefore it is not so (not different from the other elements).

Brahmans have been told by European Logicians that they could have all this more cheaply, by saying, "Whatever is odorous differs from the other inodorous elements;" "Earth is odorous;" "Therefore earth differs from the others;" But the Vaiseshika stops us at the very first word, he does not admit the "Whatever," because it is not a "Whatever," but only one single case. It would be impossible to give instances, nay, to give a single instance for the Vyâpti, proposed by the European Logicians, except earth over again.

The third case is, where the Vyâpti admits both of positive and negative instances, as in the hackneyed syllogism of the volcano. Here we can say, Wherever there is smoke, there is fire, as in culinary hearths and the like. And wherever there is no fire there is no smoke, as in the lake.

So much for the instances added to the third member, which were supposed to vitiate the syllogism.

Still more unfounded is another objection. It was said that the formalities of the Science of Logic were perfectly satisfied with three out of the five members of the Indian syllogism. Of course they are, and the Hindús knew this 2000 years ago. We have seen that the five-membered method was employed when a person, after having himself arrived at conclusive knowledge, wished to persuade somebody else of the truth of his belief. Now, if "the sole object of Logic is the guidance of our own thoughts, and the communication of those to others is under the consideration of Rhetoric," it is clear that the scheme of the five-membered syllogism belongs to Rhetoric and not to Logic. Whether or no the five steps as they follow one another, according to Kanâda, represent what does actually take place in a well-conducted argument, we may leave to Rhetoricians to decide. But, in order to show that even this far-fetched objection would not take the Brahman philosopher by surprise, we quote the following passage from the Vedânta-paribhâshâ: "Inference is twofold, intended either for ourselves or for others. The former has been explained. As to the latter it is to be accomplished by means of an argument. An argument consists of several members. And *real* members there are only three; assertion, reason, proposition; or proposition, assumption, and deduction. Not five; for three are sufficient to exhibit the pervading rule and its two members, the other two can therefore be dispensed with." Now, in the first case, which would give us "the mountain is fiery, for it smokes, all that smokes is fiery," it must be admitted there would be a want of all syllogistic arrangement. The first two members might be called an Enthymema, but then the third would be superfluous. But the fact is that Hindú philosophers never use the three members in this succession; and if they say, that the three first are sufficient for a conclusion, they take no account of their successive collocation, but simply mean that Proposition, Reason, and Assertion would form a syllogism as well as Proposition, Assumption, and Deduction. But, although the Hindú Logicians admit, in common with their brethren in Europe, that a complete syllogism consists of three members, they do by no means restrict themselves to the use of the three-membered syllogism. Gotama, for instance, says there are three kinds of syllogism, from cause to effect, from effect to cause, and from the Special to the General. Thus we infer that it will rain from the rising of clouds, it has rained from the rising of rivers; we infer that a thing is substance because it is earth. But, with the exception of the last case, it would be impossible to frame an absolute proposition, or a vyâpti, from which the deductions could be established.

So much in answer to objections which have repeatedly been made against Indian Logic. I should like to see the Brahmans themselves take up the gauntlet and defend their Logic against the attacks of European critics. Till very lately they entertained a very low opinion of European Logic, some account of which had been supplied to them from the popular work of Abercrombie. The European style is to them not sufficiently precise. The use of an abstract, instead of a concrete term is enough to disgust a Brahman. Besides, he wants to see all results put forward in short and clear language, and to have all possible objections carefully weighed and refuted. By the exertions of Dr. Ballantyne, the Principal of the Sanskrit College at Benares, some of the best English works on Logic have been made accessible to the Pandits, and at the present day we might hear the merits of Bacon's Novum Organon discussed in the streets of Benares. Indian Philosophy therefore should not be attacked at random. Thales or Empedocles can be criticized in the schools with impunity, but Ka*n*âda and Gotama may find champions in India, if not in Europe.

INDEX.

INDEX.

THE END.

CPSIA information can be obtained
at www.ICGtesting.com
Printed in the USA
LVHW040341110522
718423LV00001B/266

9 783375 007980